Praise for
THE FIRST LADY SLEEPS

Much like the prolific British mystery writer P.D. James who clearly probes her characters, Mullally's characters are faceted, warts and all. The characters create various startling plot events as the warts change the pattern of their lives. To describe the tumultuous events is to take away the drama of Mullally's ingenuity. By the end, you applaud his ingenuity.

—*Fran Schattenberg, PhD., White Lake Beacon*

DENTIST TURNS NOVELIST

40 years of dentistry brought Mullally to a deep appreciation of people. He gives the reader an extra benefit: a touch of the classical, philosophical and literary world that is prophetic in the book's modern world. A sequel is planned and will be available in 2013.

—*Journal of the Michigan Dental Association.*

POSSIBLE BEST SELLER

If you read books by Grisham, DeMille or Baldacci, you will enjoy *The First Lady Sleeps*, a White House thriller. It is an intense saga of obsessive love and extreme wealth verses governmental power. His characters are well done and the story has several unexpected twists. The author grabs your attention and holds it to the end.

—*Louise Matz, Senior Perspectives*

AUTHOR WRITES A REAL PAGE-TURNER

Mullally has a writing style which could be referred to minimalist. He rarely uses the literary device of foreshadowing. Instead circumstances change suddenly and startling events occur in rapid-fire succession, occasionally requiring that a key paragraph be reread. Allusions to science (especially to medicine), the classics and philosophy abound.

—*Cynthia Price, Norton-Lakeshore Examiner*

THE
FIRST LADY
Meets Azee

THE
FIRST LADY
Meets Azee

JOHN MULLALLY

John Mullally

All Novels Publishing, LLC.

The First Lady Meets Azee

All Novels Publishing, LLC.

Allnovelspublishingllc@yahoo.com

© 2013 by John Mullally

All Rights Reserved

ISBN: 978-0-9837808-4-7

Finished cover and text layout:
Amy Cole and Amy Landheer, JPL Design Solutions

Printed in the United States of America

I am solely responsible, for better for worse,
for the contents of this totally fictional novel.

www.thefirstladymeetsazee.com

Dedication

To John Patrick Mullally

Our Ninth Grandchild,
May you help us to
Rediscover the
Fountain of youth

Prologue

Terrorism and war usually are waged to conquer another country unless you are the billionaire super-terrorist, Azee, who was simply trying to re-win the heart of his high school lover, now the first lady of the United States. His meticulous plans to kill the president during a campaign stop in Detroit went astray as the president survived an attack. Instead, the pregnant first lady was rendered unconscious with her condition progressing to a hopeless coma leading to the title of the exciting novel, *The First Lady Sleeps.*

The stories of the homegrown terrorist Azee, related in *The First Lady Sleeps* and *The First Lady Meets Azee,* take place well before the 9/11 tragedies. Tom Gleason, the failed Secret Service agent who took personal responsibility for the Detroit attacks on the first family, determined that Azee was the treasonous perpetrator of these attacks and that he would singlehandedly bring Azee to justice.

Fabricating a devious plan from Azee's play book, Gleason convinces Azee to bail out of his allegedly doomed private jet in the middle of the Atlantic Ocean leaving Gleason to relax in the jet's cabin with the hope and expectation that Azee has jumped to his doom.

I

The trap door in the floor of the Flying Mole's fuselage, where the deluded Azee jumped out, automatically closed. Tom Gleason, the White House's senior Secret Service agent, rested his weary head on Azee's streaking Bombadier Jet's seatback. With closed eyes, he uttered the simple prayer, "Amen." Azee's treasonous bombings of the first family in Detroit were avenged. The country would be better off without the protracted trial that would be necessary to convict Azee of the crimes of the century—the maiming of the first lady and the attempted assassination of the president. Gleason could feel the Flying Mole's steep climb trying to regain the lost altitude needed for Azee's hasty departure from what he considered a doomed plane because of Gleason's threatened self-detonating bomb in his stowed bag.

Gleason was relieved that the pilot, Taajud-Deen, did not immediately put the Flying Mole into a steep dive that would have doomed him and the pilots to the same uncertain fate in the mid-Atlantic that Azee had just chosen for himself when he parachuted out of the Flying Mole. Gleason, with his ex-wife's helpful philosophical profile of Azee, had gambled that Azee would elect to take control of his own destiny, trying to save his own skin by bailing out of the allegedly doomed Flying Mole, rather than deal with the uncontrollable possibility of Gleason's threatened latent bomb.

Gleason was wagering his own AIDS shortened life that a mega egomaniac like Azee would chose to risk drowning in the mid-Atlantic over being blown apart by a stowed bomb. Gleason provided the final bait Azee needed to make his jump when he gave him a remote detonator that would blow up the bomb stowed in the fuselage as he evacuated the plane.

The one major variable crucial to his own survival that the control freak Secret Service agent Gleason was unable to forecast, was the reaction of Taajud-Deen, and co-pilot Abdul, after Azee bailed out of the doomed Flying Mole over the busy international shipping lanes. All Azee's employees had a fanatical loyalty to their boss, so Gleason's life was in the hands of highly proficient yet unpredictable pilots. Gleason was still restrained by his seat belt and shoulder harness combination that was electronically locked closed like a deadbolt, preventing him from getting out of his seat and moving around the jet's cramped yet luxurious cabin.

During his life and death game of chicken with the ever manipulative Azee, Gleason had used a prearranged, elementary form of Morse code on his CIA rigged Walkman to secretly communicate with Colonel Neil Gibson in his trailing F16 CIA surveillance jet. However, now he had nothing to lose and perhaps everything to gain if the pilots of the Flying Mole overheard their conversation.

"TG to NG," he shouted at the Walkman to overcome the Flying Mole's screaming engines. He realized that Colonel Gibson would be totally preoccupied piloting the most sophisticated piece of equipment in the CIA's arsenal of high tech toys, so he repeated his simple salutation, "TG to NG. Come in NG."

"NG here. Nice to hear your voice. I was concerned if you were still alive."

"Azee took the bait and bailed. I heard your cannon fire, just before he jumped."

"I pulverized the parachute of the survival raft and saw a small report flash of the remote detonator as his parachute was starting to fill. I didn't want to risk losing you by circling back to destroy his parachute if I could even find him in the heavy cloud cover."

"Get the exact location where Azee jumped. He should be shark bait unless he crashes onto the deck of a freighter. I'm restrained in my seat and can't get to the cockpit."

"Got the location where I destroyed the survival pack. Since leaving Annapolis we've been flying over the international shipping lanes to Europe, so there are probably ships in the area. Should I put out a SOS for Azee?"

"Hell no! He's on his own."

"Good point. I'm ordering your pilots to land at our Sigonella naval air station in Sicily. We don't have to notify the Italian government as we have carte blanche to come and go. This will be the test of Azee's contingency plans if the pilots cooperate with my orders to land there."

"What's the ETA? I don't want to mess up this beautiful interior so you'd better radio the pilots to release my restraints for a potty break. I'm still wearing the neoprene suit that shielded me from the electrical charge built into the seat, so I have probably sweated away most of my body fluids."

"Will do. Don't worry about the pilots. They see me on your wing and I have radio contact. They should follow international protocol and land at Sigonella in an hour."

"Hope you're right, but I'm sure Azee and the pilots have contingency plans for any emergency. Though our main objective is accomplished with Azee choosing his own fate, my order is still in place to shoot down the Flying Mole if the pilots don't cooperate."

After too long a pause without a reply, Gleason felt compelled to summon Colonel Gibson, "NG, did you copy my last transmission?"

"Affirmative, but I don't agree with it anymore. There's nothing to be gained by shooting you out of the sky with Azee gone. We'll deal with it if the need arises."

Although Gleason felt that he was in charge of this bizarre and clandestine mission, he recognized that Colonel Gibson had all the power. He wasn't sure why he reiterated this suicidal order. He knew that he was mentally, physically and especially spiritually exhausted and wasn't reasoning properly. Did he want to die a hero's death and not the slow embarrassing death that his AIDS was going to force on him? As he was pondering this morbid dilemma, the pilot Taajud-Deen opened the cockpit door and stood menacingly over him, brandishing a pistol that he recognized as a thirty-eight caliber police issue revolver.

He'd only said a polite hello to Taajud-Deen on boarding in Annapolis when he handed him his small duffle bag to stow in the forward hatch. Taajud-Deen's stern appearance conveyed the message that he was not pleased that Gleason had snookered his departed boss with the now patently false threat of a stowed self-detonating bomb. Taajud-Deen's hand slid off the pistol's grip to the black metal barrel. Gleason crouched down in his seat preparing to be pistol whipped into a state of unconsciousness or even death.

"I have been ordered by your pilot to surrender my sidearm," Taajud-Deen meekly proclaimed while pushing it into Gleason's still restrained hands. Taajud-Deen sat in Azee's plush starboard side recliner and began clicking a sequence of switches that Gleason worried would restart the electrical generator, giving him the high flying hot seat that Azee had futilely tried. His perspiration saturated neoprene suit would offer little protection now against the seat and shoulder harness' deadly 440 volts of built-in electrical current. Instead, a loud click of the waist buckle released the restraint that had kept him prisoner while Azee parachuted into the foreboding Atlantic. "What's our ETA at Sigonella?" Gleason asked the pilot as he was returning to the cockpit.

"About an hour if your pilot doesn't shoot us out of the sky. All is now in the hands of Allah and your demon pilot."

Gleason tucked the newly acquired pistol under his soggy waist band and stood up while bracing himself on the chair backs. He shuffled to the cramped head to relieve himself and to peel off the life saving but now moisture laden suit. Even though no one else was in the passenger compartment, he locked the bathroom door as he sought a hiding place for his silver dollar sized transponder that he smuggled onboard, which would allow the Flying Mole to be tracked anywhere in the world. Removing the fiberglass service panel behind the toilet he was able to wedge the transponder between two overlapping struts.

"TG, you still okay? I just heard this awful sucking sound."

"Sorry! I just flushed the toilet—should have turned off the radio."

"Let's hope that's our only snafu before landing. I heard your pilot give an ETA of an hour to the approaching Tripoli control tower and that's pretty accurate if he doesn't try any funny stuff."

"I think he's going to be okay. He willingly gave me his sidearm and released my seat restraint, which is about all that we can expect at this time. I suppose his co-pilot also has a side arm, but I won't try to retrieve it."

"Good idea. Don't precipitate an airborne shooting incident. Remember: the pilots are still loyal to their departed boss and his terrorist causes."

Feeling more comfortable and relaxed after his visit to the head and shedding the sweaty neoprene suit, Gleason opted to sit in Azee's starboard throne, just in case the pilots could activate the passenger seat frying pan from the cockpit. He closed his eyes to compose himself just like his fifteen minutes of morning meditation during his seminary days. He suddenly jolted upright in a state of heightened awareness. Things were not adding up. The pilots were being too cooperative. By training and culture they should be avenging Azee's death by killing him, even if it meant dying in the process.

Gleason was startled back to reality when his Walkman squawked, "NG to TG. I've been recording multiple short radio transmissions from your pilots. Can't understand them as they are in a foreign language and need translation. One was on the emergency frequency like an SOS. Should I jam all transmissions or order radio silence?"

"Keep status quo and record them. We might be able to

learn their contingency plans. How long will it take to get them translated?"

"Depends if the proper language expert is on duty at Langley. I'll have to break radio silence with Langley. Okay?"

"Do it."

II

Gleason discovered a soft black velour robe with gold braiding and piping running the length of the arms hanging in the small closet across from the head. He slipped it on over his sweat drenched t-shirt and boxer shorts. His supercharged personality was never conducive to cat naps, especially in planes, and today was no exception as hard as he tried to drift away for a few moments of surcease. The cop in him wondered whether he should get up and conduct a search of the plane's small cabin to see what other surprises Azee might have tucked away for unwary passengers. It wouldn't matter if he found another gun or two as he already had one too many, at least for use while airborne. Finally his tired mind rationalized that anything found could be construed as evidence and was better left to FBI experts to process after they landed.

"NG to TG," Tom again heard on his Walkman transmitter just as he was starting to doze off. "I have word from Langley about the translation of the messages."

"Let's have it."

"Didn't mean to get your hopes up. They said it'd be about fifteen minutes before the translator finishes his work. This shouldn't be a problem as we still have an ETA of forty-five minutes at Sicily."

"Great. I was just about asleep when you roused me with this non-news. By the way, have you talked to the pilots to make sure our fuel supply is adequate?"

"Sorry. I can't sleep while piloting this star wars plane so I figured the same for you. I'll call them about your fuel level. Your plane should be okay on fuel, probably better than this high tech hog I'm flying. Azee had the Flying Mole retrofitted with auxiliary fuel tanks to fly non-stop transatlantic." Gleason was trying hard to doze when the disconcerting message came through to him, "The pilots aren't acknowledging my radio contacts."

Immediately, the cockpit door flew open and a scowling Taajud-Deen emerged brandishing a pistol, similar to the one that he had surrendered earlier. He shouted, "Hands up, behind your head! Get in the other seat and click closed the harness buckle." With the black thirty-eight special inches from his face and his own pistol ripped from his waistband, Gleason had no choice but to comply. Taajud-Deen sat in Azee's chair and began fiddling with the bank of chair-side switches. Gleason heard the distinctive dull clunk of his harness being electronically locked and wondered if next he would hear the exterminating hum of the 440 volt generator that would turn his seat into the deadly high flying electric chair since he was now without his protective neoprene suit.

From his regained prisoner seat he thought, *they must want to keep me alive otherwise the electricity would be surging through me.* He tried to figure out why Taajud-Deen let him keep his Walkman radio that allowed him to stay in touch with the escorting jet. Taajud-Deen was too much in charge to have simply forgotten to take the Walkman radio from him. He wanted him to talk to the escorting jet so he'd better speak cautiously.

"TG to NG. I'm restrained again in the hot seat."

"We have a problem developing. The plane is deviating from the flight plan to Sigonella. The pilots still aren't responding to my radio messages."

"Wish I could help but I'm just along for the ride. All I can do is pray...to whom? Allah, since He's the god of our deviant pilots?"

"This is no time to joke! I'm just getting back the translation of your pilots' messages. Give me a minute. They requested permission to enter Libyan airspace for an emergency landing at Tripoli. Permission was granted and they have changed their flight pattern to that direction."

"No surprise there. Azee has an office in Tripoli and is buddy-buddy with Qadafi. If I weren't restrained in this seat I'd bail out like Azee, using the second survival pack and parachute in the closet. We can always do our Emergency Plan One, and you return home unscathed."

"We talked about this! Azee's off the plane, so E.P. One isn't an option. We're only one hundred miles from Libyan airspace and I'm sure they're scrambling their jets to meet us."

"What's the problem, Colonel? The Libyans fly old Russian Migs, don't they?

"I probably could take them all-out, but it would take a while. Meanwhile, you would have landed in Tripoli. I can't land this bird in enemy territory to extricate you when I wouldn't be able to take off with you aboard. I have to decide real fast as Libyan air space is only fifty miles ahead and I don't want to give their jets a reason to fire on me."

"Agreed! Peel off! You have enough taped evidence of Azee's treachery to establish his guilt in the Detroit bombings. Give my love to Cindy and sincere regrets to the president." He spoke with a profound melancholy, not knowing if these would be his final words for the two people that were his reasons for wanting to live.

III

"Hell of a time for Gleason to take a vacation," the exasperated president complained to his vice president, Hubert Taylor. "And what's the story on his car which he reported stolen to 911 burning up on the Bay Bridge at Annapolis? Why's everything unraveling around here just when I need help with the new baby and planning Kathy's funeral?"

"You know, Archie, he's a career governmental employee. He can take his vacation whenever he wants. When did he put in for this vacation and did he say where he's going? He's not going very far with his burned out car and his littered government car parked backwards in the wrong spot at his condo. It's not like him to leave us in the lurch like this."

"Hubert, don't give me this governmental employee bull shit. He's part of the family who just happens to work for the Secret Service. You could say that we're blood brothers since he gave me his blood for my emergency arm surgery in Detroit. This is the first vacation where he ever filled out the paper work. He usually just took a day here or there to play golf with some of his priest buddies from their seminary days. Not having any kids, he didn't have to go to Disney World during spring break like everyone else."

"Is it verified that it was Gleason on the 911 call reporting his car stolen? The caller said that he couldn't come in to fill out the stolen car report because he was going overseas. Gleason always said that he had enough foreign travel with you on Air Force One."

"No shit," the frustrated president replied. "Of course it was Gleason making that 911 call. By making that call he was telling us something just as his uncharacteristic fast food littered car pulled into the wrong parking space at his condo is speaking to us. My personal White House mail box received a short note from him saying that he'd be in touch shortly and that he was sorry for his role in the Detroit disaster and especially for the way that it will continue to unfold. What the hell does he mean by that? He must know something that the rest of us don't."

"I know that he feels terribly guilty about Detroit, like he's personally responsible for the failure of the Secret Service to prevent the Detroit bombings that injured you and will soon take Kathy. His ex-wife, Cindy, left a message with my secretary saying that she received a strange note from him. She wants us to call her if we know where he's going."

"Since Detroit he's done everything possible, especially for Jason and Eric, to make up for his guilt. Speaking of guilt, Hubert, how do you now feel about your firing of Jameson as our Secretary of Treasury during your first and last cabinet meeting as acting president?"

"I'd probably be feeling more guilt about it if Jameson hadn't made that crude, disrespectful remark as he was leaving the cabinet room."

"That must be the blank space on the meeting transcript that the secretary couldn't decipher."

"Probably better that she couldn't figure it out."

"For the record Hubert, what did Jameson say that we couldn't understand on the tape? I suppose that we could send the tape over to the CIA for their expert analysis."

"That's not necessary. He mumbled our old Princeton fraternity Greek password: Eis Aidou, which means, go to hell."

"That's funny and probably very appropriate given the tension in the cabinet room."

"At the time, Mr. President, I didn't think it was funny. I was the acting President of the United States conducting an important cabinet meeting to show the country that everything was still functioning normally while you were having your arm surgery in Detroit."

"Normally! When Kathy and I were hospitalized the country needed the appearance of stability, not some damned college fraternity charade. In case you haven't heard, I'm not accepting Jameson's resignation as Secretary of the Treasury, at least until the investigation of the bombings is completed. Just because the Secret Service is under the Treasury Department doesn't make him personally responsible for what happened in Detroit as you alleged in the cabinet meeting."

"Mr. President, do you want my resignation, too? You could just fire me and name a younger candidate to run with you on the ticket."

"You aren't going anywhere with the election only weeks away. You and Jameson have to make up. We have enough problems without you two fighting old battles. I'm putting you in charge of finding Gleason and figuring out what the hell is going on. Any questions?"

"No, sir. I'll stay in close contact with your office."

IV

In the days since the pregnant first lady had been transferred from Detroit to Bethesda Naval Medical Center on Air Force One, after the terrorist's bombing attack severely injured her, it was determined that the hyperbaric oxygen treatments were not waking her from her deep coma. Moreover, the hyperbaric oxygen treatments could possibly be harming the eight-month-old fetus. Hyperbaric oxygen treatments were used by the Navy to treat cases of the bends from submarine and diving mishaps. This treatment forces more healing oxygen into the patient's red blood cells. Its use was experimentally broadened to other medical conditions such as strokes and traumatic brain injuries, where it was thought that increased levels of oxygen would aid in recovery. The first lady was being treated by the Navy's hyperbaric oxygen expert, Dr. Nancy Schmidt. The process was cumbersome, at best, as the comatose first lady had to be put carefully into an iron lung type chamber for the treatments.

Dr. Schmidt had arranged numerous consultations with trauma and neonatal physicians, both military and civilian, and it was the consensus that a C-section should be performed sooner rather than later. The fetus appeared viable and it might help the first lady to be free of the burden of carrying the baby. The president was in agreement after being reassured that Kathy's already hopeless condition would not be worsened by the C-section. With the upcoming election, he did not want to give the impression that he was pulling the plug on his wife if she died during the C-section.

The C-section, delivering a healthy baby girl, was performed by a team of specialists at Bethesda Naval Hospital. The president and his two sons, Jason and Eric, were shielded from the ravenous press to allow them to act like a normal family as they enjoyed the simple joy of the baby's birth. Fortunately, in a rare moment of late pregnancy intimacy, Kathy had indicated to her husband that she loved the name Melody, so the naming decision was easy. The president and his advisors decided to wait twenty-four hours before releasing photos of the baby. This news blackout allowed time to see what happened to the condition of the comatose first lady as well as the baby. This delay also built up suspense for the maximum political effect this close to the election.

The president took consolation from the loving care that he and his sons were receiving from Dr. Schmidt as she continued her treatment of the first lady. She was as relieved as the president to have the baby delivered safely. She still had the job of keeping the comatose first lady alive. Professionally, she knew that the first lady should be declared dead with an unchanging Glasgow score of three, which meant she had no detectable brain waves and was unresponsive to external stimuli.

However, even more disconcerting to Dr. Schmidt was the accusation by a CIA internal affairs investigator that her well concealed affair with a Russian spy from twenty years ago could ground her skyrocketing Navy career. Incriminating twenty year old surveillance photos of her and Andre, a Russian attaché, frolicking naked in a hyperbaric whirlpool were recently shown to her at the Watergate Hotel by an alleged CIA internal affairs investigator. She was wracking her brain for any method, legal or illegal, to try to establish the identity of this pseudo CIA agent.

She ultimately realized that the president was the only one who could order the CIA to reveal what, if anything, they knew about her serious indiscretion and the identity of her accuser. This presidential request for help would have to wait until after the first lady's death. Most assuredly, there would be a quid pro quo required of Nancy that she was not yet prepared to deliver. Her feminine intuition coupled with her medical education told her that there was something mysterious going on around the nightmarish presidential circus that was above her pay grade to know. Otherwise, why did Gleason order her to provide him with a vial of the president's blood and to wait until after the election to perform his annual physical?

Dr. Schmidt was a board certified psychiatrist in addition to her internal medicine training. This allowed her to closely monitor the effects of the hyperbaric treatments on patients' behavior. Her psychiatric training also put her on guard to analyze the reasoning behind people's decisions. She was caught completely off guard by the president's change of heart in asking to keep the first lady on indefinite life support after the baby was delivered. His reasoning was of a nature that she had never heard before. All the political pundits privately were saying that he was afraid to turn off the life support systems because of the negative political fallout for his reelection campaign. Knowing the president, this probably was one of the factors in this life prolonging decision.

However, she was speechless when he stated that he wanted the first lady kept on life support after the baby was delivered so that in adulthood Melody would not feel any guilt about her birth being the cause of her mother's death. This was a softer, more considerate side of the president that she never knew existed. Equally surprising was his additional line of reasoning that he didn't want to deprive his sons and himself of the joy of the baby's birth by having to immediately plan the required large state funeral if life support was simultaneously disconnected. She was willing to continue compromising her medical ethics by letting the first lady remain in her vegetative state until the president gave the order that the time was here.

V

Colonel Gibson's prediction came true as the Flying Mole was greeted by a squadron of aging Libyan fighter planes. Gleason was hopeful, since Gibson had chosen not to engage them, that the Libyans would provide a friendly escort to Tripoli. He was relieved as his ears started to pop on their rapid descent to land.

The wheels of the Flying Mole stopped rolling in front of a large hangar with wide open doors ready to swallow up the small Bombadier Jet. Out of his small porthole window Gleason could see a battered, squat tow truck approaching to provide repositioning services. He knew that the Flying Mole would be moved inside the hangar to get it away from the ever-seeing satellite cameras and the high altitude U-2 spy planes that nearly ignited World War III with the Russians. Unless Gibson had been able to immediately radio the proper government agency, Gleason was sure that there would be no actual photo verification of the Flying Mole's exact location.

It would be just a matter of time until the transponder he had hidden in the head behind the toilet panel would be discovered. Then, undetected, the Flying Mole would be able to fly free as a bird anywhere it wanted. This provided no consolation as he would be locked away in a medieval Libyan torture chamber. The slight jerk of the tow truck engaging the jet's towing bar jolted him into the realization that he was alone and restrained in his seat to face a life threatening predicament of his own choosing as he had elected to singlehandedly take on Azee.

The Flying Mole was quickly moved inside the oversized airplane hangar and was dwarfed by an assortment of aging Libyan military aircraft that he knew would be no match for the United States' high tech machinery—if there were a need for a military confrontation. However, he was relieved that Colonel Gibson had not stayed to fight the approaching Libyan jets as it would have made his current confinement a certain death sentence to avenge the downed pilots.

After the Flying Mole was shoehorned between two Russian Mig fighters and the wheels blocked, Taajud-Deen emerged from the cockpit with his pistol now holstered. He twisted open the door's safety latch and pushed the open button to allow the door's hydraulic system to lower the plane's stairway. Before sitting in Azee's seat to activate the switches that would free Gleason from his electronic jail he drew his pistol and pointed it at Gleason with the frightening declaration, "You will wish that you bailed out like Mr. Azee."

"Thanks for the advice, but it's a little late." Gleason had sat in on countless White House CIA briefings that always ended with the un-actionable conclusions that Libyan leader Colonel Muammar Qadafi was certifiably crazy, totally unpredictable, and a threat to the civilized western world. Now Gleason was going to be his guest.

He pondered that he might be better off making a move on Taajud-Deen and getting shot in the plane, rather than subjecting himself to the diabolical whims of the madman Qadafi. Before he could activate that suicide plan, two Libyan officers appeared in the cockpit, hoisted him from his seat and dragged him out the narrow door and down the steep stairs.

He quickly scanned his perimeter, as if he were still guarding the president. He counted ten Uzi toting guards inside the stifling hangar. No one seemed in charge of this welcoming committee until he heard a shrill, high pitched order from behind him, "Kneel down, hands behind your head!" At the same time, he felt the nose of a rifle firmly jabbed into his back. From his knees he looked up and saw a petite woman carrying a rifle nearly as tall as she was. "Who are you and what are you doing here?"

"I'm Santa Claus and I'm looking for Mrs. Claus. Have you seen...?" before he could finish his ill timed attempt at gallows humor, the butt of her rifle crashed into the side of his head, knocking him off his prayer bones into a semiconscious fetal position.

"Get up and answer my questions unless you want me to hit the other side of your head even harder."

Struggling to upright himself, Gleason was starting to develop an appreciation of the Geneva Convention Rules which required only name, rank and serial number be given to your captors. In the dimly lit hangar he could barely read the small plastic name tag above her left breast that said *Afshaa*. He knew the name of his tormentor and he didn't plan to forget it if he survived his stay in Libya. "I am Thomas Gleason, a United States citizen and a low level employee of the United States Government." He decided not to reveal his Secret Service job as he knew that they would discover it soon enough.

"Answer my question. What are you doing here?"

Good question, he thought. "I was being held prisoner on that airplane over there that just made an emergency landing." He had no time to brace himself for the crushing blow of the rifle butt on the other side of his head.

"Up! Get Up!" He barely heard this shrill order through the fog of his semiconscious state. He felt two hands digging into his arm pits as someone from behind tried to aid his return to the kneeling position. "Again, why are you here?"

Before he could mouth another answer, that would likely earn him a third and possibly lethal blow, he felt himself teetering from side to side and rocking from front to back. His world went black and silent as he collapsed into a nose plant that would make an Olympic skier proud.

"Get him to the hospital," the diminutive Afshaa ordered, as she withdrew to interview Taajud-Deen on his role in what was most assuredly going to escalate into a major international crisis.

If Taajud-Deen and his co-pilot, Abdul, thought that they were going to have an easier time with the seemingly all power-ful Afshaa, they were sorely mistaken. "Give me your weapons. Answer my questions honestly, and you will at least walk out of here to jail." Handing over their pistols, Taajud-Deen and Abdul stood at attention while Afshaa looked them over from head to toe. "Search them," she barked to the two guards standing behind the confused pilots, who were expecting a hero's welcome. Satisfied that they were weapon free, she repeated the same instructions given to her previous victim, "Kneel down, hands behind your heads. What caused you to violate sovereign Libyan airspace?"

"We were being chased by a United States fighter jet that was trying to force us to land at their base in Sicily."

"I know that from your radio transmissions. Why were they doing this? Your plane is registered in Lebanon."

"The passenger, whom you hopefully just killed, is the top Secret Service agent protecting the president of the United States. He forced the owner of the airplane to bail out of the plane into the Atlantic."

"His name is Azee, right?"

"Yes. He's a friend of Colonel Qadafi."

"I know. Please stand. We have to be careful who enters our peaceful country. Many don't like our leader. Do you know where Azee bailed out of the plane?"

"The location is recorded in the plane's log. An SOS was sent to all the ships in the area when he bailed out."

"There isn't much we can do from here to find him. We'll take you downtown to our security ministry for debriefing and then to a hotel."

"The owner of the Corinthia Hotel is a friend of Mr. Azee. He always provides us with the Presidential Suite where Colonel Qadafi has dined many times with Mr. Azee. The view of the

Mediterranean is spectacular."

"You and the plane must stay in Libya until Colonel Qadafi
decides what to do. The United States government won't be happy
that we captured one of their top officials."

"We must stay in Libya until we learn Mr. Azee's fate. I'm sure
that Colonel Qadafi will contact us. He and Mr. Azee are business
partners as well as good friends."

VI

Vice President Taylor set about fulfilling the president's directive to find out what was going on with the MIA Gleason by sending memos marked urgent to anyone who might know anything about his possible overseas vacation plans. Not making much headway with a given problem was nothing unusual to the stuck-in-the-mud, wheel-spinning vice president. When his secretary interrupted his afternoon siesta with frantic hand gesticulations and highly animated voice, he surmised that something important was happening. She informed him that the reclusive CIA director, Elliott Hayden, was headed to the Oval Office for a meeting on the whereabouts of Gleason. The vice president and the secretary of treasury were ordered to be there immediately.

This impending meeting was the first substantive issue that the president was dealing with since the birth of Melody. The first lady was still in her comatose limbo, and he would be forced to deal with her grave situation sooner than he wanted. He was waiting in the oval office for the others to arrive, rocking Melody under the vigilant eye of a hovering White House nurse. One by one Vice President Taylor, Secretary of The Treasury Jameson, and the unflappable CIA Director, Elliott Hayden, arrived. They all offered their perfunctory *oohs* and *aahs* at seeing the first baby for this premier showing. The president reluctantly passed the baby to the nurse, so that this unpleasant meeting could begin.

Knowing that he was on the hot seat, CIA Director Hayden started by passing out the PDB, a succinct one page top secret Presidential Daily Briefing from the bowels of the CIA's Langley campus. Usually the PDB spanned the globe with small pictures and multiple one or two line summaries of the world's hot spots. Today there was just one hot spot listed: Tripoli, Libya, with two familiar pictures of Tom Gleason and Azee.

After giving everyone a chance to digest the PDB, which essentially stated that Gleason was being held prisoner in Tripoli, Hayden started to fill in between the lines acknowledging that most of the information on Gleason came from the F16's pilot, Colonel Gibson, and his recording of Gleason and Azee's final conversation in the Flying Mole.

The CIA operatives on the ground in Tripoli spent most of their time tracking the unpredictable and ever dangerous Colonel Qadafi, so they would need time to refocus on finding Gleason and the grounded Flying Mole.

A moment of awkward silence was broken by the president with the question that all knew was coming, "Why wasn't I informed of this mission sooner? Like, before it happened?" None of the three subordinates had the nerve to pick up this hot potato, because they knew that whoever answered would be held responsible and pulverized by the president's legendary temper. So the president began a monologue. "This is the worst possible news before the election. It can wipe out all the positive press that Melody's birth has generated. What will the media say about this rogue Secret Service agent, who works for you, Jameson; being tailed by our most sophisticated and irreplaceable CIA spy plane, Hayden? All the while trying to solve and avenge the crime of the century outside normal judicial circles? Don't mean to leave you out, Mr. Vice President: how many times have you been on that damned plane with your now departed buddy, Azee? I'm sure the press will answer that for us in very short order."

"Excuse me, Mr. President, but I must speak my mind for the first time since I've been your vice president." Everyone started to squirm and twist in their chairs, especially the president, at what might come out of the mouth of the newly animated vice president. "Let me start my remarks by saying that my resignation can be on your desk when this meeting concludes, or you can fire me, Mr. President."

"Hubert, get to the point. We're trying to get the facts of this public relations nightmare before we talk to the press."

"Thank you, sir. I was introduced to Azee by the first lady at one of your early fundraisers before you formally announced your candidacy for the presidency. I believe it was just after Kathy returned from her Greek Isle cruise with Azee that she wanted to take before the glare of the media was on you as a presidential candidate. Over the years my friendship with Azee deepened, as we all know. However, I've never done anything illegal. I remember you saying that Gleason called you the night before he disappeared, but you were too busy to talk to him. The White House phone log confirms his call, just as it shows that Dr. Nancy Schmidt was visiting you at the same time. Perhaps he intended to inform you of his plans for the next day, but I guess we'll never know."

Mortuary stillness engulfed the oval office. The president, staring at the soothing alabaster oval ceiling, was fuming on the inside, but he had to control his anger for once, as he knew that his aroused vice president was right and had to be placated, or at least not attacked again.

"Mr. President," Hayden gratefully broke the embarrassing silence. "I agree that we must get at the facts as we know them today. Most of what we know is from the recording that Colonel Gibson made of Gleason's and Azee's final conversation on the Flying Mole. I'm sure that our knowledge will grow from day-to-day, but here are the essential facts. First: Gleason is in Tripoli. We don't know if he's dead or alive. He has AIDS. Second: Our CIA F16 and Pilot Colonel Gibson are safe in Sicily. Third: Colonel Gibson did not violate Libyan airspace. Fourth: the Flying Mole is in a Tripoli hanger with a hidden transponder in place. Fifth: the Flying Mole's pilots are in Tripoli, condition and location unknown. Sixth: we have Azee's recorded confession as the mastermind of the Detroit bombings. Seventh: Azee implicated Iraqis, Quebec and Irish terrorists as co-perpetrators. Eighth: Azee and the Russian Andre are trying to sell Russian nuclear material to Iraq. Ninth: Gleason only pretended to partner with Azee for the ten million dollar presidential killing fee to get Azee's confession. Finally, Azee voluntarily evacuated his plane over the mid-Atlantic and is presumed dead. Obviously, not all of these facts should be released to the press. Probably only the first three should be in the initial press release."

"Thank you, Hayden, for this concise summary," the somewhat placated president responded. "I'll work with the press secretary on a press release that doesn't reveal too much. We have to notify the Pentagon to put them on increased military alert. Qadafi will try to maximize the embarrassment of the United States. The main questions I have pertain to the first and last items. What's this with Gleason having AIDS and why can't we be sure that Azee is dead?"

"Since I sign Gleason's paycheck let me try to answer the first item," the previously reticent Jameson jumped in. "This is painful for me to discuss, so please bear with me," Jameson began with a halting voice. "He contracted AIDS from a prostitute in Detroit, whom he later discovered was associated with Azee. He was in Detroit for the Thirty Day Prior meeting, coordinating all the various agencies for the ill-fated Detroit campaign stop. Knowing Gleason, the fact that he has an AIDS death sentence emboldened him to go on this suicidal mission to personally bring down Azee, thus sparing the country the turmoil and uncertainty of a protracted trial."

"All in this room know that I love Gleason as a brother and as a surrogate father to my sons. That being said, what he's done is wrong, and he has left the country and my reelection campaign in a real pinch. What about the final item that we can't be sure if Azee is dead?"

Jameson was happy to have the CIA Director back on the hot seat. "Sir, here's what we have been able to piece together of Azee's final minutes before he bailed out of what he thought was a doomed airplane. He donned a custom made Kevlar survival suit with integral flotation and a built in transponder. The pilots sent an SOS to all nearby Libyan flagged freighters in the shipping lanes below. Azee put what he believed to be the remote detonator for Gleason's stowed bomb in his jump suit's breast pocket. He shoved his survival raft out of the trap door and Colonel Gibson destroyed it with a burst of cannon fire. Azee then bailed out, pushing the remote detonator to blow up the departing Flying Mole. Colonel Gibson saw a small report flash from the detonator on Azee's person, but he wasn't positioned to destroy Azee's parachute. Circling and finding the parachuting Azee in the cloud cover would be iffy and time consuming and he didn't want to let the Flying Mole escape with Gleason aboard. There were three foot waves in the Atlantic. We can't verify if Azee is dead or alive."

The president reluctantly informed the three still uncomfortable participants that Azee was a former Navy SEAL and always prided himself on being in the same fighting shape as his service days. "How much explosive was in the detonator and who made his Kevlar survival suit?"

"Our explosive technicians were limited in how much bang they could put in a small garage door opener detonator. However, they assured me that it would be strong enough to seriously maim or possibly kill the person holding it. His Kevlar survival suit obviously was made to fit his short stature. We are contacting every firm that could make such a suit to find out how many layers of Kevlar would be over his chest area and how much blast protection that would provide."

Everyone was pondering the possibility that Azee could have survived in spite of the usually lethal CIA and Gleason's best laid plans. No one wanted to verbalize this nightmare scenario.

The vice president let his mind drift back to the serious problem of Gleason's AIDS. Gleason's ex-wife, Cindy, would be devastated to learn of his indiscretion and resultant AIDS, especially in view of their renewing friendship. However, a greater problem sailed right over the president's head: the two units of blood that Gleason gave to the president for his surgery in Detroit. The vice president wasn't about to throw that personal presidential problem into the current boiling cauldron of political and international turmoil they were considering. *Dr. Schmidt can earn her pay by explaining this to the president*, he thought.

"Everyone stay close to their office and have no contact with the media," the president ordered as he struggled with his casted left arm to extricate himself from the oversized leather couch. "All publicity will come from the White House Press Secretary to minimize the collateral damage of too many agencies talking. Any questions?"

The three participants could not leave the oval office fast enough. They knew the president temporarily spared them the forty lashes they deserved for not informing him of this rogue mission that could bring down his presidency.

VII

Gleason regained consciousness during the bouncy ambulance ride from the airport to the hospital in squalid downtown Tripoli. His last memory was of disembarking from the Flying Mole inside the dimly lit hangar and being greeted by a short attractive woman named Afshaa. His retrograde amnesia worked its welcomed miracle erasing the memories of that meaningless interrogation and unnecessary beating administered by the diabolical Afshaa. He knew that something bad must have happened because he had a pounding headache and he could feel swelling on both sides of his skull under the bilateral ice packs held in place by a tight elastic wrap. He could also feel ankle cuffs securing him to a stretcher. The absurdity of the ankle cuffs brought a painful smile to the corners of his mouth as he certainly wasn't going to jump out of the moving ambulance and escape.

When the ambulance slowed to turn into a driveway he read the name, Al-Afia, on the side of a very contemporary building. He was relieved that it didn't appear to be a jail with bars on the windows. As the ambulance backed into a ramp to unload its soon to be internationally famous patient, he could see armed guards and green scrub suited medical personnel through the ambulance's narrow windows.

The first person to enter the ambulance's open back doors was an armed guard who roughly slapped on handcuffs. *They must think that I'm somebody really important,* Gleason thought as the metal cuffs clinked around the stainless steel rails of his litter. A white sheet was pulled over his face, like he was already dead, before he was wheeled out of the ambulance. When the sheet was pulled down, he scanned the sterile confines of his emergency treatment room and was surprised to see a wide array of modern medical equipment lining the walls. An armed guard was in each corner of the room.

A masked, gloved and fully gowned person, whom he assumed was a doctor, led an entourage into the room carrying a clip board with the beginnings of a medical chart. "Hello. My name is Dr. Rahmat. You had a bad fall. You were unconscious when they put you in the ambulance so you probably have a concussion with a brain bleed. Very serious problem. We need to take x-rays to see if you fractured your skull."

Gleason was struggling to understand this heavily accented preamble to what he knew was going to develop into his nightmare of nightmares. "No doctor, I didn't fall. I think that I was knocked out by a woman cop."

"Don't talk. I need to check you," the doctor ordered as he was un-wrapping the ice packs. "Bad swelling on each side of the head from the fall," the doctor said as he pointed to the notes from the ambulance driver.

Being shown the notes meant nothing to Gleason as they were written in Arabic, so he again tried to set the record straight by saying, "I didn't fall. I was..."

"Stop talking. I need to listen to your heart before you go for x-rays. We'll keep you in the hospital for observation of a possible brain bleed."

I'll settle for a few days in the hospital versus jail, Gleason fantasized, as his litter was being wheeled down the hall to the x-ray department. He knew that a best case scenario of a prolonged hospital stay was not going to happen even in the nirvana world of perfect dreams.

. . . .

With their police escort of flashing strobe lights and blasting sirens, pilots Taajud-Deen and Abdul quickly traversed the thirty-five miles from the airport to the downtown governmental office complex that was home to the Libyan internal security office for their debriefing.

The pilots felt momentary relief entering a conference room and seeing at the head of the table the coolly efficient greeter at the airport hangar, Afshaa. To their surprise she was not asked nor did she ask any questions. Two nameless and nearly faceless bureaucrats, behind their dark sun glasses, led the discussion. The pilots were told to give a verbal narrative of their flight from take-off in Annapolis to their landing in Tripoli. They were interrupted and asked for more details and clarification concerning Azee's exit from the Flying Mole. Taajud-Deen felt that these desk detectives wanted all the details of Azee's bailout to bolster their preconceived opinion that no one could survive such a foolhardy jump. *They don't know Azee*, Taajud-Deen thought.

The debriefing concluded with Taajud-Deen asking the bureaucrats to notify Colonel Qadafi of his good friend Azee's serious plight and requesting any help that the Libyan government could give in finding and rescuing him. The Colonel would know that they were staying at the Corinthia Hotel and could contact them there.

VIII

Every day Dr. Schmidt had a late afternoon consultation scheduled with the president concerning the first lady and the newborn first baby. Since the baby was now at the White House in a specially equipped neonatal nursery with round-the-clock nursing care she wasn't primarily responsible for the baby like she was for the first lady at the hospital.

Whenever she could, she tried to placate the president with a phone consultation, but there were times when he insisted that she come to the White House for dinner, usually just the two of them, although she always tried to include Jason and Eric to minimize the president's appetite for more than the food on the table. All her training as a psychiatrist was called upon when she visited the White House to deal with the president's loneliness and the boys' increasingly dysfunctional behavior because of the absence of their mother, their main caregiver and pillar of loving support.

The president's secretary had left Dr. Schmidt a curt phone message that she must come to the White House tonight and be sure to bring the first lady's latest test results, which she recognized as a thinly disguised excuse for tonight's meeting. This summons sounded like a direct order from her commander-in-chief, so she felt that she had better not beg off tonight like she usually tried to do.

Since she was a frequent visitor to the White House and had the proper color and numbered bumper sticker on her spiffy red Mustang convertible, the young Marine guard gave her a crisp salute and opened the heavy cast iron gate into the White House VIP parking lot. Once through the gate she looked into her rear view mirror and was delighted to notice the young Marine guard crack a smile. *Boys will always be boys when they see a pretty girl in a hot car*, she thought. She surmised that the guard house notified the inside security desk of her arrival because she was always greeted at the visitor's side entrance and escorted to wherever the president wanted to meet her.

She dreaded the day when she would be escorted directly to the presidential bedroom and she would have to use all her guile to preserve what little was left of her dignity. Today she was escorted into the oval office and directed to a corner sofa while the president, whom she was instructed to call Archie, short for his hated given name of Archibald, continued to talk on the phone. After a few moments he closed a thick folder that he'd been studying and greeted her, "Didn't mean to be rude and ignore you, Nan, but I have a big problem. I mean all of us, the whole country, has a problem! I need a drink! Can I fix you something?" he offered, turning to the mini bar concealed in the ornate credenza behind his massive desk. "You sure get the young bucks at the guard shack excited when you drive up in your hot car. Your code name when they notify the inside desk is *the red convert*. 'The red convert is here,' is the way they put it."

"Thanks for offering, Archie, but I'm the officer of the day for after hours hospital problems, in addition to monitoring the first lady around the clock, so I need to keep a clear head. You go right ahead as you look like you need a good stiff one. By the way, the young bucks at the guard house keep asking for a ride in the red convert. I tell them that they'll have to clear it with you."

"Fat chance I'll do that! Some night we'll have to sneak out of the White House and take a little spin. By the way, it's ridiculous, Nan, that you have to stand call for officer of the day at the hospital. I'll call the admiral at the hospital to get you relieved of this. How often does your turn come up?"

"It comes around only one day every two weeks, so it's not so bad. I wish you wouldn't call the admiral. Everyone at Bethesda thinks that I have it pretty soft already with only one patient and, of course, they're jealous of my White House access."

"I guess you're right, at least for now. That's a small problem compared to what the press secretary is going to announce shortly," the president said, as he handed her the copy of the PDB with Gleason's and Azee's pictures on it and the terse CIA analysis of Gleason's serious predicament.

"Oh my God!" The startled president jumped out of his chair at Nancy's scream. Her soft sob, as if having trouble catching her breath, soon escalated into a bone wrenching, chair shaking grand mal seizure.

The alarmed president put his hands on her shoulders, more to keep her from falling out of her chair than as a comforting gesture. "Don't worry, Nan, everything will work out. Gleason will be okay."

"It's not Gleason. It's him!"

"What do you mean, 'it's him?' Gleason is my only concern. Azee's a lost cause whether he survived his jump or not. The CIA has my unconditional approval to appropriately handle Azee if and when he's ever found. You have my solemn word on that."

"That's great, but can I have a piece of him before the CIA?"

"You know Azee? He's the one I was referring to when I asked you at the hospital if Kathy had any un-logged visitors."

"He sure as hell never visited the first lady. However, I met him under the guise of a serious national security problem. Posing as an internal affairs CIA agent, he ordered me to meet him in the presidential suite at the Watergate Hotel."

"So, what happened? Did he get fresh with you?"

"I wish he had. That would have been easier to handle than what went down," she softly replied, as she continued sobbing.

"We don't have to talk about this now, or ever, if you don't want to. I have to get ready for the big announcement of Gleason's capture and you still need to update me on Kathy."

"I'll be brief since you have bigger problems. Twenty years ago, I was romantically involved with a junior Russian diplomat who later was determined to be a spy. Azee had incriminating photos of Andre and me that he was using to blackmail me to postpone your physical."

"I don't have time now to get into all his threats and the photos. I'll call the real CIA and have them debrief you. Details could be important for their investigations of the bombings and making the case against Azee. Why did he want you to postpone my physical? That bastard was always sticking his nose into mine and Kathy's life."

"He didn't give a reason for the postponement. I got the distinct impression that I was toast if I didn't cooperate with him."

"Don't worry. He's now the one floating like a piece of soggy toast in the middle of the Atlantic. You can stay at the White House if that'll make you feel more secure. We have plenty of room."

The veiled shack-up invitation from the president was the reality check that she needed. "Thanks, Archie. Now that I know who threatened me I'll be alright. I wish that I could say the same for the first lady. Fortunately, the C-section delivery of the baby didn't harm Kathy as no anesthesia was used. She only needed two units of blood, which of course were double screened for any possible problems such as AIDS or hepatitis. She has enough problems without running the risk of contracting these. We still draw blood daily to monitor her blood chemistries for any changes."

"She's getting the best possible care. Even though I received two units of blood from Gleason, I'm sure that they didn't have the time to test them as you mentioned."

"Kathy's end is near, whether we pull the plug or not. You could pick a date to remove her life support. It's never going to be easy."

"You're right on selecting a date. We'll see how this situation with Gleason plays out. We'll use Kathy's death as a diversion from any bad press that develops because of Gleason's ill-fated solution of the bombings."

IX

Gleason was pleasantly surprised that he hadn't been subjected to another beating or interrogation at the hospital. He was being treated more as a patient than as a prisoner except for the constant ankle and wrist cuffs to the bed or chair that allowed him to move only one leg and arm in a search for comfort.

Once his head swelling decreased a photographer came to his room with a fingerprint technician to perform what he would refer to as *booking procedures*. Multiple photographs were taken, both in his hospital room and outside in a lush hospital courtyard, wearing an unwashed brightly colored flowered shirt that he hoped hadn't been worn by too many other prisoner patients. He knew that the tropical photos were for propaganda purposes to show that he was well treated.

He kept his left eye partially or completely closed in the photos as a covert sign that all was not as it seemed in the innocuous photos. The CIA had instructed its agents and other high ranking government personnel to do this as a simple code that harkened back to the Latin word for left, sinister, which in English still conveys the desired message that all is not okay.

Dr. Rahmat appeared with his support staff and an ever bulging chart that Gleason thought could not be all medically related.

He was apparently the only English speaking member of the medical team taking care of him. The doctor repeated all his dialogue with Gleason in Arabic for the rest of the entourage. "Your head seems to be getting better, with no more brain bleeding that we can detect. We always worry about a subdural hematoma for the first few hours and days after severe head trauma. Do you have any dizziness or blurred vision?"

"Everything's okay with my head. No headache after the first day. However, my knees are still sore from the fall," Gleason said, with an Irish twinkle in his eyes.

Rahmat lifted Gleason's gown and gently palpated each knee. "They seem fine," he said, smiling from ear to ear.

At least he has a sense of humor, Gleason thought. It really mattered little at this stage of the game. Indeed it was a game, whether he was beaten or fell down the airplane's stairs. What was important was that Rahmat knew that even though they were playing this game with international repercussions, good patient care would not be compromised. "Any problems with my blood tests, like my cholesterol level?" Gleason asked, as if his cholesterol numbers made any difference in the reality of his present dire situation.

Rahmat moved closer to the head of the bed while nervously flipping through the chart looking for something. "Cholesterol, no problem, but we have an unexpected result in another area. Very serious."

He noticed that Rahmat had stopped translating into Arabic and was barely speaking above a whisper. Gleason tried to steel himself for what he knew was coming.

"The blood tests show that you have AIDS. We can repeat the tests to be sure there's no mistake. Do you know this?"

The patient rested his head on the pillow for a brief moment before nodding his acknowledgement. "That's why I did what I did on the airplane with Azee. I have nothing to lose."

"We have a high incidence of AIDS in Libya among the prostitutes and the poor, so we have much experience treating it. The medicines are very expensive and in short supply here. However, I'm sure Colonel Qadafi will insist on treating you since you are his guest."

The mention of the word prostitute engulfed Gleason in a flashback of draconian proportions. His one night stand, more correctly a thirty minute fling, with the beautiful casino hostess from Windsor, somehow associated with Azee, was the dumbest moment of his life. His emergency donation of two units of blood for the president's arm surgery thirty days later had elevated his personal folly to a national tragedy. Gleason realized that his very private disease was going to become public knowledge in the high stakes poker game that was probably already going on between the United States and Libya. He felt remorse that the president and his ex-wife, Cindy, were not going to learn of his AIDS firsthand from him, to say nothing of the president being told of his own possible AIDS.

"Unlike in the United States, AIDS is on the decrease in Libya. Do you know why?"

"Don't have a clue. Just for the record, I contracted it from a Canadian woman."

"Country wide we are using the ABC program we got for the U.S: Abstain. Be faithful. Condoms."

"Guess I should have known my ABC's. However, having AIDS empowered me to take on Azee, so it's not all bad."

"Who's this Azee? All the hospitals in Tripoli are on high alert, which only happens when an attack is imminent or someone very important is arriving. We were told to expect a severely injured patient transported from an ocean freighter via helicopter. Could this be your friend, Azee, who jumped from his airplane?"

Gleason was speechless. He turned as white as his bed sheets at the doctor's suggestion that Azee is alive. *My nightmare will get worse, if such a thing is possible*, he thought. He felt a dismal failure for botching the one job that he needed to do well.

Rahmat, noticing Gleason's change to a pale white appearance, abruptly ordered, "Take his blood pressure stat!" While waiting for the blood pressure cuff to be put on, color started returning to Gleason's face. Rahmat quickly countermanded his previous order, "Skip the BP. Take it later with his other vitals."

"Are you going to be Azee's doctor, too?" Gleason was barely able to ask.

"I'll probably be assigned to both of you by Colonel Qadafi since I'm the only European trained, board certified, ER doctor in Tripoli. You're recovering quickly from your fall and you won't be requiring much care, except for the AIDS. I'll talk to the colonel to see if he wants me to treat your AIDS. It's possible that doctors from Europe could be imported to take care of this arriving VIP, who has very serious injuries according to our radio reports."

"Why don't they lock me up in jail if I won't need hospital treatment?"

"In case you haven't noticed, you are locked up. You're just wearing a gown with a hole in the back, instead of striped pants and shirt."

"I kind of get that feeling with the wrist and ankle cuffs. It's not that bad as long as I have an arm and a leg free."

Rahmat moved within inches of Gleason's head as if checking the swelling. "I'll keep you here as long as I can. Libyan prisons are hell. Remember me when you get back to the U.S."

Gleason gave an understanding wink of his right eye to the doctor as he backed away from the bed, while at the same time reserving the right to remain skeptical of the true intentions of his ingratiating remarks. After all, his boss was the unpredictable Qadafi, an avowed enemy of the United States.

X

The press secretary read a prepared statement to the clamoring news room that a Secret Service agent, on a mission to catch the mastermind of the Detroit bombings, was being held captive in Libya by Colonel Qadafi. The president scheduled another meeting with Vice President Hubert Taylor, Secretary of Treasury Bart Jameson and CIA director Elliot Hayden. The Chairman of the Joint Chiefs of Staff, five star general Mitchell Jackson and FBI director James Fairborn were also included. These two additions, especially JCS chairman General Jackson, reflected the growing seriousness of the international crisis, where a military option would be a definite consideration if Colonel Qadafi started rattling his scimitar rather than negotiating a settlement.

Hayden requested the emergency meeting to share the latest developments that his agents on the ground in Tripoli had unearthed. He was always amazed that the old adage, *money talks*, was still one of the pillars of the intelligence business. *The poorer the country, the louder money talks*, was the CIA's mantra for their successful sleuth business. In Tripoli's hospitals the below subsistence level pay for housekeeping and maintenance jobs provided fertile ground for CIA money to grow information. The true talent of any local CIA operative was not the random distribution of U.S. taxpayers' dollars, but the ferreting of the facts from the fiction from these overeager informants.

CIA Director Hayden had a good news, bad news dilemma that he needed to bring to the meeting. The good news was really an update from reliable hospital sources that Gleason was resting comfortably in the hospital without any apparent serious injuries from the unplanned, but routine, landing of the Flying Mole in Tripoli. However, the oval office became hushed when Hayden reported the bad news of Gleason's probable AIDS. The diverse, highly intelligent group in the oval office could only be stalled off for so long by CIA double talk and obfuscation.

Finally, the president, having been subjected to many a CIA run-around, demanded to know if the hospital in Tripoli had done reliable blood tests that reconfirmed Gleason's AIDS. Hayden recognized the need for a direct answer to his boss so he quietly confessed, "His blood tests in Tripoli reconfirm that he has AIDS."

The stunned silence was awkwardly broken by the president, "Are they treating his AIDS over there?"

"Our hospital spies say no treatment yet. AIDS takes at least thirty-days to show up in a blood test after the initial exposure." Hayden was aware of Gleason's blood donation to the president at the time of his arm surgery, so he closely watched the president's body language that would betray his successfully connecting the medical dots between Gleason's blood and his own. Not seeing any telltale signs of the president making this potentially fatal connection and after the room reached the unpleasant consensus that they were powerless to help Gleason until he got back home, they broke into idle chit chat, assuming that the business portion of the meeting was over.

Reluctantly, Hayden rhetorically asked if the group still had the stomach for the worst, most surprising news of the day as he passed around copies of today's PDB with a picture of Azee.

"Do we have a choice?" the president needlessly asked, while everyone silently read their copy. The president looked up, disgustedly shaking his head in disbelief. The PDB succinctly stated that Azee had been picked up at sea by a Libyan freighter that was in the immediate area of his bailout from the Flying Mole. His jet had put out an SOS with the exact coordinates of his bailout and the frequency of the emergency transponder built into Azee's survival suit. The odds of this perfect rescue scenario in the middle of the Atlantic Ocean were miniscule, but the PDB gave a one hundred percent level of certitude that Azee was alive.

However, the PDB went on to equivocate on the type and severity of his injuries. A CIA planted maintenance worker, buffing the hospital floor, observed Azee being moved in the emergency room. The only visible injury was one arm in a sling with the hand wrapped in a large bandage. Colonel Qadafi had issued a total information blackout on both Azee and Gleason under the threat of immediate firing squad death for anyone leaking information. Everyone knew that this threat was real, so the CIA had to spend more money to get credible information from those willing to take this risk of certain death.

The president led the roundtable discussion on Azee's situation with the same inconclusive conclusions that there wasn't much that could be done until an international political solution started to rear its serpentine head. The United States had no extradition treaty with Libya, or with most of the other Arab countries for that matter, including Lebanon, so the chance of Azee being voluntarily returned to the United States to face trial for his admitted crimes was practically zero. Hayden assured everyone that this was not a problem since his agents could and would be able to get to Azee anywhere in the world whenever the president gave the word. Like in the days of the old west, Azee's return, whether dead or alive, mattered little to the CIA cowboys on the ground.

General Jackson asked for and received permission to station a naval battle force from Sigonella, Sicily, including a nuclear armed aircraft carrier, in international waters off Libya. The naval forces would make no incursions into Libyan air or water space unless provoked by hostile Libyan action, which our vastly superior naval force would welcome as justification for annihilating the* weaker attacking forces.

The discussion on Azee opened the door for FBI director James
Fairborn to give an update on the ongoing bombing investigations
in Detroit and Windsor. The perpetrators of the bombings were
professionals, so very little hard evidence had been found at the
three sites in Detroit. Fairborn began by praising the organiza-
tion skills of the mastermind who could coordinate these three
nearly simultaneous bombings that tore apart the very fabric of
our peace-loving society.

The president abruptly cut short this laudatory line of reasoning by reminding Fairborn that the first lady was comatose on her
death bed, he had a severely fractured arm and the Ambassador
Bridge between Detroit and Windsor was damaged. He insisted
that Azee be dealt with as a hated, villainous traitor, not as a genius
mastermind of the worst attack on America since Pearl Harbor.

Fairborn mentioned that Gleason's and Azee's airborne conversation, captured by Colonel Gibson in his surveillance jet, was
strong evidence and they could wrap up their preliminary investigations in a day or two. Also, the Flying Mole made incriminating
stops when Azee left the country after the bombings, heading to
Beirut for a two week holiday with his wife and children. Hayden
suggested that they might be able to procure the Flying Mole's log
book from the cockpit of the grounded plane in Tripoli. Skepticism
about the veracity of the plane's log book was expressed by most
until Fairborn mentioned that the intact log book on the destroyed
Aqua Mole yacht appeared to accurately represent the travel and
guest history of the yacht over the past two years. Azee was fanatical about documenting everything, oftentimes in a crude classically
based code, so there is a good chance that the airplane log book
would corroborate their other findings. Hayden was authorized to
procure the Flying Mole's log book by any means necessary, short
of creating another international crisis on top of the current fiasco.

Fairborn continued his investigation update with the first
Detroit bombing, the explosion of the van on the center span of the
Ambassador Bridge downriver from the docked Aqua Mole. He
commented that this incident seemed to serve no useful purpose

and was a calculated risk for the terrorists because if the timing were not perfect and it went off too soon, the first lady's party would have had time to take shelter before the bomb in the dockside limousine was detonated.

The FBI, working with American and Canadian customs and immigration officials, identified the vehicle that picked up the driver of the destroyed van as it exited the bridge on the Canadian side. This was a laborious process of eliminating one vehicle at a time with license plates checks of the exiting vehicles captured on the bridge's video cameras. A big break came when a car that matched one of the bridge's still unidentified vehicles was found abandoned in the Windsor airport parking lot. The car was stolen in Detroit and was clean of any evidence except for one thumbprint on the parking ticket that the bombers carelessly left in the car confirming their entry into the lot a few minutes after the bombing. Passenger lists of all departing commercial flights and private planes from the Windsor airport were being analyzed.

"Good work, Fairborn. However, we don't know if identifying the bridge bombers will lead us to the actual perpetrators of the other two bombings so don't divert too much attention to it. What do we know from the investigations of the other bombings?"

"Mr. President," Elliott jumped in, "at our next meeting I'll have transcripts of Gleason's and Azee's conversations on the Flying Mole before Azee bailed out. We'll also try to reconstruct the unrecorded events that took place inside the cockpit. This process always takes longer than it should because we need to recover and enhance every word of their conversation due to excessive background engine noise. The recorded pilot communications are also proving to be difficult to translate into English. I'll bring all this to our next meeting," Elliott concluded, trying to reestablish the primacy of the CIA in another inside the beltway turf war.

"Let's hold the rest of the information on the other bombings until tomorrow's meeting. I need to feed and change the baby." The smiling president used the fallacious, but totally unassailable, baby excuse to terminate the meeting that required many more meetings.

XI

Gleason was awakened from his nap by the unmistakable sound of an incoming helicopter. Since his head had been covered by a sheet for his unceremonious admission to the hospital's ER, he didn't notice a helipad for medevac flights. His guards took turns going out into the hall, only to return and share their information in Arabic, which was of no use to Gleason. He could only guess at what they were saying to each other, but it must have been very important as the hall became a beehive of activity.

Dr. Rahmat examined an exhausted Azee and ordered x-rays and a battery of blood tests. Azee was surrounded by loyal and highly trained guards from Colonel Qadafi's personal protective force when he was transported from his ER admitting room to a corner hospital suite reserved for Colonel Quadafi and his VIP guests.

Compared to these skilled professionals, akin to the Secret Service, Gleason's security was more like the rent-a-cops at the county fair. This suited him just fine as he didn't feel endangered in the hospital confines and he didn't want hovering guards monitoring his every twitch and move.

Gleason kept the old black and white television tuned into the local Arabic speaking stations just to give his guards something to focus on beside him. CNN was not one of his channel options and the low budget local stations were not reporting his arrival, nor that of the recently landed helicopter, probably because of the Qadafi ordered news blackout. He had joked with his guards using hand gestures pointing to himself and the TV, asking that they alert him if the TV news reports were about him. At some point he knew that one of the pictures taken of him would be shown on the local TV news when his capture was being reported and the price of his release was being negotiated.

Rahmat presented Azee with his preliminary findings, with the preface that he was one lucky person whom Allah spared to live another day. Azee didn't know or care what role Allah or any other supreme being played in his survival. He trusted more in his own preparedness and the miracles of modern science that created the bomb-protecting Kevlar in his survival suit and the transponder that facilitated his quick rescue from the turbulent Atlantic. His multi-layered high tech Kevlar survival suit had blunted the lethal force of the garage door opener bomb in his breast pocket. His resultant broken ribs, though excruciatingly painful, had not penetrated or collapsed his lungs, otherwise he would not be alive to worry about his severely injured hand that had pushed the bomb's detonator button.

Rahmat showed him the x-rays of his mangled right hand and his aching chest. The broken ribs were difficult for the untrained eye to detect on the chest x-rays, but you didn't have to be a doctor to see the shattered fingers and metacarpal bones. Many of the small wrist bones were fractured and dislocated and probably had micro fractures too small to be detected on the x-rays. Looking down at his unwrapped, dangling appendages that once were functional fingers, Azee wondered aloud, "Am I going to lose the hand?"

Before answering, Rahmat did simple neurological needle sticks at multiple locations where he could find intact skin while observing for any pain response. The vascular and nervous systems in the severely traumatized hand had to be assessed accurately if there

were to be any chance of saving it, to say nothing about it returning to normal function. There was still some color in all the fingers even with much of the skin on the gripping side shredded or
blown away. Rahmat made the gross clinical assessment that the
blood supply, though compromised, was still present and could
hopefully support the surgical reconstruction necessary to save
Azee's hand.

Getting appropriate positive pain responses from most test sites
in this basic neurological needle test, he felt confident in saying,
"The prognosis for saving your hand is fifty-fifty, so that means
that we must pull out all stops to save it. As for the return to normal function, only time will tell. The neurological and vascular
systems are working even with the large amount of swelling present. The problem is that we don't have a qualified hand surgeon in
Tripoli to perform this delicate reconstructive surgery. We have..."

"No problem. I'll get on my airplane and be anywhere you
send me in a matter of hours and I'd like you to accompany me.
I'll pay you very handsomely."

"Thank you, Mr. Azee. I was starting to say that over the years
we have imported doctors from the best medical centers in Europe
to perform surgery on your friend, Colonel Qadafi, and other high
ranking officials. Our operating facilities here at the hospital are very
good. We just lack the best doctors to perform this delicate surgery."

"I'm sure you're right and I'm impressed by your expertise.
In the United States we're encouraged to get a second opinion. I
would still like to fly somewhere else to get that second opinion."

"Get me a telephone," a bruised ego Rahmat barked to an
attending nurse.

"Whom are you calling?"

"I'm getting your second opinion. I'm calling the Colonel."

In an instant Azee knew that he was in a no-win situation
both medically and politically. His friend, the Colonel, wouldn't
release him because of what he had perpetrated in the United
States. "You're right, Doctor. Let's do it here. My hands are in
your hands."

A relieved smile crossed Rahmat's face as he didn't want to make that phone call any more that Azee wanted it made. "One of my trauma rotations was at a hospital in Zurich. The best known hand surgeon in Europe was on the staff. We have stayed in touch and have worked together on a few cases, although nothing as severe as yours."

"How soon can he be here?"

"We need to wait at least forty-eight hours for the swelling to go down and we must put you on IV antibiotics to prevent an infection. I know the pre-surgical protocol that we need to follow for the best chance of a successful outcome. We have to clean and irrigate the open wounds and then use wet to dry dressings every four hours to minimize chances of infection. The fact that your wounded hand was essentially pickled in the clean waters of the Atlantic until your rescue by the Libyan freighter is in your favor. We also have to be on guard that the palm does not fold over and pinch off the blood supply to the fingers, making any reconstructive surgery impossible. Then amputation would be our only option. This forty-eight hour delay is medically necessary and it'll give the doctors time to clear their schedules and make their flight arrangements to come here."

"Flights aren't a problem. My plane can pick them up and bring them here."

"That will appeal to the doctors, flying non-stop in your jet to Tripoli versus the two or three airline connections needed on commercial flights."

"Doctors? Who else is needed besides the hand surgeon?"

"I should have mentioned that I'd feel better if we avoid general anesthesia with your broken ribs, so we'll need an anesthesiologist experienced in giving cervical nerve shots to block the nerves to the arm. The anesthesiologist and the surgeon will have to evaluate if your arm is strong enough to use a Bier block anesthesia procedure, which involves a tight tourniquet above your elbow that restricts the blood flow in your wrist and hand area so that the local anesthetic works better. In the cervical and

Bier block procedures anesthetic drugs, like your dentist uses to numb your teeth, are injected. We use mostly prilocaine anesthesia here and in Europe, whereas xylocaine is more commonly used in the United States. They'll want to bring the latest Zeiss surgical microscope and all the necessary wires, pins and screws for bone fixation. Finally, we need a thoracic surgeon to give a second opinion on your broken ribs just to be on the safe side. How big is your plane?"

"That's three doctors and their equipment. No problem. I usually only have luxury seating for two. However, we can carry eight passengers, which is what I need when my family flies back and forth to Lebanon. I appreciate your concern for getting me the best doctors."

"In spite of being viewed as a third world country by the western media, we take good care of our citizens with our limited resources. The colonel has ordered the hospital to spare no expense on you and our other American patient. Since the doctors are coming at your expense, they insist on being paid before they come. Will this be a problem?"

"Hardly. My insurance won't cover their fees, especially considering how I sustained the injuries." Azee asked if the colonel's elite guards could step out into the hall before he continued. "How would it be if I transferred five million U.S. dollars from one of my accounts in Zurich to a new medical account in your name and you handle all the specialists' fees and expenses. Anything left over stays in your name for your professional services rendered."

Azee detected a relieved sigh from Rahmat as he'd been uncomfortable dealing with the monetary aspect of his care. "That should be more than enough to cover everything. One final detail, I need your pilots to take copies of your medical records and x-rays to Zurich a day early so that the doctors can evaluate them for bringing any special supplies and instruments that they might need."

"They'll be coming later today and you can explain all the medical details of their flight to Zurich."

XII

When Dr. Schmidt saw the blinking light on her answering machine she assumed that the president had left a request for a personal update on the first lady's condition later at the White House. However, she was pleasantly surprised when she discovered that it was not another presidential summons. The message was from a woman named Cindy, who identified herself as Tom Gleason's ex-wife. She was requesting a meeting to discuss an unspecified medical issue. She racked her brain for any clue of what this issue could be as she returned the call and Cindy resisted any of Dr. Schmidt's subtle attempts to discover the true purpose of their meeting. Cindy wanted a neutral site for their get-together, but yielded to the doctor's busy medical schedule, agreeing to come right over to her office at the hospital.

After a phone call from the security desk in the hospital lobby getting clearance, Cindy was escorted to Dr. Schmidt's makeshift office near the presidential suite where the comatose first lady was being treated. Cindy did not recognize any of the young Secret Service personnel guarding the floor, and no one acknowledged her as Tom Gleason's ex-wife, even as she was being logged into the visitor's registry.

The meeting with Cindy provided Dr. Schmidt with a welcome

break from the tedium of the continuous monitoring of the first lady. The uncertainty surrounding the reason for the meeting made it even more interesting for her curious mind. As a psychiatrist, in addition to her hyperbaric oxygen therapy expertise, she was comfortable to let Cindy do the talking with minimal questions for clarification, and of course numerous head nods of understanding.

The public news of her ex-husband's captivity in Tripoli was upsetting to Cindy as she used many tissues from the box that Dr. Schmidt pushed across the table. Knowing Tom's great sense of personal loyalty to the president and his sense of indestructibility, she was not surprised that he undertook this secret mission to catch and punish the perpetrator of the Detroit bombings. Cindy recounted in great detail their last meeting at the Old Ebbitt Grill. At the time of their last conversation many things did not make sense and his written note, which she received the day he went AWOL, was equally ambiguous. She brought it to show Dr. Schmidt.

Dr. Schmidt mentioned that it should be given to the Secret Service or the CIA, even though it seemed to contain nothing unusual. Cindy agreed, but wanted to keep it as a last memento from Tom, as he had seldom sent her anything that arrived on time such as a birthday or anniversary card.

The note authorized her to remove any keepsakes from his condo from their years of marriage, or anything else that she wanted. Curious as to why he would make such a strange request, she visited his condo the day the note arrived. Getting out of her car she was immediately put on guard as his government car was pulled head first, not backed into the parking spot he always used for his personal car which had burned on the Bay Bridge. Inside she noticed that the condo was in a state of chaos totally out of keeping for the obsessive neatnik Gleason. The sewing needles, thread, metal zipper and buttons on the dining room table were a complete mystery, as she knew that he didn't have the patience to thread a needle, let alone actually sew anything. Confused and upset, she left without taking anything.

Still holding the note, Dr. Schmidt looked up at Cindy. "What's he mean by his P.S.? *I will explain the circumstances of my sickness if I see you again. I'm sorry.*"

By now Cindy was openly sobbing. "I don't know what illness he's referring to. He was healthy as far as I know. At our dinner the night before he disappeared he mentioned that he had blood drawn for what I assumed was his required yearly physical. You would know about that, wouldn't you?"

"The president has appointed me Chief White House Physician. Our medical office schedules all the required yearly physicals of the Secret Service agents assigned to the White House. We didn't order any blood tests for him."

"Returning from Detroit in the White House jet, he called to set up our dinner date for that evening. Could he have had blood tests done in Detroit? Don't you need a doctor's order to have blood work done?"

"That's the usual scenario but he could have gotten a doctor's order in Detroit." She didn't want to mention that in most big cities there are store front clinics where patients can be tested for hepatitis, AIDS, or sexually transmitted diseases. Just then she remembered that same morning, under great duress, she had given him a vial of the president's blood for testing, as he said, for top secret government reasons. He must have taken it to Detroit to be tested. "Are you okay?"

Cindy was about to repeat the question back to the visibly shaken doctor reaching across the table for a tissue for herself.

"I'm sorry, Cindy. I don't know what it is. I'm too young for hot flashes. Let me make you a copy of Tom's note. I'll give the original to the Secret Service with the understanding that you get it back after they run the needed tests." They exchanged cell phone numbers, planning to stay in touch.

Schmidt stayed in her quiet office staring at Gleason's note, especially the P.S., hoping against hope that the worst case medical scenario would not become reality. She made a copy for herself and another one she put in a sealed envelope marked, *Personal, The*

President, and gave it to a young Secret Service agent in the corridor, knowing that it would be on the president's desk as quickly as it could be driven from Bethesda to the White House. The original she put in an envelope labeled, *Personal, Bart Jameson*, which she would personally deliver to him, so he could get into the proper hands for the needed analysis. Then, for a switch, she called the White House requesting to see the president later today.

XIII

Dr. Rahmat made his late afternoon rounds visiting his two patients. All other emergency patients, regardless of their condition, were transferred to lesser trained doctors. He had made the necessary phone calls to Zurich arranging for the best European medical specialists to come to Tripoli. Azee's pilots were leaving with copies of his medical records and x-rays for the high powered specialists to review before packing their medical supplies. If everything met their approval, they would be in Tripoli within forty-eight hours. The specialists seemed especially pleased when Rahmat informed them that one half of their professional fees would be immediately transferred to their Swiss bank accounts and the other half, plus a sizable bonus, would be transferred after the surgery.

While doing Azee's admittance physical, Rahmat noticed something that troubled him along with the seriousness of the bomb injury. He asked the guards who were lingering near the door to please step outside so that he could talk privately with his patient. Azee gave a dismissive wave to the reluctant security people to reinforce the doctor's request. The doctor struggled how to broach the delicate subject with Azee. "Libya, as a third world country, still has many of the diseases that you have successfully eradicated in your country such as syphilis. I have seen and treated many active cases of syphilis."

"What are you getting at? Are you saying that I have syphilis? I have killed people for less than that." Azee strained to sit upright in his bed, giving the doctor an angry stare.

"Not exactly, but we need to talk about your teeth."

"I know. I must have broken off a back tooth when I jumped out of the plane. It had a crown on it and now the roots are sharp and cutting my tongue."

"I noticed that broken tooth. A dentist will fix it after your hand is taken care of. The teeth that I am concerned about are your other molar teeth. Their biting surfaces have many small round enamel bumps that make them resemble a plump mulberry and not the usual four or five tall sharp cusps. Thus, they are called mulberry molars. Also, your front incisors have groves in the biting edges. The third thing is that your forehead is rather prominent when looking at your face from the side."

"Big deal. I've always been this way. Didn't you do blood tests for syphilis?"

"Your blood test was negative for syphilis. Was your mother healthy her whole life?"

"She died in her late thirties. All that my dad ever said was that she died of a blood disorder. What's that have to do with me? It's not going to stop my surgery, is it?"

"These three things I mentioned are consistent with you having congenital syphilis, which means you were exposed to syphilis before you were born."

Azee wondered what other good news he would get. "You said my blood test for syphilis was negative, so my surgery will still go ahead, right? You know who I am and the power I have. Why didn't a doctor ever tell me this?"

"Most American doctors have never seen or treated a case of congenital syphilis in babies. I see it often. You must have been treated for it as a newborn as you have no other signs except these three anomalies that were formed before you were born. Mr. Azee,

I certainly know who you are. That's why I'm telling you about this syphilis issue. You have a right to know. I'm sorry to upset you."

After a long uncomfortable pause, Azee laid back on the bed. "Doctor, I respect you for not being afraid of me, for telling me the truth. Most of my friends and advisers aren't like that. What else should I know?"

"What we can say is that your mother had syphilis while she was pregnant that caused your triad of symptoms. Whether as a newborn baby you had syphilis, we can't say. I didn't mean to say bad things about your mother. However, this could be what caused her to die at such a young age."

"Now it's making sense why she always warned me not to mess with a girl until I was ready to be married because the costs were too high. Now I know what she meant."

After a few seconds of profound silence, Azee motioned for the guards to go completely into the hallway. He did not want them to know that he was betraying their confidence that they had told him about the other American that was a patient in the their hospital.

Rahmat wondered what deep, dark secret would spew from Azee as he called him closer to the bed, just inches from his whispering mouth. "I'll double the money in your Swiss bank account if your other patient has a fatal stroke or heart attack. Shouldn't be too hard, some kind of lethal injection."

"Mr. Azee! I would certainly need the colonel's permission to do that. My orders are to keep him alive as a bargaining chip in the international poker game that's going to allow you to safely leave Libya."

"Don't worry about the colonel. You probably aren't aware that my company keeps a Tripoli office in the basement of the air-conditioned Government Treasury Building, where my computers can stay cool. This office serves as our off-site computer back-up in case anything happens to the main computer in my Windsor office. These computers and my technicians are also the brains behind Libya's treasury and their money supply management. I know more about Libya's treasury operation than the colonel, although I'd never tell him that. I stop here monthly on my way to visit my family in Beirut. I've done some pretty interesting things for the colonel over the years. You might say that he owes me."

"I'd still need his permission, just as I did for your specialists to come from Switzerland. Not much happens here without first talking to him. I know that if something happens to my other patient, I'm all done as a doctor in Libya, maybe even dead like the patient. My main concern is you being treated by the best doctors from Europe."

By the time the shaken Rahmat visited his second patient, Gleason was restless and questioned the need for the constant ankle and wrist restraints, even though they were rotated daily from right to left and back again. "I'm told that you are a trained killer so we have to keep you shackled to the bed," Rahmat spoke loud enough for his entourage to hear. As he approached closer to remove the head bandages, a faint smile told Gleason that the doctor didn't believe his own words. Leaning close he whispered, "Not safe here. Must discharge you stat."

Gleason nodded. "How's the swelling, Doc? I'm feeling fine. No headaches or dizziness."

"That's good. Luckily, your fall wasn't too serious. I'm very busy with my other patient so I am discharging you to the custody of Qadafi's own security staff who will keep you healthy for your return to the states. Being discharged to a Libyan jail you wouldn't survive the first night."

"You mean I'm going to a five star resort."

"Not exactly five star, but at least you won't be eaten alive by rats or two legged monsters. Not everyone wants you alive. I'll arrange your immediate discharge."

"Will you continue taking care of me?"

"I've taken the Hippocratic Oath and I try to live up to its tenents of saving every patient's life, regardless of the politics. I'm sorry, but the results of your blood tests have made the local media, so the whole world will shortly know about your AIDS. The colonel isn't happy about this leak." Rahmat led his entourage out of the room. Gleason hoped that this wouldn't be the last time that he saw the ethical doctor struggling to save two disparate lives.

The CIA agents shadowing the pilots at the plush Corinthia hotel were relieved to follow them to the hospital as Azee had predicted. This provided a needed window of time for other agents to do their airport work of procuring the Flying Mole's log book. With the pilots at the hospital getting their orders from Azee and Rahmat, the CIA operatives were able to use their established contacts at the airport to gain access to the hangar where the Flying Mole was being held out of the spy satellite's view. The plane's log book was quickly discovered in the co-pilot's seat back pocket. Rather than remove the log book, they photographed each page as well as the interior of the aircraft. Not sure what other evidence they should be looking for, they did a perfunctory cabin search, hoping that something significant would jump out at them. They were unaware of the transponder that Gleason had wedged behind a fiberglass panel in the head, so they couldn't verify that it was still in place.

Azee used a lengthy departing embrace with his trusted pilot Taajud-Deen to quietly order him to make a coded radio/phone announcement once airborne. Taajud-Deen did not question his boss, as he knew that this was an urgent message that the recipient would understand and act upon.

XIV

Dr. Schmidt called ahead to make sure chief White House nurse, Monica Mason, would be available to meet before her scheduled time with the president. Monica was the nurse assigned to accompany the pregnant first lady on the tragic Detroit campaign stop. She had cradled the bleeding unconscious first lady against her white Navy uniform while awaiting the arrival of the medevac helicopters. The CIA and FBI had debriefed her numerous times about the explosion of the dockside Canadian limousine that had rocked the Aqua Mole, causing the first lady's head injury and coma.

Dr. Schmidt was hoping to learn more from her about the illness that Gleason had alluded to in his note to Cindy. Unfortunately, Monica was unable to shed any light on his medical condition.

However, she got her answer from the president's secretary when she was given a small packet labeled "*Libya*" to read until the president was free to see her. Two paragraphs were highlighted in yellow. The first on Gleason's AIDS had a large red question mark in the adjoining margin. The second on the survival of Azee had a bold red exclamation mark in its margin. She hardly had time to assimilate these two shockers, when the door to the oval office opened. She was seldom caught speechless as she just nodded to the president seated behind his cluttered desk.

"Any change in Kathy's condition?"

"There's certainly no improvement, at least that we can measure with lab tests. We are not doing daily blood draws anymore as the labs results are remaining unchanged and it is difficult to find good veins under her dry and friable skin. We have to guard against needle poke infections. We are still waiting for your word when this ordeal can be over." The president was too deep in thought to reply, so she changed the subject. "How's Melody doing? Are you getting any sleep?"

"She's doing fine. The White House nurses are proving to be excellent nannies. She and the boys are the only things that keep me going. Our CIA sources at the Tripoli hospital have confirmed Gleason's AIDS. Wait until our media gets ahold of this little tidbit. That bastard Azee surviving his jump is unbelievable! Where's the justice? I have a broken arm, just inches from being killed. The first lady is a vegetable, soon to die. He's alive! How many good people were killed in the explosions, leaving behind shattered families while the guilty party is resting in a hospital bed? I applaud Gleason for trying to take Azee out. It almost worked."

"You certainly have a lot on your mind and it's likely to get worse as you try to capture Azee and get Gleason out of Libya. Do you want some pills to help you sleep?"

"Thanks for your offer. However, like a good father, I want to hear Melody when she wakes up even though the nanny does the night bottles. I can't do newborn duties with just one hand. Mainly, I need to be alert twenty-four-seven with the Libyan situation changing by the minute."

"Everyone is worried about you. A new baby, a comatose wife, and two young sons would be enough for most people, and you still have the overwhelming responsibilities of your office."

"Well-intentioned people are treating me with more deference than usual, which I don't like. Now a little TLC from you, that's another matter—perhaps later."

She was relieved that the president postponed his standing invitation for a White House sleep over. "We'll talk tomorrow about the first lady and I'll do a little research on Gleason's AIDS."

XV

Gleason was securely cuffed, hands and feet, and blindfolded for the short bouncy van ride to his new detention site. After being strip-searched, he was given a change of clothes that any well-dressed Libyan would be proud to wear. The colorful attire would certainly allow him to blend in with the natives, if somehow he could escape his new confines. However, once in his cell he realized that an escape wasn't going to happen. He had one barred window the size of a shoebox that overlooked the well manicured courtyard of a Moroccan style villa. The heavy metal door with a slot for passage of a food tray told him that he certainly wasn't the first detainee to occupy these quarters. The metal bed, straight back chair and relatively modern indoor plumbing, alerted him that he had all the necessities for a long stay. He reasoned that the colonel would have nothing to gain by mistreating or torturing him. He'd done nothing to Libya, outside of being American. He was kidnapped by Azee's vengeful pilots and delivered unannounced to the Libyans. Still, he feared the all-reaching influence of Azee, who could bribe one of the guards to poison his food or arrange another pseudo-fall that would break his neck or fracture his skull.

His small window to the world allowed him to hear and see planes arriving and departing from a major airport that he assumed was where he had landed. He tried to distinguish the tail markings of the various airlines servicing Tripoli. Passing time, staring out the small window, he thought for sure that he saw the Flying Mole take off. He had no way of knowing that the Flying Mole was headed to Zurich to pick up the medical specialists who were going to treat Azee. Of course, he fantasized that Azee was aboard and was secretly escaping to some remote outpost beyond the reach of U. S. authorities. He was hoping that the transponder, if still hidden in the plane's bathroom, would allow the CIA to thwart this escape plan.

The Flying Mole had no problem getting clearance to take off from Tripoli with a flight plan destination of Zurich. Once airborne, it was picked up by the Naval Receiver Transmitter Facility at Niscemi, Italy near the naval base at Sigonella. A squadron of F16 jets scrambled to await orders from Washington. After NRTF's message that the Flying Mole was airborne was given to the National Security Council, an emergency conference call between FBI Director James Fairborn, Joint Chief of Staff Chairman Mitchell Jackson, CIA Director Elliott Hayden, and the president, was quickly patched together. All options were considered while Hayden awaited a report from his agents in Tripoli on the Flying Mole's surprise departure and, more importantly, who was aboard.

The president and the CIA did not want the trailing F16's to shoot down the Flying Mole as long as it stayed on its flight plan to Zurich. Hayden reassured the president that the plane and its occupants would be under close surveillance from the moment it landed in Zurich. They all expressed a curiosity about why it was headed to Zurich. The president broke the tension by opining that Azee was going to Switzerland to pick up a couple billion dollars cash for pocket money while on the run.

The Flying Mole radio communications were being monitored and recorded with the problem that many of the transmissions were again in Arabic. The meaning of the one transmission that was readily understood as the first and last letters of the Greek alphabet, *alpha* and *omega*, remained baffling to the interpreters at Langley. Instantaneous translations and continuous location updates were being provided on open lines to all the involved agencies as the Flying Mole followed its flight plan to Zurich. There was a collective sigh of relief when the Flying Mole touched down in Zurich and taxied to the fixed base operation's hangar. As expected, the Swiss government was proving to be easier to deal with than Libya. CIA agents and Swiss gendarmes, disguised in dark blue work coveralls, appeared ready to service the arriving jet as it came to a stop. Shortly the plane's door opened and the compact stairway folded down. The pilots casually descended, each carrying an over-night bag. They were directed to an inside service counter to complete their temporary visa applications, present their passports and have their luggage inspected. Even though they answered two as to the number of people arriving, the plane was closely monitored until the pilots left for their hotel.

A joint team of Swiss and U.S. agents, with guns drawn, cautiously ascended the narrow steps into the small plane. A delayed shout of, "all clear!" from inside the plane allowed everyone in Zurich and Washington to breathe a little easier, but still wonder what was going on with the ever devious Azee. The review of the pilots' temporary visa applications gave a little hint. The purpose of the visit was answered as medical consultation and length of visit was twenty-four hours.

The president was starting to thank everyone on the conference call when Hayden interrupted with an urgent message from the Windsor office of the Royal Canadian Mounted Police. The RCMP had Azee's Global Construction Technology office under surveillance as the scenario in Tripoli was unfolding. Their initial report indicated that an explosion had ignited a fire that was engulfing the GCT office building. Basement walls collapsed from the initial explosion and certainly there would be the loss of life of GCT's employees working at the time.

The conference call continued without much additional

information to share. Fairborn was instructed to put FBI agents from the Detroit office immediately on the scene of the Windsor explosion to work closely with the Canadian authorities.

The group was at a loss to explain why anyone would risk blowing up Azee's office building when he seemed to be neutralized in the hospital in Tripoli. The president expressed the opinion, based on years of simmering disdain for Azee, that he was sure Azee was behind this bombing of his own building. He felt that it was more than coincidental that the explosion occurred shortly after the radio transmissions from the Flying Mole. He wanted every word of these transmissions scrutinized for any possible clue. Hayden mentioned that the one obviously suspicious message, *Alpha-omega* was given like a SOS message across open airwaves. Anyone could have received it, so it was not traceable to any one recipient.

Fairborn asked everyone on the conference call to hold for a minute while he received additional information coming in on another line from his Detroit office. Momentarily, he came back to the conference call almost breathless. "Wow! You'll never guess what else is happening."

"With Azee, anything is possible," the president chimed in.

"The rural township fire department, where Azee has his large estate, has issued an all points alert asking for help in controlling a large fire. The surrounding grassy marsh land and the large castle-like house are ablaze. They can't get at the house fire because it is on an island surrounded by a moat. The connecting drawbridge is destroyed so they are using boats to get across the moat which is too deep to wade. It will probably be a total loss by the time they are able to get water hoses to the house fire."

"It's pretty obvious that some pyromaniac is trying to destroy evidence! One guess who?" Hayden needlessly asked.

The president answered the rhetorical question with a quiet reflection. "Kathy saw Azee's estate in the final stages of construction. She said it was over the top, typical Azee. Maybe Azee's telling us by destroying his office and his house that he's not returning.

Let's change those plans and get his sick ass back here to sit in the electric chair."

"I'll get another crew out to the estate fire to learn what they can," Fairborn interjected, "and I'll keep you updated on both sites."

The president thanked everyone on the conference call and closed with the angry logic that, "the more shit that continues to happen, the more reasons we'll have to fry Azee."

XVI

The CIA and Swiss authorities had the pilots, Taajud-Deen and Abdul, covered like the proverbial blanket from their touch down in Zurich. Their hotel suite was bugged and they were discreetly followed into the hospitals and doctors' offices that Dr. Rahmat had arranged. While the pilots were thus preoccupied, two bugs were put in the Flying Mole: one in the cockpit and another in the passenger area. Since the transponder that Gleason had hidden in the head was still functioning, the Flying Mole would remain under close scrutiny.

The pilots did nothing suspicious during their short stay in Zurich. Being long term employees of Azee, they were used to playing things close to the vest like their boss. However, the CIA was able to add a new name to their watch list when Taajud-Deen phoned Shakoor at Temenos, Azee's fortified sea side villa in Beirut. Shakoor offered to put Azee's wife, Hasnaa, on the phone, but Taajud-Deen declined, saying that he'd have Azee call her when they returned to Tripoli. The pilot asked Shakoor if Azee's important message came through and Shakoor replied that they should watch CNN. It was of special interest to the CIA when Taajud-Deen closed by saying that Azee was planning to return home to Temenos to recuperate from his planned hand surgery.

After the CIA learned the names of the doctors going to Tripoli, extensive background checks were run. None of the three doctors appeared to have any terrorist connections. Assuredly, they were being highly paid to forsake their own busy medical practices to treat someone they didn't even know in a foreign country. All were respected by their medical colleagues throughout Europe. Indeed, Dr. Ludwig Lamonte had a reputation as one of the best hand surgeons in the world, treating many star athletes and musical virtuosos who needed their hands for their livelihoods. Dr. Lamonte, whom his friends called Jake, had an interesting background, as his three names might indicate, that gave the authorities a little pause. He was Jewish and born in Alsace Lorraine to parents who were university professors. The residents of Alsace Lorraine, depending on who won the last war, were either a part of Germany or France. Hence his name, Ludwig Lamonte, reflects both these heritages.

When relatives started to go missing from the Warsaw ghetto, the family fled to Switzerland. They found refuge in Zurich and his highly educated parents were able to eke out a living as substitute teachers and school custodians. Following the war, their living conditions improved. Jake and his siblings were entering high school so the family decided to make the peaceful and cosmopolitan Zurich their permanent home. Jake, excelling in the sciences and with a strong desire to help people, was steered toward a medical career by his parents and teachers.

After receiving his medical training, Dr. Lamonte started making frequent trips to Jerusalem and Tel Aviv to help train Israeli surgeons in the latest reconstructive hand surgery techniques. The tragic suicide bombings in Israel provided more emergency surgical cases than the Israeli trauma surgeons could treat, so a triage system had to be devised and implemented.

The only question mark that the CIA could discover in Lamonte's background check involved him chairing the Israeli medical triage commission that established the basic triage guidelines for emergency treatment during a mass casualty event. The triage guidelines of the International Red Cross were accepted, but Lamonte's commission reserved the right to use nationality as a factor in the triage protocol to determine who first received emergency care. This created an instantaneous uproar from the non-Jewish residents of Israel, many of whom were legal citizens like their Jewish friends and neighbors. The commission, chaired by Lamonte, did not bend to international pressure and kept this controversial nationality provision in their triage guidelines.

Ultimately, in an attempt to solidify this controversial point, Lamonte went on the record that injured Israeli citizens would be treated before a more seriously injured bomb toting terrorist. The Arab media immediately labeled him and the government sponsored triage commission as anti-Arab. Since suicide bombers usually die when their bombs detonate, no one has been placed in the difficult position of delaying treatment of a more seriously injured non-Israeli to treat an injured Israeli citizen. The CIA analysts, sitting behind their desks at Langley, tried to envision every possible scenario and expressed a little curiosity as to how he would respond to his injured patient in Tripoli, who by nationality and name might be considered an Arab terrorist.

The background checks of the other two doctors flying to Tripoli raised no red flags. Dr. Henri Beauchamp, a well respected thoracic surgeon, viewed the x-rays showing Azee's broken ribs, but there was no substitute for palpation and auscultation to determine if anything different than the tincture of time was needed for their healing. The generous fee arrangement appealed to Beauchamp as he was building an extravagant ski lodge in the Alps.

The need for the anesthesia services of Dr. Martin Lyman was perhaps a case of overkill by Dr. Rahmat. There certainly were anesthesiologists in Tripoli who could numb the ulnar nerve and give intravenous sedation to keep Azee quiet for the surgery. However, he wanted Lyman to bring the latest Stryker pressure pumps and disposable tourniquets, imported from the United States, for attempting the preferred Bier block anesthesia procedure. Use of contaminated reusable tourniquets and unreliable pressure cuffs was not an option for treating Azee. Since money was no object, Rahmat wanted to cover his backside, so Lyman was added to the team. Lyman's background check revealed that fifteen years earlier his hospital privileges were suspended for three months while he sought treatment for substance abuse issues. His record has been clean since and he is known around the hospital as a fervent green tea drinker who is going to live to be one hundred years old.

The medical equipment and supplies loaded aboard the Flying Mole would do any third world operating room proud. Once airborne, Taajud-Deen was overheard at Langley on the hidden cockpit microphone telling his co-pilot that they were being followed on each wing by two jets, most assuredly U.S. military aircraft. He did not expect any problems on the flight; otherwise they would not have been given clearance to take off from Zurich.

The three doctors seated amidst the lashed down boxes were having a friendly discussion on their latest vacations and general medical topics. Lamonte nervously steered the conversation to the difficult case that they were going to treat. Beauchamp agreed to scrub in as his assistant to suction and provide retraction while Lamonte did the delicate work of putting Azee's hand back together. Just as Lamonte was starting to talk his way through the steps of his planned surgical procedure, starting with the irrigation and debridement of dead tissue, Lyman said, "What's this?"

A collective, "Oh shit," was the response in Langley's monitoring room, as the bug in the cabin was discovered on the floor beside a box. The hastily placed bug obviously had been dislodged from its hiding place during the loading of the airplane.

Lyman viewed himself as an electronics expert as he built a kit radio as a teenager and was in the process of assembling a super computer, more powerful than one out of the box. He said, "It's obviously a bug planted to listen to us." He raised his finger to his mouth and for the rest of the flight they talked about the simmering beauty of the Mediterranean below and the billowing cumulous clouds on the horizon.

THE FIRST LADY MEETS AZEE

The president, against the advice of all his advisers except Gleason's boss, Secretary of Treasury Jameson, ordered a full squadron of F16's from Sigonella to pick up the Flying Mole and shadow it into Libyan airspace to visually verify its landing at Tripoli. Libya was given notice of this impending incursion on its airspace at the same time that it was reminded of President Reagan's air to ground missile attack that missed killing the colonel by a matter of minutes. The diplomatic efforts to resolve the current crisis of a high ranking government official held hostage in a hostile country that was also providing refuge for a fugitive guilty of trying to assassinate the president and the first lady, were moving too slow for the president's patience.

The president was playing hardball trying to quicken the release of his friend and failed protector. Should the feeble Libyan Air Force be foolish enough to attack the superior planes, they would be destroyed and the Flying Mole would be shot out of the sky also. If this incursion into Libyan airspace went unchallenged, the president knew that he was in the driver's seat in getting Gleason released, as the Libyans did not want to escalate this into a major conflict.

The squadron of F16s buzzed the Tripoli airport uncontested at one thousand feet as the Flying Mole landed. The unusual noise of multiple jets in the air brought Gleason to his window. He was able to make out the friendly markings on two of the jets banking for their return to Sicily. He didn't know the details of what was going on, but he smiled at the knowledge that something pretty serious was being done to release him.

XVII

The president's secretary left a message for Dr. Schmidt to be at the White House for dinner and a medical update at seven. Trying to think of any excuse to distract the president from his secondary agenda of seeing her alone, she replied that she was bringing an important guest with her. She kept checking her messages the rest of the day to see if the White House had any objection.

Her bright red Mustang convertible, with its top up in the early fall chill, got the usual drooling scrutiny from the young Marine on duty at the White House VIP parking lot. She went through an unnecessary introduction of Cindy Gleason seated in the passenger seat, as the sentry remembered her from her days married to Tom Gleason when he was head of the Secret Service White House protective unit. The radio to the inside security desk crackled, "The red convert is here with a guest."

They had the choice of riding the elevator or taking the beautiful spiral stairs up to the second floor family quarters where the president was meeting them. This was Dr. Schmidt's first climb up the spiral staircase. She was glad to have Cindy running interference as she had attended a tea for Secret Service wives that the first lady held in the first month of their presidency. At the top of the stairway they were escorted into the large living room to await the president. On seeing the single bowl of peanuts waiting on a coffee table, Cindy whispered the little known fact that the president has to reimburse the government for the food that is served in the family's private living quarters, "So don't be surprised if we are served mac and cheese like Jason and Eric."

They were still giggling when the president, humming an unrecognizable lullaby, arrived, cradling Melody in his good arm. He warmly kissed Cindy and handed Melody over in the same motion. "Fortunately, Melody is good with everyone. People are fighting to hold her so she isn't hurting for attention." When the president left to fill their wine requests, Melody was handed to Nancy for her motherhood fix.

Cindy recalled to the president's delight how much Tom always enjoyed being with the boys, and he often commented that if they ever had kids he wanted them to be just like Jason and Eric. Many times he would come home with dirt and grass stains on his best suit pants from playing with the boys on the south lawn. The president mentioned that the boys were having a sleep over tonight with some of their classmates from Friends School and they could check on them after dinner.

Seated at the dining room table, the president apologized for the simple cuisine. The kitchen prepared his favorite meal, southern fried chicken with all the trimmings. During the dessert of pecan pie he gave a cryptic CIA type update on Tom and Azee. When Tom was in the hospital, the CIA was able to closely monitor his condition with their reliable informants among the hospital staff. However, now the CIA was out of the minute by minute loop after he was relocated to his new detention site.

Nevertheless, the local CIA was still monitoring Azee's general activities and sending reports to Langley. Dr. Schmidt was appalled at the fugitive Azee's world class treatment when the president explained the European specialists that were arriving to treat him.

The president boasted of the show of strength when the squadron of F16's shadowed the Flying Mole uncontested into Libyan airspace in the ultimate game of international chicken. He felt that it would just be a matter of days until details of Gleason's release would be worked out, since Qadafi had nothing to gain by continuing to illegally hold him hostage. Azee's return to the United States would be a topic for another day after Gleason's release.

The president, against the advice from the Pentagon, had notified the United Nations that unless Gleason was released within seventy-two hours, the United States would act unilaterally, using whatever means were at its disposal, to secure his release. Pentagon generals objected to giving Qadafi too much time to prepare his defenses and secretly move Gleason again, even to another country. Cindy expressed fear that if we attacked Libya to free Gleason he would be killed to get even with the hated United States. The president reassured Cindy that the situation would be resolved diplomatically before things got that far.

The president was personally anxious to get Gleason back to the United States to begin treatment for his AIDS. "I don't know how to ask this delicately, Cindy, so I'll just get it out. Have you been tested for AIDS?" Both ladies dropped their forks and stopped eating their pecan pie in shock at the president's bluntness. Cindy could feel her face turning the color of the California Rose' they were drinking. "I'm sorry, Cindy. You don't have to answer. I just don't want you to get hurt or be surprised."

Dr. Schmidt broke the awkward silence with a medical perspective. "We have to explore the details of how he contracted AIDS. The incubation period of AIDS is at least thirty-days from initial exposure before it would show up in a blood test. I checked his medical records and he is due this month for his yearly physical including blood work. Last year's blood tests were normal."

"Speaking of physicals, Mr. President, we're overdue on yours." Dr. Schmidt was mentally connecting the medical dots from the timetable of Gleason's AIDS to his giving two units of his blood for the president's emergency arm surgery in Detroit. She was also silently remembering Gleason's shakedown of her for a vial of the president's blood for testing because of an alleged serious national security issue after her traumatic meeting with Azee disguised as a CIA internal affairs agent in the Watergate Hotel. All this would have to be shared with the president, but not tonight with Cindy present.

"I know, I know. We've postponed it with everything else going on. We'll get it scheduled once this Libyan crisis is resolved."

Cindy could feel her complexion and blood pressure returning back to normal. "I'm sure that I'm okay as Tom and I have only been together for lunch or dinner since our divorce a year ago. Recently we've been starting to grow closer, almost like we might try to get back together. The Detroit tragedy deeply affected him. Now that I think about it, he really seemed different starting with his return from the Thirty Day Prior meeting. I can't explain it, but it's like he wanted to tell me something that he just couldn't get out. Maybe it's just a case of my hyper-tuned feminine intuition."

"I don't think so, Cindy. My psychiatric training tells me that these deep seated feelings are usually reliable. Maybe we should start our inquiry with the Thirty Day Prior meeting. How should we go about this, Mr. President?"

"Just what I need, another problem! Even as president I can only do so much with the new baby and the dying first lady, along with Gleason's plight and bringing Azee to justice. I'll pass this off to his boss, Jameson at Treasury, so why don't you meet with him to tell him what we know and suspect. He'll get to the bottom of this—soon I hope."

"You're right. You've got more than enough to deal with. You mentioned the first lady. I wish that I could bring you even the slightest glimmer of hope. Soon we should stop her futile hyperbaric oxygen treatments. Forgive me, but I'm starting to feel that I don't care about the politics of the final decision on the first lady. I've heard that attorneys from the Hemlock Society have been snooping around the hospital to get information on her condition. The rumor is that they are going to petition the Courts on her behalf to allow her to die. Hospital security has been told to run them off. They're like pit bulls, afraid of no one."

"Bastards! Is nothing sacred anymore? Too bad they can't be shot like pit bulls. Let's go see the kids where everything is good!"

XVIII

Upon landing in Tripoli, the three doctors were brought to the hospital to evaluate Azee for surgery the next day. The pilots stayed with the plane to supervise the unloading of the medical cargo into a waiting van, which they would accompany to the hospital. They were under strict orders to not let the valuable cargo out of their sight even though local security was everywhere. The black market in Tripoli would instantly swallow up the drugs and medical supplies without a trace and tomorrow's surgery would have to be cancelled.

Dr. Rahmat primed the doctors on Azee's background and friendship with Colonel Qadafi. A warrant for Azee's arrest had been issued by the Federal Court in Detroit, so he was now classified an international fugitive. Dr. Lamonte, having been associated with Israel's medical and legal issues of treating terrorists, had the most questions. Also, as it turned out, he had the most answers for this team operating by the seat of their pants on the medical ethics and legal implications of treating an international fugitive terrorist. At one point, Lamonte suggested that a Libyan lawyer knowledgeable in international law, could be brought in to advise them. Rahmat's phone call to Qadafi's office seeking advice generated a terse reply to proceed with the planned surgery and let the colonel take care of everything else.

Libya, like many Middle Eastern countries including Lebanon, had no extradition treaty with the United States, so nothing could be done legally to force Azee's return to the United States. Rahmat's promise of an additional six figure bonus post surgery for each of the doctors was the stimulus needed to get the doctors away from the conference room and into Azee's room to begin their examinations.

Rahmat made a formal introduction of the specialists to the mildly sedated Azee. The doctors in their pre-exam conference agreed that the thoracic surgeon, Dr. Henri Beauchamp, would examine him first to be sure that his broken ribs would not stop the sedation and anesthesia needed for the hand surgery. As they were reviewing the latest chest x-rays, Azee became quite animated waving his injured right hand to show that was what he was most concerned about, not his broken ribs.

Dr. Beauchamp, thinking he was still in the cool mountains of Switzerland, needlessly hand warmed his stethoscope while explaining in heavily accented English, the need to be certain that Azee was healthy enough to remain sedated on the operating table for the long hand surgery. "Oui, oui," Beauchamp exclaimed, as he hung the stethoscope around his neck. "You have very painful broken ribs, but you are okay for the surgery tomorrow. Your Kevlar suit prevented more serious internal injuries and saved your life. Fortunately, you were in good shape before the accident."

While at Azee's hand, Lamonte took great care unwrapping the moist gauze strips that served as a stabilizing splint for Azee's dangling digits, as well as a dressing to sop up the straw colored fluid oozing from his open wounds. Lamonte performed the same basic needle prick neurological tests as Rahmat with the same results. He had Azee open and close his fingers to test for bone, ligament and muscle integrity. Azee winced with pain as he tried even the slightest of finger and hand movements. "What do you think, Doc? Can we start the operation right now?"

Dr. Lyman had been slowly inching toward the bed to get a

better look at Azee's arm. The forearm above the wrist seemed uninjured except for the black and blue edema developing. "We can try the Bier Block tourniquet anesthesia as I know you would prefer to operate with reduced blood flow at the operative site," he commented to Lamonte.

Lamonte recovered the mangled hand with a sterile towel. "I agree that it would be best to do the Bier Block anesthesia. Sorry, Mr. Azee, didn't mean to ignore you. I know you're anxious to begin and so are we. I've done thousands of hand operations and I'll be honest with you, most doctors wouldn't attempt what we are going to do. I always ask myself, if this injured hand was my hand, what would I want done? To be honest, yes, I'd want to try surgery, but I'd still be a little afraid that it may not work out. Not trying to scare you. I just want you to know all the facts."

"I appreciate that. In the U.S., doctors might not do it for fear of getting sued or maybe the patient's insurance wouldn't pay for it. Here in Tripoli, we don't have to worry about either of these. Do your best."

"Tomorrow I'm going to try to save all your fingers. However, I can't be sure how everything will work until your hand heals for a few weeks. Before we even do tomorrow's surgery, I assure you that you will need additional surgeries to help restore more function. Somehow, we must arrange to check you within a month, in case we have to do some minor touch up work."

"No problem. I'll be returning to my compound in Beirut and you can come there to check on things."

"As you may know, I'm in Tel Aviv every month doing surgery on Israeli terrorism victims. I will need to see you at the hospital clinic in case we need to do anything."

"I have a lot of contacts in Israel. By then I'll be more than ready for a little escape from my wife Hasnaa and the kids at Temenos."

"We'll work it out later. Tomorrow we'll start with the wrist where I'll have to fuse two or three small bones, which will restrict some of your future wrist movements. I've given up trying to figure out exactly how many pins and screws we'll use. Wires will be used to hold the bones in place. After the wrist is stabilized, we'll begin with your thumb and work our way to your small finger, one digit at a time. Our opposable thumb separates us from the apes, so I'll do everything I can to save this important function. As we proceed from finger to finger, we sometimes have to borrow a little bone, muscle or tendon from one place to use somewhere else. We just hope we don't run out of these natural replacement parts before we get to the last couple fingers. The most challenging aspect will probably be to find enough healthy skin to cover the open wounds. We'll do multiple small flaps and skin grafts to achieve as good a closure as possible."

"Sounds complicated, Doc. My life and job have always dealt with the uncertain and the difficult so I know what you're facing. I have one large business deal pending, so let's get on with it."

"Okay, Mr. Azee. Get a good night's sleep and we'll be back at the crack of dawn."

The four doctors returned to the sparse conference room with the x-rays and the ever thickening medical chart. Rahmat made sure that the door was securely closed. They breathed a collective sigh of relief as they collapsed into their chairs around the well-worn Formica conference table. They were all thinking and feeling the same thing with no need for anyone to verbalize their thoughts and emotions until Rahmat sighed, "Well?"

The onus to respond naturally fell to the surgeon, Lamonte, who silently surveyed his tongue-tied fellow doctors. "What can I say? The most important thing we should talk about might be the departure time of tomorrow's first flight back to Zurich. Mr. Azee is one scary person. He's agreeable before the surgery. Everyone always is. After the surgery it will be a different story, especially if it doesn't work out perfectly." His fellow Swiss doctors nodded their assents.

Rahmat's jaw dropped. "You're kidding, right? Qadafi will have something to say about an early escape tomorrow."

"You mean that we're just as much a prisoner as the patient we're supposed to treat? I've never before operated under the gun.

You put us in a very tough position. If Azee was a terrorist in Israel, his hand already would be in the biopsy pail. I don't think he deserves the impossible, which is what we're being asked to perform."

Rahmat was sorry, but not surprised, that his esteemed mentor so soon had cut through all the international intrigue to realize that he had committed himself and his team to something they didn't feel comfortable doing. Rahmat started dialing a number on the black rotary phone in the center of the table. "Maybe you can explain to Quadafi your religious and political views that prevent operating on his good friend." Rahmat dialed only five numbers of Quadafi's phone number, not the needed six, allowing Lamonte a chance to respond.

Lamonte raised his hand as a signal to Rahmat to stop dialing before he answered. "It's more than religion and politics. It's mainly medical. He could slough some or all his fingers or even the whole hand after the surgery. I don't want to be here in Tripoli if that happens and have to deal with the wrath of the colonel and Azee. Is that unreasonable?"

With that modest breakthrough question Rahmat hung up the phone. "In my communications with you, Dr. Lamonte, I was totally honest about the difficulty of this case. However, I wasn't aware of your feelings about operating on terrorists. As far as Qadafi is concerned, I'm now part of your team. Now it's the four of us. I will explain to him again that we will do all we can to save Azee's hand, but we can't do the impossible. The results will be in Allah's hands."

"I hope Quadafi understands that. We'd have a better chance for long term success if Azee came back to Zurich with us, so we could closely monitor his healing and watch for infection."

"That can't happen. The United States would shoot his plane out of the sky. Your flight here on the Flying Mole was shadowed by U.S. planes from the time you left Zurich until you landed in Tripoli. I have no doubt that if your pilot had deviated from the flight plan you wouldn't be sitting here today. Please take Azee's treatment one step at a time. The long term post-surgical concerns can be addressed later. Tomorrow we must proceed for better or for worse. I beg you to put aside your reservations about treating Azee because he's a terrorist. He's a close friend of the colonel."

The three Swiss doctors stared silently at each other until Lamonte again was the spokesman. "This whole scenario is more than we signed on for. I'm scared and I don't scare easily. We will do our best tomorrow. However, the three of us had better fly back to Zurich on a regular scheduled airline when we leave. Azee's plane will be followed wherever it goes. Our surgical supplies and the medical equipment, especially my surgical microscope, can be flown back to Zurich on his plane without us aboard."

"That's probably the safest plan for your return home. The colonel was okay with you leaving forty-eight hours after the surgery. Lucky you! You'll be safely home if any delayed post-surgical problems arise and I'm here to take the brunt of the colonel's and Azee's wrath."

XIX

Dr. Schmidt went about her morning routine at Bethesda Medical Center awaiting the call from Bart Jameson's office about the president's mandated meeting to try to discuss the details of how Gleason contracted AIDS. It was becoming harder and harder for her to continue supervising the fruitless hyperbaric oxygen treatments on the unresponsive first lady, who had to be moved from her bed into an iron lung type apparatus for every thirty minute pressurized oxygen perfusion treatment. Dr. Schmidt had prevailed upon the president to do the treatments only once a day rather than the original four times a day that were showing no results and were probably harming, rather than helping, the systemically fragile first lady. The mid-morning message to be at the secretary of treasury's office at noon, where lunch would be available, accelerated her planned morning activities.

She debated whether to wear her civilian clothes or her dress Navy uniform with all the medals and ribbons dangling on her chest and the gold stripped epaulets squaring up her shoulders. Never one for military protocol, she nevertheless opted to wear the seldom used dress uniform, hoping to impress the secretary of treasury. The attendant in the hospital guard shack gave the red Mustang a crisp salute as the white wooden bar raised, freeing Dr.

Schmidt to join the noon D.C. traffic madness. The all-too-famil-
iar drive to the White House and the adjacent Treasury Building
allowed her to crystallize her thoughts on the limited contacts she
had with Gleason. Reluctantly, she came to the conclusion that
she had to tell the Secretary about her encounter with Gleason
in the fast food restaurant across from Andrews Air Force Base.
She knew that this information would be passed to the president,
probably before she got back to her car.

She found her way to the secretary of the treasury's office after
clearing the countless security check points guarding the treasury
office. Jameson's secretary escorted her right in to see him with
the quiet comment, "Lunch is being served." He apologized for
seeing her during lunch, but that was the only time available when
the president called with the request that they meet today. A white
coated aide wheeled in a cart with a small smorgasbord of meats,
cheese and bread to make sandwiches. She was glad to have the ice
breaker of a quick lunch before she had to make her confession.

Jameson had put his staff to work reconstructing Gleason's
involvement with the *Motor City Blitz* to clarify the origin of
his AIDS. They started with the Thirty Day Prior visit, where all
the involved agencies met to coordinate their preparations for
the planned presidential visit. Gleason's official White House
log revealed that he was picked up at Detroit City airport by his
friend, Detroit Chief of Police, Jefferson Hawkins. He handed Dr.
Schmidt this log entry and a copy of the hotel receipt from the
Detroit Renaissance Hotel as he explained, "Everything appears
to have been done according to the book. The one thing that's
missing is a receipt for his dinner the night that he arrived. Our
Secret Service agents, when working on the road, faithfully turn
in all their reimbursable receipts, but I find nothing for his dinner
that night. Excuse me. I'll call Chief Hawkins in Detroit. They
must have dined together."

Jameson turned to use the phone on the credenza behind his
desk, so Dr. Schmidt could hear very little of the hushed conversation. The frequent nodding head and the slowly sinking, drooping

shoulders of the normally take charge Jameson told her more than the few words she could decipher. As the conversation was starting to conclude with the usual pleasantries, Jameson reached for a tissue as he banged the phone into its cradle. It seemed like an eternity before he turned around with tearing eyes. Dr. Schmidt struggled to remain silent until the person in charge was ready to talk. "I don't know what to say. I'm shocked, hurt, betrayed."

She wanted to refocus the problem, whatever it was, away from the new victim across the desk. "What can I do?"

After another long, pensive delay, an angry response came. "You can tell the president that he probably has AIDS."

"I know. I've suspected that since it was announced in Libya that Gleason has AIDS. Did Chief Hawkins give any details on how Gleason contracted it?"

"Yes, very reluctantly I might add. The basic facts are that Gleason met a hostess during dinner at the Windsor casino. Later she came to his hotel and they did what couples do. She has since tested positive for AIDS."

"That's shocking, totally out of keeping with the Gleason I know. The timetable certainly is right for the president to be exposed to AIDS as he received two units of Gleason's blood during his arm surgery a month later. It all makes sense. Excuse me, now I need a tissue." She retrieved a quick handful from the box on the credenza. She was crying by the time she sat back down.

Jameson easily empathized with her and gave her a few moments to gather herself before he spoke. "The one thing that Chief Hawkins said that I don't understand is that the recent Detroit test on the president's blood was inconclusive for AIDS. I should have questioned him on the president's blood being tested in Detroit. How was that possible?"

"Unfortunately, I can explain it. Before the Detroit bombings, the White House was undecided about performing the president's yearly physical before or after the election. After the Detroit bombings when he and the comatose first lady returned to D.C., there was consideration to do the President's annual physical and publicly releasing his good results before the election. I drew multiple blood specimens to send anonymously to the lab so the results would be back at the time of his physical a few days later. Naturally, Gleason was aware of this blood draw. He insisted because of national security considerations that I give him a vial of the president's blood for independent testing so I gave it to him outside Andrews Air Force base where he was preparing to make a quick trip to Detroit to check on the bombing investigations."

This information helped Jameson and Dr. Schmidt to refocus and regain their composure. "Gleason was out of line in asking you for the president's blood specimen. Unfortunately, I'll have to recommend Gleason's dismissal from the Secret Service when, or I should say if, he returns from Libya. What did you do with the other blood specimens?"

"They were sent to the lab at Bethesda for testing where we always use pseudonyms for the president. The lab sent a note indicating a slightly elevated lymphocyte count, so they recommended retesting in three months. This elevated count could have been related to his bombing injuries or as we now know the start of AIDS."

"I guess it didn't take us long to answer the presidential mandate about Gleason's AIDS. The president has always thought of Gleason as a brother and a second father to Jason and Eric. The president has to be informed of what we know. I don't want to leave a paper trail of Gleason's one night fling in Detroit, so I'll schedule a meeting with the president tomorrow. I'd like you to be there to cover the medical issues involved."

"I hope that the president has started to make the association of Gleason's AIDS and his blood donation, so what we tell him tomorrow won't be a total shock."

"I doubt that he's made the connection. He isn't terribly introspective, although recent events have started to change him. See you tomorrow."

On the drive back to Bethesda, Dr. Schmidt felt relieved that the act of her giving the president's blood sample to Gleason was out in the open. However, she was sure that there would be repercussions and professional sanctions, possibly starting tomorrow with the presidential meeting. On a woman to woman level, she would have to think about how she would inform Cindy of Tom's indiscretions before she heard it second hand from the Beltway grapevine.

XX

The behind the scenes international negotiations surrounding Gleason's release were intensifying, but without any palpable results. France was the intermediary since the United States and Libya did not have diplomatic relations as reinforced by President Reagan's surprise missile attack on Quadafi that just missed its mark. The CIA operatives in Tripoli, still in the aggressive mode, suggested a car bomb attack on the hospital the morning of Azee's surgery since Gleason was already removed from the premises. Fortunately, cooler heads prevailed. The collateral loss of innocent civilians would probably trigger a death sentence for Gleason.

Dr. Rahmat slept at the hospital in the same locked room with all the imported medical supplies and expensive surgical equipment to insure their safekeeping until Azee's morning surgery. Looking at the doctors' inventory list, he realized that they didn't bring any disposable sterile needles from Switzerland.

His heart raced when he realized it was near the end of the month and the hospital could be out of their meager supply of sterile needles. When that happens, which is nearly every month, except perhaps the shortened month of February, the hospital cleans and tries to sterilize needles for reuse until next month's supply arrives. Many third world countries consider it an unnecessary luxury to use needles only once. He checked with the operating room nurses and, as suspected, there weren't any sterile needles.

Behind a picture of Colonel Qadafi in his private office was a small wall safe that had an affixed official government memorandum proclaiming: PROPERTY OF COLONEL QADAFI. The safe contained a small supply of emergency medications and sterile supplies, including the precious needles. Every emergency room in Libya was ordered to have these sterile supplies strictly for an emergency involving the colonel or his family. As he removed the dozen needles from the safe, he was sure that the colonel would approve their use for his friend, Azee.

The surgical team arrived well before the scheduled surgery. They changed into their scrubs and supervised the set up of the operating room and their surgical trays. Lamonte personally unpacked his Zeiss surgical microscope, making sure that the critical magnifying optics were clean and properly installed. He saved all the packing material and plastic bags back in their proper boxes for repacking after the operation.

Lamonte had his first run-in with the always territorial operating room supervisor over his request to have classical music played during the long operation. She informed him that it wasn't possible to play any music in the operating room since there was no intercom or speakers. Rahmat came upon the tail end of this potential meltdown and told Lamonte that he would find a cassette player and some classical tapes to help soothe the hours of Azee's surgery. He reasoned that it was better to deal with an irate nurse than a frustrated surgeon holding a scalpel.

Their surgical instruments arrived from Switzerland in sterile packs, but Lamonte insisted, against the operating room supervisor's wishes, that they be given a quick sterilizing flash to insure their sterility. Luckily, Rahmat didn't have to mediate this more serious issue as Lamonte ultimately got his wish without blood being shed. Infection was the major complication of this delicate reconstructive operation that required the surgical sites to be open to the air for the hours of the micro surgery and Azee's injured hand already had been open since the explosion days ago.

Azee reported to Lamonte that he slept well after making a few phone calls. The CIA was unable to record these calls, except one, as they were made on his secure satellite phone that the pilots brought from the Flying Mole. The one call that they were able to monitor was to Temenos, his family compound in Beirut. Azee had chosen to use the land line into Temenos, knowing that it would be recorded, to talk to his wife and children, for the first time since his injury. The CIA analysts at Langley were surprised at the warmth and love he expressed to his family, especially his children. The analysts dissected every word with the expectation of discovering some hidden message or code. Nothing sinister was detected, although they were again intrigued by Azee's mention that he'd be back to Temenos very soon. Surely Azee wasn't naïve or deranged enough to think that the United States would allow safe passage for him to return home to Beirut.

The president was faxed a verbatim copy of this loving conversation. After reading it and becoming angry at Azee's saccharine hypocrisy, he balled it up and threw it into the burning fireplace to be consumed, in the same way he hoped Azee would be consumed in the fires of hell.

The operation began as planned with Lyman administering the I.V. sedation and cervical nerve block anesthesia. Everyone would have preferred general anesthesia, but Azee's broken ribs and the extended length of the very tedious surgery negated this option. Beauchamp scrubbed in as an assistant along with a local scrub nurse. Rahmat, besides being the disc jockey, was available to fetch items needed from nearby shelves and bins. Azee's shattered wrist bones were first aligned with screws and wires to provide a stable foundation for the hand reconstruction.

The surgical field of the wrist and hand was so small that Dr. Beauchamp's retraction instruments always seemed in the way. Lamonte methodically called out, as in a medical school cadaver dissection, the name of every bone, muscle, tendon and nerve located as he attempted to put the pieces of the jigsaw puzzle back together. Beauchamp marveled at the patience and precision of Lamonte as he was often dealing with tissue smaller that a thread through the surgical microscope. At least in his field of thoracic surgery, even though dealing with many life and death situations, he usually was able to see what he was working on with the naked eye.

Lyman was informed when there were ten minutes of final suturing left so that he could start tapering off the sedating IV drugs. "About what I expected, an hour a finger," Lamonte announced, as he peeled off his bloody gloves. "The wrist was a little more involved than I anticipated. Nevertheless, five hours isn't bad, considering the assistant I had."

"Be careful or I'll push you off a cliff the next time we're skiing," Beauchamp retorted, to ease the pervasive operating room tension.

Lamonte followed Azee's litter back to his room and helped slide him back onto his bed. He was writing post-op nursing orders when Rahmat motioned for him to step into the hall where he was handed a phone. "Hello, Doctor, thank you for fixing my friend's hand. Dr. Rahmat tells me that it was a very hard job, almost impossible. Stay in Libya as long as you want as my guest."

Before he could answer, Lamonte heard the click of the line going dead. "Was that Colonel Qadafi? I'm sorry that I didn't thank him for calling."

"He's a man of few words. Most don't get a chance to talk to him; they listen. Even as his personal doctor, we communicate on a very limited basis."

"He said that we could stay indefinitely as his guest, but I think that we should depart in two days as planned."

"I agree. I'll treat any post-op problems." Rahmat took the surgical team around the corner from the hospital for a late lunch. "Best food in Tripoli," he bragged as they were seated at an outside table hoping to bask in the warm sun and unwind from the pressures of the operating room. Everyone enjoyed each others' company since their difficult mission was now accomplished. They almost had to take a number to get a word into the animated, far reaching discussion. They all grabbed for the check from the hesitant waiter, but Rahmat won the battle by telling the waiter to put the bill on the hospital account.

When they returned to the hospital to start repacking their things, Lamonte took personal charge of his baby, the Zeiss surgical microscope. He didn't notice that a few plastic bags and some of the packing material were missing. He was mainly concerned that all the parts got into their proper foam lined boxes. Once everything was repackaged, it was moved into Rahmat's office to await transport to Zurich on the Flying Mole.

XXI

Jameson and Dr. Schmidt were seated in the oval office before the president came down from the upstairs living quarters. Dr. Schmidt quietly expressed her nervousness about how to tell the president that he could have AIDS. Jameson gave the sage bureaucrat's advice to always let the person in charge lead the discussion and a window would open up. He mentioned that the president was more perceptive than most people, especially the media, want to admit. Contributing to this false perception of dullness was his managerial style to freely delegate responsibilities. However, to reinforce the notion that he was in charge, he often reminded his cabinet, quoting his presidential idol Truman, "The buck stops with me." Jameson mentioned that the president always gives his subordinates enough rope to hang themselves. Dr. Schmidt couldn't help but wonder if this were the scenario developing around continuing the futile hyperbaric oxygen treatments of the first lady where she ultimately would be held responsible for the first lady not recovering.

"Good morning, Nan and Bart. Thanks for coming over this early. Haven't had my morning coffee yet," the president announced, as a not so subtle hint to his secretary to bring coffee for everyone. "Melody had a restless night. Thank God for the wonderful White House nurses. Any change in the first lady's condition overnight?"

"No change, sir. The once a day hyperbaric oxygen treatment seems to be keeping her stable, but with no improvement. There's no need to go back to the four treatments a day, which didn't help her."

While the secretary was out getting the coffee, Jameson mentioned to the president that he would feel more comfortable discussing the matter at hand behind closed doors. This government lingo for requesting no shorthand transcriber and no recording device activated caught the president by surprise. It typically was his prerogative to request meetings behind closed doors because it was usually reserved for top secret national security issues. However, he nodded his assent and summarily waved off the secretary, after she served coffee, and ordered her to turn off the *electronics* as they referred to the recording device in the oval office.

"Bart, what's the bad news on Gleason? I'm ready for anything!"

"I hope so. Most of the information is from his long time friend, Jeffrey Hawkins, Detroit's Police Chief. He painted a big picture of deceit with Azee right in the middle of it, which shouldn't be a surprise."

"Don't need to hear that. He's already ruined my life. What's the story on the AIDS?"

"The long and short of it is that Gleason slept with a casino hostess, a former stripper, the night before the Thirty Day Prior meeting in Detroit. She has since tested positive for AIDS."

"That's it?"

"I'm afraid so. The fallout and repercussions personally affect all of us."

"How so? Things can't get any worse," the president commented.

Jameson glanced at Dr. Schmidt and she knew that, unfortunately, the stage was hers. She had the foresight to clench a crumpled tissue in her hand. "Mr. President, you remember that we drew blood samples for your planned physical? As usual, I sent them to our lab at Bethesda, but Gleason insisted on taking one specimen out of town to Detroit for testing, as we have since found out. As I told you, the Bethesda test results were a little suspicious and the lab wants to retest your blood in three months."

"What the hell was Gleason doing with my blood in Detroit? Do we know the results of this test in Detroit?"

Dr. Schmidt reluctantly continued, "Your blood test in Detroit was inconclusive, the same as ours in Bethesda. However, it was tested at a clinic in Detroit that has much experience in diagnosing AIDS. We learned yesterday from Chief Hawkins that this lab indicated that your blood test is consistent with early AIDS, but not necessarily totally diagnostic. With that in mind, I have requested Bethesda to reevaluate your blood work." Dr. Schmidt did all she could do from breaking down as she wiped a tear from her eye waiting for the president to reply.

The hard-nosed businessman serving as secretary of treasury also started to tear-up before the president broke the oppressive silence. "We probably should have a good cry, we'd all feel better. Sorry, but I'm all cried out, too numb to even care about myself anymore. You said that Azee is in the middle of this?"

Jameson was glad to speak to counter his deepening depression. "This hostess, Misty, worked for Azee, entertaining his big shot clients and foreign dignitaries. There's apparently a little black book with names and phone numbers of former clients. The chief is starting to notify all of them to be tested for AIDS. This list could prove interesting and embarrassing. I've requested a copy."

After a moment of silence, the president loudly promised himself, Jameson and Dr. Schmidt, "I will get Azee for this. He will pay with his own life. Nan, what do I need to do? Sounds like my fun days are over."

"We need to take it one step at a time. I'll submit a new blood specimen to the NIH Research Institute," Dr. Schmidt quietly answered. "They are working on a new test that confirms AIDS at an earlier stage. We need to get blood specimens from Gleason and the casino hostess to see if they have the same virus. If your test is positive, it should match their virus."

"We're going to evaluate the Secret Service policy requiring agents with the same blood type as the president to always be at his side, like Gleason was in Detroit," Jameson interjected, relieving Dr. Schmidt of some of the presidential scrutiny.

"We're just starting to scratch the surface on what we know about AIDS," Dr. Schmidt said. "There's an Air Canada flight attendant whose AIDS has been traced to over two hundred victims in San Francisco alone. I'd be curious if he ever flew into Windsor."

"All that crap is good for the researchers, but where the hell does that leave me, a father with three kids and no wife? I'm screwed big time, and don't forget Gleason, if we get him back alive."

"Mr. President, let's wait to get a definitive diagnosis from NIH. We'll deal with Gleason when he's back home," Dr. Schmidt said.

"Needless to say, today's discussion can't leave the oval office before the election. My lead in the polls would instantly evaporate and we'd all be on the streets looking for a job."

"Mr. President, that's why I requested this closed door meeting. Gleason's AIDS is public knowledge. Knowing him like I do, I'm sure that his AIDS emboldened him to singlehanded try to take out Azee. Unfortunately, he failed. So now our situation is even more complicated."

"As you know, Jameson, I barely tolerated Azee because he was the first lady's friend for reasons I'll never know. The cruise on his damned yacht was her idea. Azee has been meticulously planning these bombings for a long time starting with the idea of the peace forum that would bring me to Detroit and put me on the expressway so I could be blown up. I applaud Gleason's actions trying to kill Azee outside the United States since it now gives me more choices to deal with Azee outside the country. Once Gleason is back home, all options to get Azee are available."

Jameson was alarmed at the president's bravado. "Don't forget, Mr. President that we're still engaged in your reelection campaign.

I agree our number one priority is getting Gleason home safely and quickly. Azee's mega ego will open the door for us to snatch him later and bring him back for trial."

"I know what you're saying. I'm just venting as I occasionally need to. Kathy was always my sounding board, who bounced me back to reality." The president was interrupted by a buzz on the intercom from his secretary. He knew it had to be important, so after listening to her he said, "Send him right in." The president arose to greet FBI Director Fairborn hurrying into the oval office with a thick folder under his arm. "You have some interesting information on the fires back in Detroit?" the president asked.

"Let me start with the office explosion and fire," Fairborn began. "Two GCT employees were killed. There would've been more deaths if it hadn't started with a loud explosion in a concrete subterranean vault that warned most employees to evacuate before the fire spread. Fortunately, the explosion was mostly self-contained in the reinforced basement vault, but the fire soon engulfed the whole building."

Fairborn went on to describe how the vault imploded and that everything inside was reduced to ash except two charred items that the forensic experts are calling *two human teeth with gold caps*. The fire marshal found evidence of explosives and a petrochemical accelerant. The employees interviewed didn't even know that the vault existed. Azee was the only one with access to the vault via a private elevator from his top floor office suite.

The Otis Elevator people in Bloomington, Indiana were reluctant to discuss it. "Finally, they gave us their as-built blueprints," Fairborn said. "Otis signed off on the elevator before completion when Azee insisted that his own electronics expert would do the final wiring hookup to an alpha numeric key pad that only he could activate. The FBI is trying to determine the identity of this phantom electrician. Azee is brilliant, but he would have needed help rigging this sophisticated security device to the explosives inside the vault."

"Is the fire extinguished so that evidence gathering can begin?" the president wondered.

"The fire is out, but it's still too hot to search for evidence. We know that GCT's computers were destroyed. However, a computer technician volunteered that the last thing he did every evening was back up GCT's data to an off-site location in Tripoli. This unsolicited comment provides a hint at why Azee made frequent stops in Tripoli as the plane's log book shows. The log book mentions refueling as the reason for these stops in Tripoli. However, the four to five hours on the ground were much longer than needed to refuel the Flying Mole. Azee obviously had an additional agenda for these layovers."

"I'll call Hayden at Langley to have his agents on the ground locate the GCT computers in Tripoli," the president said. "We can take out these computers by a missile or something less lethal on the ground. A less satisfying way to destroy them would be to use the Pentagon's hacking experts. They could just hack into Azee's Libyan computers to procure GCT's files and then destroy their data. However, there'd be a little poetic justice in seeing the computers blown up on the evening news."

"The fire at his suburban estate leveled the main house before the firefighters were able to get across the moat to put it out," Fairborn resumed. "General Hodgechis, the director of the Michigan National Guard, stopped by to survey the damage. Fortunately, my agents were there at the time to talk to him."

"I remember his name. Gleason had a major run-in with him planning the security for our Detroit visit. I think he's a good friend of Azee, so I don't trust him. Why don't you run a background check on him?"

"Consider it done, Mr. President, but let me continue. His National Guard heavy equipment operators did the estate's site preparation work for a training exercise, including digging the surrounding moat, which he said was a minimum of eight feet deep, so there was no wading across it to get at the fire. The house burned to the ground, destroying any possible evidence.

The general offered the information that Azee has a hunting and fishing lodge in Northern Michigan on Drummond Island, only a short boat ride from Canada. So far this property hasn't burned down. It must have good lightning rods."

"It'll take more than lightning rods to stop Azee's torches," the president replied to the restrained laughter of the others in the room. "Maybe when this whole ordeal is over, the government can make this property a national historical site or a northern vacation White House. I'm sure that it's *over the top*, as Kathy would say."

"Actually, the local sheriff and my agents that have already seen it say it's rustic, more of a male hunting camp. There's a local caretaker, Drummond Island Joe, also known as D.I. Joe, who watches over it. He was close mouthed, easy to do since he only has a few broken off teeth, until the local sheriff arrived and took him out to the woodshed for a little common sense reasoning that involved the sheriff sticking his pistol into D.I. Joe's large belly that was overflowing his tightly constricted Harley belt buckle. When they returned D.I. Joe opened up like an erupting volcano. He willingly showed the agents a site in the back of the property where a football field length of a thick reinforced concrete road had been poured and later blown up. D.I. Joe volunteered that he thought it was stupid to build and then blow up a good road. That comment brought a smile to the oval office.

"Maybe not so stupid, looks like a practice run for Detroit," Jameson said, trying to move the meeting along as he had to get back to his busy schedule. "How close is Drummond Island to Canada?"

"That's my next point. Azee keeps a number of boats at this camp. Some smaller aluminum fishing boats, a master craft ski boat and one high speed cigarette boat, apparently painted an ugly black to make it less visible at night. D.I. Joe was in charge of maintaining the boats and he said many mornings when he got to work he had to gas up the cig, as he called it, because of late night cruising, probably to Canada to smuggle back their cheaper cigarettes that all the natives on the island like to smoke."

"That cheap bastard, Azee! Smuggling cigarettes!" It was a few moments before the four of them stopped laughing at the president. "Sorry, Fairborn. Any other island news?"

"D.I. Joe reported that the cig has been missing a couple days, which wasn't unusual. His buddy from the marina in Canada, where Azee keeps a slip, called to report that the cig appeared abandoned, poorly tied up and without a mooring cover and that the old truck that Azee kept there was missing. D.I. Joe's well-intentioned offer to make a midnight cigarette smuggling run to retrieve the cig was politely rejected. D.I. Joe reported that one of Azee's Detroit SUVs was parked in the garage and he showed them Azee's small office that was ransacked with a hidden wall safe left open and his computer missing. We surmise that whoever started the Cripplegate estate fire drove up to Drummond Island from Detroit, cleaned out Azee's office and fled to Canada on the cig. They probably didn't want to draw attention to their escape by torching the hunting lodge. The Canadians weren't too happy to find out that a couple of dangerous terrorists could be roaming around their peaceful country."

XXII

After checking one final time on Azee's post-surgical healing, Lamonte supervised the loading of the medical boxes into the van that would transport them to the airport for the flight back to Zurich aboard the Flying Mole, while the doctors flew back to Zurich by commercial airline. In a rush to get to their departure gate, the doctors left a large tip and the medical boxes with the boss of the fixed base terminal to load aboard the Flying Mole once the pilots arrived from their final visit with Azee. The pilots had to retrieve a briefcase from Azee that was urgently needed in Zurich.

Dr. Rahmat waited at the airport terminal until the Swissair flight to Zurich was airborne with the three doctors aboard. Lamonte, as the de facto leader of the group, did not want to tempt fate by returning in the Flying Mole, as it would be shadowed from take off to landing by a possibly vengeful and certainly heavily armed U.S. Navy flight squadron. Colonel Qadafi approved the doctors' departures since Azee was doing well and Rahmat would supervise his post-surgical care.

The two casually dressed businessmen who boarded the flight after the doctors didn't arouse Rahmat's suspicion any more than the two airport workmen washing windows in the gate area. The

CIA had this routine departure well covered. The doctors would have a formal greeting party awaiting them in Zurich where they would be debriefed, willingly was the CIA's hope, about the condition of their patient and their knowledge, if any, of Gleason. The CIA working with Swiss authorities had a couple surprises planned after the doctors' plane and the Flying Mole made their separate landings.

Rahmat carried his black medical bag when he went to visit Gleason in his new place of confinement, in case he had any minor medical needs. When the heavy metal door to Gleason's cell opened, Rahmat discreetly flashed his finger across his mouth as the universal sign of don't talk unnecessarily, as he was sure that the cell was bugged. While taking his blood pressure and listening to his heart, Rahmat engaged Gleason in idle conversation about his improving condition. Gleason, in his most sincere manner, asked how Azee's operation went.

Rahmat didn't give the answer that he would have loved to hear, that Azee died on the table. Instead, he mentioned that the operation went so well that the Swiss doctors departed this morning and they probably flew right over his cell.

Rahmat offered to bring AIDS medication, even though it was not the cocktail of newer medications that were being used in the U.S. Gleason mentioned that it might depend on how long he was going to be in Libya whether he should start taking it. Rahmat prefaced his remarks with a smile by saying that it depended on the United States' willingness to negotiate with a smaller, weaker country and not continue to play the role of the international bully. He also mentioned that Colonel Qadafi was now personally involved in the negotiations and ordered this medical check-up to be assured that Gleason was being well cared for.

Even though the colonel and Azee were friends, the colonel realized that he was in an international public relations game that he couldn't win while harboring the wanted terrorist, Azee, and illegally detaining Gleason. Rahmat had no way of knowing that negotiations were heating up as all parties saw the mutual benefits of getting Azee and Gleason out of Libya. However, the colonel had to save face by not appearing to be intimidated by the United States into releasing Gleason too early.

XXIII

The Flying Mole's non-stop flight to Zurich arrived well before the doctors arrived, due to their need to transfer in Milan. After deplaning, Taajud-Deen and Abdul were asked to wait until the medical cargo was unloaded and inspected by Swiss custom officials and covert CIA agents. The pilots were impatient and not used to waiting for such a routine inspection. Taajud-Deen pleaded to no avail that he had to be at Azee's bank with the briefcase before it closed for the day and their filed flight plan called for their immediate return to Tripoli.

The unhurried customs officials found and opened the largest medical box for inspection. After rummaging around in the packing peanuts they brought out a shoebox size package. They showed it to the pilots and asked if they recognized it. The pilots pleaded ignorance as they had nothing to do with the medical boxes except flying them back to Zurich. They put the package on the ground and brought over their drug sniffing canine, which got a positive hit on the small box. Opening it revealed drug paraphernalia and hashish in multiple plastic bags with medical symbols and terminology on them. Taajud-Deen looked at Abdul with a look that said *we're screwed*.

The customs supervisor was called and read the pilots their

rights but they were not placed under immediate arrest. They were being held until the doctors landed and could be brought over to the fixed base terminal to shed some light on this serious drug smuggling issue. However, the Flying Mole was impounded for an indefinite period, so the return flight to Libya was cancelled. The Swiss authorities informed the pilots that forfeiture of the plane could be a penalty for attempted smuggling.

The three doctors picked up their checked bags from the baggage carousel in Zurich before they were approached by unsmiling customs officials, who escorted them to the fixed base terminal for a search of their personal bags, which proved negative for any contraband. Then they were shown the incriminating evidence found in the medical box. As Swiss citizens, the doctors were escorted into a private conference room where they were read their rights. The pilots were being detained to observe the rest of the medical cargo as it was unloaded. The authorities went through the motions of having each medical carton sniffed by the canine cop, knowing they would find no more contraband.

The doctors could see their prestigious careers disappearing before their eyes, if they were charged and convicted of drug smuggling, as the questioning customs and CIA agents suggested. The plane's owner, the pilots, and the owner of the cargo could all be charged with smuggling when the contraband was presented to the government prosecutor. After the doctors had the *feces scared out of them*, as Lamonte commented, the pilots were brought into the room with the three doctors. This potentially hostile five-some was closely monitored and videotaped through a two-way mirror. Lamonte broke the ice by asking, "What have you done to us?"

Taajud-Deen, as a man of few words, threw the amended question back to the doctors, "You packed your boxes! What have you done to us?"

The hidden observers watched with a certain amount of satisfaction as the two groups threw recriminations back and forth and speculated how the drugs got inside the medical box. The observers didn't expect to hear a confession from either of these unknowing groups. The CIA was mainly interested in how strenuous Lamonte was in protecting his impeccable reputation, so that he could continue his medical work at home and in Israel.

Once the overly animated discussion in the room settled down, the observers re-entered with the airport's security supervisor. He had a cameraman with him who took a mug shot of each of the humiliated conspirators, with the box of contraband on the table in front of them. All five of them had to sign a form stating they would not leave the country and that they would be available for further questioning once the seized contraband evidence was reviewed. Everyone's passport was collected to reinforce this travel prohibition.

As he was asked to open his briefcase on the well-worn table, all Taajud-Deen could think about was where Azee was when he needed him. He sat there with his arms crossed and unresponsive until the request was repeated more firmly. Reluctantly, he rotated the small dials of the integral combination locks and flipped up the two brass tabs. He was asked to unload everything onto the table. The agent seated next to him repeated *everything* and Taajud-Deen warily removed a 9mm Glock pistol from one of the concealed pockets in the upright lid.

This was the perfect opening for the government officials to go ballistic about trying to smuggle firearms into the peaceful, pacifist country of Switzerland on top of the already seized drug contraband. The customs supervisor dramatically slammed shut the briefcase and informed the speechless pilots that they were holding the briefcase, and all its contents, as evidence of their drug and gun smuggling activities.

In reality, the authorities wanted to hold the briefcase to make copies of its contents, hopefully shedding light on Azee's far flung business activities. Now, of course, there was no point in the pilots going to Azee's bank without the contents of the briefcase. The supervisor also reinforced the notion that the pilot of the plane, like the captain of a ship, is responsible for everything on board and that the plane can be forfeited for such illegal smuggling activity.

Taajud-Deen and Abdul were relieved, even without Azee's important briefcase, to go to their hotel rather than to a jail cell for their unexpected night in Zurich. They were not looking forward to calling Azee with the news that he no longer has an airplane and that all GCT's computer information from the briefcase was now out of their hands. They were supposed to deliver this private business information to Azee's banker in Zurich as another back-up in case something happened to his primary back-up site in Tripoli. Azee was essentially on the run now that his headquarters in Windsor was destroyed and he would soon be gone from Tripoli. His bank in Zurich was his final choice as a safe haven for the GCT computer records, and now Taajud-Deen would have to inform him that this plan was negated.

XXIV

The CIA did not initially realize the treasure-trove they lucked into with Azee's briefcase as they set about copying all its computer discs and papers. They gradually discovered that they now had the inner workings of Global Construction Technologies in their hands. When this drug smuggling charade was hatched in Washington, the main objective was to get some leverage over Dr. Lamonte with the trumped-up drug charges. The briefcase and its valuable contents were an unexpected bonus. The CIA planners at Langley surmised that the two superegos of Azee and Lamonte would want and need to get together for post-surgical care in the near future. The CIA wanted to be part of that meeting.

The triangular negotiations between the U.S. and Libya, with France as the mediator, were not proceeding fast enough for the president, so he wanted something to get Qadafi's attention like President Reagan's unannounced, and nearly successful, missile attack. When informed of the briefcase's valuable contents, the president was hit with the idea that this would be the perfect time to take out Azee's back-up computer site in Tripoli as an irritant to both Qadafi and Azee. His only instruction to CIA Director Hayden was that no innocent civilian lives should be lost, since the United States is a principled country fighting an undeclared war against lawless terrorists.

The CIA operatives in Tripoli had no trouble finding a source for enough car bomb explosives to wake up most of Tripoli in their attempt to destroy Azee's back-up computers in the basement of a government office building. Hayden laid down the basic presidential parameter of no civilian casualties. He let the local field agents use their training in explosives to achieve a successful mission.

Gleason was jolted from an already restless sleep in the middle of the night by the car bomb that sounded like it was just outside his villa's white stucco walls. In reality, it was blocks away and the deep quiet of a slumbering Sunday night offered no dampening to the five hundred pounds of explosives parked in the alley behind the building housing Azee's computers. There was no more sleep to be had as air raid sirens awakened the city to an early start of a Monday morning.

Hayden briefed the president about the details of the bombing as the live CNN news feed was arriving on the East Coast. The president watched with a certain relish, knowing Qadafi would now be more inclined to get serious about releasing Gleason. The news media were waiting for a terrorist group to claim responsibility for the seemingly senseless bombing of a Libyan government office building. The president knew that Qadafi would not announce the fact that Azee's computers were in the basement of the now-flattened treasury building.

The president wanted to go on TV and proudly beat his chest while shouting, "*We did it!*" However, that couldn't happen until Gleason was safely back on American soil. Qadafi knew who was responsible and that was all that mattered.

XXV

The wheels of justice turn slowly in Switzerland, with their paranoia about secrecy. Often the defendants and their attorneys embrace this judicial delay, hoping that the charges will simply fade away as they proceed with their daily lives. However, in regard to the pilots and the Flying Mole, an expedited decision was preferred by the United States and Swiss authorities to allow them to quickly return to Azee in Tripoli, without any formal charges filed, but without the briefcase and its valuable contents.

There was blood on everyone's hands, as the briefcase and medical box contraband were not officially logged into the Swiss judicial system. When it became apparent that the pilots would be released without charges, the government's seizure and retention of the briefcase's important contents went unchallenged by the legally unsophisticated pilots as they were happy to get out of the country with The Flying Mole. Hayden, working closely with his field operatives and their Swiss counterparts, determined that they would prefer to fight Azee in Swiss courts at a later date, if he wanted the briefcase and its contents returned.

The CIA had the chance to re-bug the cockpit and passenger cabin of the Flying Mole with the most sophisticated microphones available, which would allow them to closely monitor

Azee whenever he departed Tripoli. The treasure-trove briefcase would be saved as evidence should Azee ever come to trial for his dastardly deeds in Detroit. If not admissible in court as evidence, because of the questionable way that it was seized, it would still provide valuable background information to help the federal prosecutors build their case.

Dr. Lamonte's next scheduled medical trip to Tel Aviv that required his passport was coming up soon. He called on his friendships with high ranking Swiss government officials in an effort to spring the little red book free so he could proceed with plans to go to his surgical clinic in Tel Aviv. He kept getting the bureaucratic run-around with promised calls back, so he was on the verge of canceling this trip.

When Hayden outlined the CIA's plans to the president to capture and repatriate Azee, he was ordered to go to Zurich to set the plan in motion. It was imperative that the talks between Libya and the United States, with France as the intermediary, yield the desired results of securing the release of Azee and Gleason from Libya very soon.

The CIA's original plan, and still the ultimate fallback solution, was to shoot down the Flying Mole with Azee aboard as it was heading back to Beirut. However, if this option were followed, the court of international public opinion would castigate the United States for not bargaining in good faith by immediately killing Azee after acquiring Gleason. Plus, the president wanted to bring Azee back to the face the public humiliation of a high profile trial in his hometown of Detroit.

The president insisted that there be no paper or electronic trail of their top secret plan to capture Azee. Therefore, Hayden left for Zurich to meet with Lamonte in a well orchestrated meeting along with the Swiss Director of Security, Jean Richard, at a debugged royal suite in the Park Hyatt Hotel.

Richard casually tossed Lamonte's passport into the center of the round glass table where they were seated. Lamonte's eyes were fixed on this obvious carrot, as a very somber Richard meticulously explained the drug smuggling charges against Lamonte and the other two doctors. The doctors' fingerprints were the only ones found on the plastic bags containing the contraband. Lamonte's previous admission that they were the only ones repacking the medical equipment for the fight back to Zurich did not help his vociferous denial of guilt either. Lamonte's request that he be allowed to have his attorney present fell on deaf ears. Richard explained that he was not yet formally charged as the investigation was still on-going and they were merely explaining the severity of the charges as a courtesy because of his prominence as a Swiss citizen.

Lamonte explained that he had important upcoming medical obligations in Israel to help the victims of terrorism, and that he would need his passport to fulfill this recurring commitment. Hayden and Richard did their best to act surprised that he wanted to leave the country while still under the shadow of the drug smuggling charge.

Hayden asked Lamonte if travel between adjoining Lebanon and Israel were possible in case he needed to see the recovering Azee. He stated that no such post-surgical visit was planned, but it would be a good idea to arrange one since Azee was in nearby Beirut. It would be better if he could see Azee at his hospital in Tel Aviv, where he would have necessary equipment and supplies for any minor follow up procedures. The hospital had a very secure roof-top helipad, as well as a ground surface helipad in a corner of the hospital parking lot that was used as a back-up when the roof-top was occupied. Richard and Hayden excused themselves and went into the suite's bedroom leaving the fidgety Lamonte seated at the spotless glass table to ponder his future while staring at the little red book so alone in the center of the table.

They returned in a few minutes smiling broadly and Lamonte took the same liberty as he leaned back in his chair to learn his fate. Richard took out some printed sheets from his briefcase. "I understand that you have some reservation about treating terrorists, at least moving them ahead of wounded Israel citizens in Tel

Aviv. Why did you agree to treat the ultimate terrorist, Azee?"

A deathly silence engulfed the room as Lamonte realized that his future medical career, and indeed his whole life, could be determined by his answer. "I have two reasons. The first is easy. Dr. Rahmat is a medical colleague of mine and I helped train him here in Zurich where we worked together on many cases. Nothing as serious as Azee's, I might add. After arriving in Tripoli and evaluating Azee, the three of us wanted to bail and return home. However, we were told that Qadafi insisted that the surgery be done on his friend. Thus, we were forced to operate under the gun, but we still should have refused. If we didn't operate on Azee we would probably still be in Tripoli, but we at least wouldn't be facing this drug smuggling charge."

Hayden was anxious to get at what really made Lamonte tick, to determine if he could be trusted with his most important operation. "How did you find Azee? Did you like him?"

"Medically he was a mess and as a person he isn't very likeable. He loves money and power more than anything else. I got the feeling that he would kill me if the operation wasn't successful. I could never be his friend. Fortunately, doctors don't have to be friends with their patients."

Hearing the answer that he needed, Richard risked his final question. "You said that you had two reasons for operating on Azee?'

"I have never been good at lying, so here's my second reason that I'm not proud of. The three of us jumped at the money we would make. It was more than ten years salary for each of us and since it was earned outside of the country there were no taxes. Ask me if I would do it again. The answer is *no, no, no!*"

Hayden and Richard nodded at each other before they laid out Lamonte's exit strategy from the legal quagmire he was caught in. He was given the name of his future boss, a high level CIA operative in Israel, who would be in touch the moment he landed on his next trip to Tel Aviv. The operative's orders and directions were to be followed without question. Once their objective was achieved, he would be flown out of Israel back to Switzerland. Lamonte snatched his passport to freedom from the center of the table as the three men shook hands to cement the make or break mission for all of them.

XXVI

Hayden's private meeting with the president on his return to Washington was off the record. He assured the president that everything was carefully planned for the clandestine operation called *ATOOL*, which stood for Azee Tom Out Of Libya. There was no need for the president to get involved in the details of the operation, at least until Azee's repatriation was imminent, as he was dealing with enough domestic problems: the election, a new baby and a rapidly failing wife. His main job was to stimulate the State Department to secure Gleason's timely release and Azee's return to Beirut, so that the main purpose of ATOOL—the capture of Azee—could be set in motion.

After the car bomb took out Azee's computers in the heart of Tripoli, Qadafi was less inclined to continue playing David against Goliath, hoping to buy additional time for his recovering friend in the hospital. However, his surprise midnight visit to Azee's hospital room changed his viewpoint. Azee prevailed upon the colonel that he would be safe at Temenos, his fortified compound in Beirut that was guarded by his wife's family militia and his own trained guards.

Azee's main worry was that he would not make it back to Beirut if the Flying Mole were shot down over the Mediterranean by the vengeful United States. Qadafi had obviously considered this possibility when bargaining with the U.S., so Gleason would not be released until Azee had landed in Beirut. The colonel knew of the president's special relationship with Gleason and that he would do nothing to jeopardize Gleason's life.

The president would certainly like to make a big reelection splash by securing Gleason's release and putting Azee on the run as his flight to Beirut would be spun to the media. When Qadafi and Azee exchanged their goodbyes, Azee held up his surgically dressed hand and asked his friend if he would kill Gleason after he was safely home in Beirut. The colonel, pushing Azee away from what could be their final embrace, turned red as his blood pressure went off the charts. "Azee, we have done a lot together. You helped me. I helped you. If I kill Gleason, Libya would be annihilated. I can't fight your fights anymore. I'll get you home to Beirut."

Qadafi had one more stop after leaving Azee. He made sure that an aide had a camera and today's newspaper with them. Gleason was aroused at this ungodly hour and told to shave, shower and get dressed. Of course, his spirits soared in anticipation of heading to the airport to go home. The newly applied handcuffs and ankle restraints would be only minor irritants until he got on the airplane. He detected more commotion than normal outside the heavy door to his cell. A large, nicely dressed guard, carrying a straight backed chair, stepped into the small room and instructed Gleason to stay seated on the edge of the bed.

Qadafi entered and shook Gleason's restrained hand. With three guards hovering over the seated colonel, Gleason did not need words to know what was happening. "I hope you have enjoyed your stay in Libya. If your imperialist president cooperates, you will be home soon."

"Why wouldn't he work with you? I'm a big distraction that he doesn't need for his reelection."

"Possibly because he will have to guarantee safe passage for Azee to Beirut before I release you."

"The president is a practical man who keeps his word. He'll deal with Azee later."

"So be it. That won't be my problem." The colonel stood up and put today's newspaper in Gleason's hands, covering his handcuffs. After a number of solo pictures, with Gleason half closing his left eye, the colonel moved beside him for a few closing shots.

The colonel turned to leave the room, but halted as Gleason teased, "Colonel, could you autograph one of these pictures as a remembrance of my vacation in Tripoli?"

The colonel smiled and gave a thumbs-up. Gleason stayed dressed as he was too excited to sleep and might as well be ready to start his countdown to a quick release.

At the break of dawn, the photos of Gleason holding a current newspaper were delivered to the French Embassy in Tripoli, along with a one page memorandum explaining the details of the departure of Azee, and then a few hours later the release of Gleason. The phone lines and fax machines at the State Department, the CIA and the White House were buzzing to bring this crisis to a timely conclusion.

The president bristled at Qadafi's dictating the terms and the timing of Azee and Gleason's releases. Fortunately, cooler heads prevailed after Hayden reminded the president that their risky ATOOL plan to capture and repatriate Azee would only work if Azee were released to Beirut. The president was acutely aware that the election was imminent and wanted to give the public impression that he secured Gleason's release against the will of a hostile dictator.

When the United States' approval of the releases of Azee and Gleason was received in Tripoli, Rahmat prepared Azee for his departure to Beirut. Accompanying Azee to the Flying Mole in the ambulance, Rahmat assured him that his hand was healing normally, but he highly recommended that he see Lamonte in Zurich or whenever he conducted his surgical clinic in Tel Aviv. Azee pointed out that Zurich was not possible as he would be arrested and extradited back to the United States. However, with his contacts in Israel, he could sneak down to Tel Aviv the next time Lamonte was there.

Once The Flying Mole was airborne, Rahmat drove over to Gleason's detention cell allegedly to give him a departure physical, anticipating his exit from Libya after Azee safely reached Beirut. He found Gleason in good spirits, happy to be heading home in spite of his failed mission of singlehandedly annihilating Azee. Gleason had some apprehension about how he would be accepted by the president and perceived by the media and, of course, what legal charges he faced.

They engaged in light hearted conversation as the physical exam concluded with Gleason being invited back to Tripoli, hopefully on a more social basis. He even managed to gain a few pounds because of better than average jail food and his restricted physical activities. Rahmat gave him an extended embrace, whispering in his ear, "Stay in touch. Hope you get him next time."

While waiting for the guards to take him to the airport, Gleason smiled at Rahmat's encouragement to get Azee next time. He made a mental note that he needed to return to Tripoli to personally thank Rahmat for saving his life, but probably not until Qadafi was out of office.

Two F16 Navy jets from Sigonella picked up the Flying Mole with Azee as a passenger as it cleared Libyan airspace. The Navy pilots established radio contact with the Flying Mole, stating that they would be flying escorts until the Flying Mole landed in Beirut. Taajud-Deen nodded to his co-pilot Abdul to acknowledge the receipt of this warning message. They knew that deviation from the flight plan could not happen unless they were prepared to die. Azee also heard this brief radio exchange and knew that his phone calls from the plane would be monitored.

When the Flying Mole touched down in Beirut, the Navy pilots radioed their home base at Sigonella so that Gleason's departure could proceed. Unlike his usual raucous homecomings at the airport, Azee's arrival was very sedate as he was only greeted by Shakoor and the armed militia in two armored Mercedes. His wife and two children were in a protective lock down inside Temenos. Shakoor informed Azee that security both outside and inside

Temenos was heightened; not knowing if other militias in the still fragmented Lebanon would try to take advantage of the situation with him in the Tripoli hospital.

It was not out of the question that America could mount a Rambo-type assault on Temenos to capture Azee, or they could hire one of the warring militias to do their dirty work for them. Shakoor, as Azee's alter ego in Beirut, had taken it upon himself to construct a subterranean survival bunker with reinforced concrete walls that were three feet thick and could survive anything short of a direct hit by a nuclear bomb.

On the ride to Temenos, Shakoor updated Azee on everything that happened while he was hospitalized in Tripoli. The U.S. ambassador showed up the first morning that he was reported missing on the transatlantic flight. Hasnaa cordially received him in a small sitting room without allowing him and his aides to tour the rest of the villa. He was very solicitous about Azee's welfare and offered the full support of the United States government. Needless to say, once Azee's role in the Detroit bombings was ferreted out, the ambassador's friendly visits ceased.

Shakoor had been in touch with their Russian arms dealer, Andre, by one of the still functioning pay phones in a Beirut hotel lobby with the cryptic message, *the deal is still on.* They were waiting for a reply from Andre that he was going to be able to hold up his end of the deal by supplying the contracted nuclear material to Iraq. Shakoor reported that Iraq's finance minister, Mustafeedh, had called twice inquiring about Azee's condition and that he would be in touch as soon as Azee returned home to finalize their business arrangement.

Being out-bluffed about the Flying Mole's stashed bomb by his pseudo partner, Gleason, was the worst hurt of Azee's life. However, Azee took consolation from the fact that Gleason would ultimately die from AIDS that he contracted from his casino hostess, Misty. If anything, he was more emboldened to pull off his largest and last payday with the sale of Russian nuclear material to Iraq. He was pleased that Shakoor had been in touch with

Andre in Russia and Mustafeedh in Iraq to keep the ball rolling toward the culmination of this world changing transaction.

When Shakoor asked what would happen with Gleason, their official enemy number one, Azee said that he was sure that he would be transferred back to the United States after a few days at Sigonella base in Sicily. Shakoor reminded Azee that the wharf restoration in Sicily at Messina, near Sigonella, was their first Mediterranean project for the Marine division of GCT. In fact, through contacts made there, it opened the door for GCT at the Institute of Religious Works, the Vatican bank that controlled renovations and preservation of the Vatican's properties. This contact with the IRW allowed Azee's firm to successfully bid on the stabilization of the Sistine Chapel foundation using its patented laser alignment system. Shakoor offered to be in touch with their friends in Messina to ferret out Gleason's accommodation at Sigonella and what could be done to arrange a special welcome for him.

Azee smiled at seeing the solitary minaret on the corner of his walled estate through the dust cloud stirred up by the lead limousine. The minaret was a source of pride for the Muslim population of Beirut, but for Azee it was merely an eye in the sky that allowed him to monitor visually and with security cameras both inside and outside the walls of Temenos.

Azee was more standoffish than usual with his wife, Hasnaa, and their children, Jamal and Saarah, because of the mental and physical scars of his recent ordeal. He was careful to keep his injured hand wrapped in a sterile dressing when his family was around, so as not to frighten them with the hideous reminder of the price he paid for living life on the edge. He took little comfort from the well-wishers that told him that he was lucky to be alive. He still had unfinished business to take care of while Gleason was in Sicily.

XXVII

The unmarked Navy jet that was going to fly Gleason from captivity in Tripoli to freedom in Sicily was waiting at a freight hangar for the call from Sigonella that the Flying Mole was on the ground in Beirut.

Gleason laughed at the thought that he would be skipping all customs and immigration procedures in Libya and the United States by flying on a military aircraft. As a matter of fact, he didn't have a clue where his passport ended up, so it wouldn't have a Libyan stamp as a memento of his forced stay in a hostile country.

As the unmarked military jet's stairway was lowering, one of the colonel's plainclothes security guards handed him two large manila envelopes with the request that the colonel wanted him to open them before he boarded his plane. Each envelope had a picture of him and the colonel taken in his cell. The guard asked him to sign the unsigned picture for the colonel as the other picture was already autographed by the colonel for him. After inscribing, *Thanks for your warm hospitality* and signing his name, he and the smiling guard exchanged a high five. He felt grateful to be leaving Tripoli with mixed memories, when at times he had worried that he'd be leaving in a wooden box. He made a mental note to remind the president that the Colonel maybe wasn't the evil demon they all thought.

He bounded up the plane's stairs like a first grader going out to recess. Inside the cockpit he was greeted by two passengers in dark suits who introduced themselves and flashed their CIA photo IDs. He was glad to have their companionship for the long transatlantic flight home since there were no stewardesses provided by the Navy. He also knew that their main mission was to debrief him in as non-threatening an environment as possible.

Once airborne, the pilot came on the intercom with the announcement that their ETA in Sigonella was at noon local time. Gleason must have looked perplexed as the senior CIA agent noticed his quizzical look and explained that his good friend in the White House wanted him to have a couple days of recuperative R and R with someone special on the warm Mediterranean beaches of Sicily, before facing the media madness back home. Gleason didn't have to ask who that someone special was as he suspected that the president would dispatch his ex-wife, Cindy, to be his greeter in Sicily. He was gladdened and terrified at the same time, knowing that his first order of business was to make peace with Cindy, before he could face the world. Score one for the president, who knew what he needed better than he himself knew.

The two CIA companions took turns asking what he considered soft ball questions, mainly about Azee's current medical condition and if he knew Azee's future plans. He spoke glowingly of Dr. Rahmat saving his life by getting him out the hospital, away from the bribing hand of Azee, who would stop at nothing to get revenge. Rahmat's hands were officially tied by the despotic colonel, but Gleason was certain that the doctor would share information on Azee if he was discreetly approached by local CIA operatives. He put a plug in for Rahmat's career by stating that anything the CIA could do to help him should be done. Gleason was glad for the companionship of the debriefing agents, even if it meant being on the hot seat for the short flight to Sigonella. He suspected that he would have a more intensive debriefing at Sigonella and back in Washington, which was the price he had to pay for his foolhardy attempt to bring down the biggest terrorist in the world.

While in the colonel's lockup, Gleason had ample time to think of the crimes he committed that could result in serious federal charges. The legal fees to defend himself against the raft of possible charges would quickly empty his modest retirement savings and, if convicted, he would forfeit his federal pension, which, of course, he wouldn't need if sentenced to spend the rest of his life in a federal prison.

The pilot's announcement to prepare for landing caught them by surprise as they were enjoying the low key debriefing that was the perfect tonic for Gleason to start shedding the burdens on his troubled soul. It kept him distracted and prevented him from formulating a game plan for his unexpected meeting with Cindy. As the plane rolled to a stop, he resolved that total honesty with Cindy was his only path to rebuilding their failed relationship, if indeed she still had the same interest. The fact that she would travel three thousand miles to greet him, notwithstanding the president's certain request, spoke louder than any words they would share. He resolved not to blow this final chance at reconciliation.

As the small jet swung around to park near the freight terminal where they were disembarking, he caught a glimpse of Cindy standing next to a high ranking officer, judging by the scrambled eggs on the bill of his cap. *Possibly the base commander*, he thought. While his two traveling companions were gathering their notes and papers, he furtively crossed himself like a batter stepping back to the plate with a 3-2 count in the bottom of the ninth inning. He was hoping and praying that Cindy would not throw him a curve ball causing him to strike out forever.

XXVIII

Gleason quickly descended the stairs and rushed into Cindy's open arms, breaking their embrace only when they heard the admiral beside them clearing his throat as if to say, *I'm here, too*. Indeed it was the base commander, Admiral Peterson, who ushered them into a small freight packing room that also served as an impromptu conference room. He picked up the phone on the well-worn shipping table and called his secretary, instructing her to notify Washington that the package from Tripoli arrived with no damage and they would await further orders on when to transfer it to Washington. When he replaced the receiver in the cradle with a loud bang, everyone in the room had a good laugh at the continued absurdity of talking in code to needlessly protect Gleason. He was back safe no matter how you said it.

Gleason was handed a packet of information on the base and the surrounding Sicilian countryside. They were provided with the VIP guest quarters next to the admiral's residence. The admiral told them, with an ear-to-ear smile on his well tanned, leathery face, that they had better be on their best behavior. Tom glanced at Cindy when the admiral made this prescient comment and she wasn't smiling. Gleason scheduled breakfast debriefing sessions, as Cindy would probably be sleeping in, as well as evening sessions, thus freeing their days to take advantage of the chauffeured car that could show them the beauties of Sicily.

On their way to their little bungalow, Tom mentioned that he needed to replenish his wardrobe at the base PX as he literally departed Tripoli with the clothes on his back. Cindy smiled and said that he should first check the things she brought for him. The admiral turned around in the front seat and blew a kiss to the hugging love birds in the back seat, a genuine wish for their happiness that the Washington big shots could not order.

When they arrived, Tom collapsed in a man-sized recliner while Cindy went into the bedroom to get him a pair of shorts and a tee shirt from the wardrobe she brought with her. Even though his body was relaxing, his mind was racing out of control trying to figure out the best way to initiate this reunion with the only person he ever loved. She made it easy for him as she plopped on his lap and put her arm around his neck. They held each other, silently snuggling for minutes before they exchanged a tender kiss. They both sobbed and cried until there were no more happy tears to shed. This was one of those mystical out-of-body experiences that they instinctively knew should not be degraded by idle conversation. Cindy finally took the pressure off him by whispering, "I was so very worried about you. I cried every time I thought that I'd never see you again."

He sighed and found a few last tears as he was only able to mumble, "I'm sorry, I'm sorry..." Cindy silenced his trembling lips with a gentle kiss that gradually increased in intensity until they had to come up for air.

She stood up and pulled him into a standing embrace, as she pleaded, "Don't do anything like that again. It will kill me."

"Me too!" They hugged and rocked back and forth in unison sealing the deal that would give them a second chance.

The CIA was good about giving them the space they needed to start rebuilding their relationship, but they still insisted on the morning and evening debriefing sessions. Gleason realized that he was often rehashing many of the same events when questions were being asked from a little different perspective by different debrief-ers, who would obviously compare his answers among themselves. Fortunately, most of his final conversation with Azee, before he bailed out of the Flying Mole, was recorded with reasonable clar-ity. Thus, the CIA could reconstruct the convoluted method that Gleason, posing as Azee's future partner, used to get Azee's confes-sion on masterminding the Detroit bombings, as well as provide a hint of his future plans to supply nuclear weapons to Iraq.

In Gleason's mind, the in-flight recordings on the Flying Mole proved beyond a shadow of doubt that he was only pretending to have sold out his country by becoming Azee's business partner. He had nothing to hide in the debriefings or any need to fabricate any details of his relationship with Azee. He remembered the time when his college Latin professor, who was also the school's feared Dean of discipline, caught a student red-handed violating one of the rigid seminary rules, saying, *Res Ipse Loquitur*, Latin for *the thing speaks for itself*. Gleason's actions were an open book, recorded on the Flying Mole, yet his motivation might be subject to some discussion. He and his CIA debriefers realized that the legal system, probably using a grand jury, would make the final decision on what charges he would face.

Gleason accepted the admiral's offer of a car and driver, so that he and Cindy could admire the beautiful coastline and rolling terrain of Sicily. It seemed like they never lost sight of the rocky coastline as they worked their way to Messina, where Cindy had cousins in the restaurant business.

She had called them when she received word from the president that she could meet Tom in Sicily. She wanted to surprise Tom with this welcome home family reunion with dozens of her rela-tives, so she didn't tell him until they were having a cappuccino in Taormina, a short distance from Messina. She had visited her father's family in this area of Sicily as a teenager for a cousin's wedding and was bored to tears with the long days of celebrating with people she hardly knew, even though they were family. She couldn't wait to get back to her friends at home. Now, as an adult, she was eager to revisit Messina and to enjoy her family like she should have years ago.

The panoramic view from the cliff at Taormina overlooking the Mediterranean matched her teenage memory, except now there were two huge cruise ships tendering in hundreds of tourists to see the local sights. As the swarms of tourists in Bermuda shorts and tank tops worked their way up the cliff to take pictures of their cruise ships out in the bay, Cindy decided they should head to Messina before they were trampled in the quaint narrow streets of the old town.

XXIX

Her family's restaurants were on or just off the Via Garibaldi Boulevard that ran along the harbor, where large freighters docked to allow access to Messina. She remembered the choppy ferry ride as a teenager leaving Reggio Calabria across the narrow straits separating Sicily from the Italian mainland and how relieved she was to reach the terra firma of Sicily. She also remembered how she was greeted at the ferry dock by her boisterous family, waving and shouting, like their home team just scored the winning goal in a soccer game.

Before going to the surprise party at her Uncle Vinnie's restaurant, she asked the young Navy driver to take them to the cathedral in the central part of Messina, where she had attended her cousin's wedding years ago.

Standing in the cathedral's expansive marble piazza, which was still the focal point of life in Messina, she told Tom to keep looking at the impressive stone campanile and clock tower to the left of church. As soon as she alerted him, three black doors opened and out popped carved wooden figures that moved rhythmically with accompanying music. Their intricate choreographed movements were somehow synchronized by the world's largest astrological clock above them that dominated the piazza. The piazza was teeming with street merchants in makeshift stalls or the less affluent peddlers selling rosaries and pictures of the saints from their bent and rusty grocery carts. After two or three more cycles of the larger than life cockoo clock, Tom gave Cindy an appreciative hug with an uncharacteristic comment, "That's cute."

The dark interior of the aged cathedral was illuminated by flickering candles and random rays of sun streaming though priceless stained glass windows. Penniless Tom borrowed a dollar from Cindy, as she was obviously the financier of this holiday, and he slid it into the slot below a large bank of blazing votive candles. He handed Cindy the wax taper so she could light the candle of her choice. They knelt down on the soft velvet kneeling pad as she lit a candle directly in front of them. They crossed themselves and held hands saying their silent prayers as one heart and soul. Walking past the dark marble baptismal font he had flashbacks to the scene in *The Godfather* where the family's joyous baptism was the cover for the brutal massacre of rival families. He knew it was time to leave church when all he could think of was murder and mayhem.

Their driver had pulled the car onto a side street, since the piazza in front of the cathedral was closed to vehicular traffic. They didn't notice that they were being followed at a discrete distance by two overly dressed men whispering into small walkie-talkies.

Cindy pulled a slip of paper from her purse with the name and address of her uncle's restaurant and handed it to their driver who nodded as he read the location where she had arranged to meet her family for Tom's surprise homecoming party. Tom suspected that something was up and it took all his self-control to let Cindy orchestrate whatever was going to happen. As they stopped in front of the restaurant overlooking the harbor, she let the cat out of the bag when she said, "I have some people I'd like you to meet."

Tom muttered, "Oh shit," as he got out of the car and they entered the restaurant to a mixed chorus of *surprise* and *he's a jolly good fellow*. Third generation American Cindy still considered herself Sicilian since countless generations of her family had lived in Sicily even though the mainland of Italy was just across the busy straits of Messina. Sicily was an amalgamation of its maritime Greek origins with the hordes of Europeans who headed south across the straits to a freer life in Sicily. The native Sicilians, like Cindy's family, always felt that they accepted the best of all the immigrants to form an even better group of people. Tom certainly wasn't going to argue that point, as he went from one bone crunching hug to another until he greeted everyone in the large restaurant.

He was good at working a room from all his White House experience, while at the same time being on guard for any suspicious behavior. When he finally reconnected with Cindy he gave a flick of his head toward two well-dressed men standing near the front door who didn't seem to know anybody or to be part of the family, with the implied question of *who are they?*

Gleason saw nothing wrong with crashing a party, as he and his buddies were old pros at doing it in their younger years. However, they usually knew someone at the parties they crashed and these two fellows looked quite uncomfortable waiting by the door as if they were guarding it against unknown party crashers. Without appearing too obvious, Tom and Cindy found her cousin Vinnie who was starting to arrange the food tables for the buffet. He didn't recognize either of them, nor did his brother Tony, who prided himself on knowing everyone in Messina, if not all of Sicily. As Tony headed over toward them to make their acquaintance they quickly vanished out the door. Tony shrugged his shoulders as he walked back to continue setting up the buffet. They look like they were from the other side of the island he thought, a veiled reference to the Mafia stronghold of Palermo.

The free flowing wine, the endless Italian buffet and the lively dancing distracted Tom from worrying about the two interlopers until they again appeared inside the door as the party was starting to wind down. They weren't smiling and they appeared nervously agitated that the party was going on so long. Tom commented to Vinnie, "Maybe they're cops getting ready to stage a raid."

Vinnie could hardly contain himself. "Sorry Tommy boy, but we are the cops along the waterfront. Still, I don't like their looks. I'll have a couple of my men from the kitchen move them outside for a little lesson on manners—you don't crash one of Vinnie's private parties. They won't be back."

XXX

The goodbyes were as involved as the arrival greetings. Each parting embrace included the mutually exchanged invitation to come visit soon, even though Cindy and Tom knew that another party like today would probably never happen. Suddenly, two of the largest men that Tom had seen in Sicily, wearing dirty, red stained aprons and brandishing long boning knives, started across the emptying room to confront the two men still rocking side to side in their fine Italian leather loafers. This time they held their ground, not backing away from the approaching knife-bearing chefs. They pushed back their dark suit coats revealing the leather shoulder holsters that obviously weren't holding super soaker water pistols.

Vinnie grabbed Tom's and Cindy's elbows. "This isn't good. Follow me."

The three of them hurriedly cut through the kitchen into Vinnie's small business office. He shut and locked the door and opened the window overlooking the parking lot. He moved aside a coffee stained, well-worn recliner that obvious had provided years of naps for the aging and hard working owner. Sliding aside a small frayed Persian throw rug he lifted up a concealed trap door, pointing to the narrow ladder leading into total darkness. "My own personal wine cellar." Cindy started down the ladder and Vinnie handed the flabbergasted Tom a small flashlight. "Don't drink too much wine. I'll be back when it's all clear." Vinnie closed and covered the trap door and moved the big recliner back to its original spot. He set the flimsy doorknob lock so that the door would be locked when he closed it.

Going back into the hot kitchen smelling of garlic and oregano, he could see through the small window in the swinging door separating the kitchen from the dining room that the two armed men had the two disarmed cooks spread eagled on the floor in front of them. Another accomplice had entered the dining room and was going from person to person having the few remaining guests empty their pockets and purses into a waste basket that he slid in front of them with his foot.

Vinnie inched back from the door and went to the once white, now tomato colored wall phone and called his cousin Reggie at his dock workers' bar just a block away. All he said was, "Bring five with the goods." Reggie unlocked and opened a metal filing cabinet under his shabby bar. He had no need for tippy tables or cozy booths. If you wanted to talk to someone along the beer varnished bar, you could see them through the smoky haze in the bar length mirror, obstructed only by a random bottle of cheap whiskey for those that wanted a shot to go with their beer.

He held up one of the guns and his other hand wide open, as he shouted to his loyal patrons, who were taking a break from their work as deck hands and stevedores on the docks across the road, "Need five." This was a fairly common occurrence for the regulars seated in their usual spots at the bar. Probably once a month a law enforcement issue arose in the working class bars and restaurants, so nobody was surprised. Everyone raised their long neck bottles, as a sign of community support, and some just wanted to get the free beer that Reggie gave them on their quick return to their still warm bar stools. Reggie was known as the *waterfront sheriff* and nobody from Messina messed with him or his burly enforcers. The undermanned police department welcomed this self-policing by a peaceful show of force to calm down a raucous bar or restaurant party. It had been years since a shot was fired, and that was a warning shot into the floor to get everyone's attention at an overflowing, out of control, coming of age drinking party. The newly deputized and armed volunteers chugged the last of their beers and followed Reggie out the front door for the short walk to their always fun second job.

Gleason stayed at the top of the ladder with his head up against the trap door to try to hear anything he could from the now silent dining room. *All was quiet, too quiet*, he thought. Cindy was tugging on his pant cuffs to come down and be with her in the eerie darkness of the small wine cellar. Their little flashlight barely allowed them to survey the dirt floor and the musty four walls of their closet sized prison that Vinnie had euphemistically called a wine cellar. He was right about one thing, the cool temperature was probably just right for storing the few dust covered vintage wine bottles they could see with the dimming flashlight. He wondered how many happy, intoxicated previous occupants Vinnie had helped up the narrow ladder once their particular crisis passed. He was hoping that they could add their name to that list of happy, not-too-drunk survivors. He didn't want to remind Cindy that he was just released from a greatly upgraded cell and he wasn't ready for another one, even with her as a bonus companion. Cindy was fiddling with her cell phone that she dug out of her purse, trying to determine if she had a signal. She was glad that she had upgraded to international coverage before she left the states, but she still couldn't register a signal in the wine cellar.

The office door banged open, as if a shoulder or foot hit the door, shattering the fragile lock mechanism. They heard heavy foot steps on the floor above them and an angry voice, "So, where the hell are they?"

The unnecessarily loud answer they recognized as coming from Uncle Vinnie, "They must have jumped out the window." Now they knew why Vinnie had thrown open the window.

Cindy started crowding up the narrow ladder beside Tom so

she could hear. What they heard next, they didn't want to hear. The same strange voice screamed, "Die pentito, die!"

The muted swishing sound of a bullet leaving the silenced muzzle of a pistol fired at close range was followed by Vinnie's reactive "Ahh..." The floor above them shook with a resounding thud. Tom instinctively clamped his palm over Cindy's mouth before she could scream their death sentence.

"Let's torch this damned place. That'll learn these stupid pentitos not to mess with us." The floor above them went silent except for the broken office door as it tried to bang shut.

The biggest enforcers from one of Palermo's finest families stacked greasy paper filled boxes on top of the blazing stove burners. Within seconds the grease in the hood and the venting ductwork gave off a distinctive booming roar, as all the oxygen was used to feed the flaming grease. Automatic fire suppression systems were not required in Messina and would have been ineffective when experienced pros were determined to torch a restaurant.

At the sound of the mini explosion in the kitchen, Gleason screamed, "We've got to get out of here—now!" Cindy backed down the ladder to give him room to work. He found one corner of the trap door that he was able to slightly elevate. He pushed, rocked, and slid the trap door until he could get one corner and then one side to reluctantly move. He knew that the rug and old recliner were on top of the door and he hoped and prayed that the 250 pound Uncle Vinnie had not, in one final heroic gesture to conceal the trap door, fallen on it. Yet, the harder he pushed, the more it became apparent that Uncle Vinnie tried to be helpful to the very end. Wisps of dark acrid smoke were starting to filter down into the pit, motivating him to push even harder.

Finally, he was able to get an arm and then his head out to survey the scene. Fortunately, the open window was sucking a lot of the smoke out of the room, but he still had to work quickly before the fire engulfed the room. He got the rug and recliner off the trap door and he struggled to push the dead weight of Uncle

Vinnie away from the opening to keep him from falling into his own wine cellar grave.

Sitting at the top of the now clear opening he hollered down to Cindy, with his best gallows humor, "Bring up a bottle of wine, but hurry!" Sure enough, she handed up a dusty brown bottle that he grabbed as he helped her up the ladder. He pushed the recliner against the shattered door to help retard the billowing smoke and increasing heat while he checked Uncle Vinnie. "He has a faint pulse. We've got to get him out the window. You go first and I'll push him out to you."

She dropped the wine bottle on the grass below the window. Even though she hiked her tight skirt above her knees, she heard a rip as she straddled the window frame for the short jump to the ground. It took all Gleason's strength to drag Uncle Vinnie over to the window, as he was coughing non-stop in the increasingly dense smoke. He was able to get Uncle Vinnie's free falling head out the window and Cindy pulled on his limp arms to try to get them outside.

Sheriff Reggie and his five joking deputies rounded the corner and could see smoke pouring out the roof and the open front door. They were nearly run over by three well-dressed patrons running up the street away from the fire. As they got closer, someone in the crowd hollered, "Stop them!" and pointed in the direction of the fleeing men. Reggie spun around, but they were gone.

Everyone on the street was coughing and wheezing trying to catch their breath. He spotted Tony doubled over steadying himself against a telephone pole to keep from falling over. "Tony! Where the hell is Vinnie?" Reggie shouted.

"Last I saw him was before the fire broke out. Two of the bad guys had pistols in his back headed for his office, probably looking for the cash box."

Reggie knew that Vinnie's office had an outside window so he took two of his deputies and raced around to the back of the smoke and fire engulfed building. Black smoke was billowing out the window and he could barely make out a tall slender woman

trying to pull someone out the window. She was frantically shouting, "Tom, you've got to get out right now!"

Reggie pushed her aside and started to pull the limp person's
shoulders. "My God, it's Vinnie!" With the three of them pulling
from the outside and Tom pushing from the inside they un-wedged
Vinnie from the window frame and his body fell like a rock to the
ground. Gleason, pale as the white shirt he was wearing, leaned
out the window gasping for air. He tried to get one leg up on the
window sill, but started to teeter and fall backward into the black
abyss as Cindy screamed, "Tom!" Reggie grabbed Tom's slumping
shoulders and roughly dragged him over the barely visible win-
dowsill to a safe distance from the doomed building beside the
motionless Vinnie. Tom coughed and retched trying to clear his
body of the suffocating smoke.

Cindy, sobbing uncontrollably, knelt beside her loving uncle
who sacrificed his life for theirs. "He had a pulse when we first got
out of the wine cellar," she wailed.

Still coughing and vomiting to purge out the nearly lethal
smoke, Tom sat up and frantically felt for a pulse in Vinnie's massive neck before screaming, "Who knows CPR?" Cindy immediately tried to blow the breath of life back into her favorite uncle
while Tom used all his strength to begin chest compressions. They
heard the fire trucks arriving out front and Reggie sent one of his
deputies to get the paramedics out back.

While waiting for help to get back to them, Reggie noticed blood
oozing onto Vinnie's shirt with Tom's every heart compression and
Cindy's lung filling breath. "Son of a bitch! He's been shot!"

"We heard the shot down in the cellar and he hit the floor like
he was dropped from a plane. We need to get the heart beating!"
Tom could hear loud gurgling and air escaping the bullet hole as
Cindy continued her hopeful expirations into Uncle Vinnie.

One of Reggie's deputies regretted asking the question after it
escaped his fading voice, "Did they get the cash box?"

Tom and Cindy were the only ones who could answer the
question, if they even wanted to dignify it with an answer. Tom

surprised Cindy with a gentle smile in the direction of the mortified questioner. "They didn't want the cash box. Uncle Vinnie took a bullet meant for me."

Tom was surprised at the effect of his words on his own thinking. He knew that Azee had ordered this contract hit as one last attempt to get even with him. Now his personal war with Azee, since Cindy was also nearly killed, was elevated to the level where there are no rules, except that the most ruthless and strongest will prevail the next time. No questions asked.

Fortunately, the EMTs arrived to relieve the physically and mentally exhausted Tom and Cindy, freeing Tom to completely break down in Cindy's arms, as the true meaning of his own words rocked his soul like never before.

Another team of EMTs arrived, hoping to transport a revived Vinnie to the hospital. Vinnie's heart started beating after the second stimulation with the paddles. Gauze was packed into the open chest wound to decrease the air loss from the punctured lung. It took all four EMTs to get the corpulent Uncle Vinnie onto the stretcher and into the back of the ambulance. When slamming the rear door shut, a rushing paramedic told the gathering crowd, "Everyone better pray real hard. Vinnie has a chance, but it's in God's hands now."

Tom and Cindy were refreshed by breathing the pure oxygen from the EMT's tank. They wanted Tom especially to go to the hospital to be checked out, but now running on a new burst of adrenaline, he resisted, saying that he felt okay. Cindy promised that she and Tom would stop by the hospital a little later to check on Uncle Vinnie and they could be examined then.

XXXI

The police were trying to move all cars and people away from the front of the totally engulfed restaurant. The fire department gave up trying to extinguish the blaze and moved into containment mode, so it didn't spread to other nearby structures. A white Fiat with *Property of the U.S. Navy* stenciled on each front door was the only vehicle still in harm's way, unmoved as all four tires were flat. Gleason bent over to inspect a rear tire that was obviously slashed when he heard kicking and thumping from inside the trunk. The heat was making the metal on the trunk almost too hot to touch. He could only imagine how hot it was inside the trunk. The missing Navy driver was likely bound and gagged inside the sweltering trunk, and quick action was needed to prevent his suffocation or the gas tank from exploding, which would kill everyone around them.

A fireman sprayed water on the car while Gleason frantically hailed a tow truck that arrived. The driver started deliberately backing over, trying to align perfectly for an easy pick up of the immobilized car. Gleason stopped him and pleaded for a simple chain to drag the hot Fiat away from the heat, so they could pry open the trunk to rescue the trapped driver.

The tow truck driver finally understood the urgency of his

request and quickly hooked up a chain behind the front bumper. Tom could hear less noise from inside the trunk as the car was pulled across the street on four flat tires. The tow truck driver realized that someone was trapped in the trunk and he pushed Gleason away, who was looking on the truck for a crow bar to pry open the trunk. "Fiat, cheap lock," the driver said, as he took a short measuring half swing with the round end of a ball peen hammer. The smash of the hammer sent the lock assembly flying inside the trunk. Sticking his finger into the lock hole, the trunk opened easily.

Gleason could see the sweat drenched Navy driver floating in and out of consciousness. He ripped the duct tape off his mouth and cut the heavy nylon ties that were used as hand and ankle cuffs. Fortunately, the driver's young age and superb military conditioning allowed him to survive his short passage to hell and back, but another couple minutes in the pressure cooker trunk would have been a different story with a very sad ending.

The rescued driver was aided out of the trunk and sat on the curb with cool damp towels over his head and shoulders. Two glasses of cold water seemed to totally revive him. "Are you and the lady okay?" were the first words out of his mouth. "I was supposed to watch out for you, besides being your driver. The admiral isn't going to like you guys nearly being killed and the wrecked car."

Cindy and Tom were again teary-eyed as they sat on the tire marked, rough concrete curb next to their young, distraught driver. "Son, don't worry about the admiral. All this: the fire, poor Uncle Vinnie, this totaled car, everything, is on me. It's all on me." Gleason knew that the driver didn't understand why he was accepting all the blame for today's meltdowns. There would be time later for explanations and he certainly didn't want to lay out the whole sordid story to the local authorities. He figured the admiral could better explain it after he and Cindy were back safely in the United States. "Let's check your car telephone to call the base to let them know what happened."

"It can reach the base from here. I was talking to them just before I was jumped by two big guys in dark suits. They threw me in the trunk. I felt the car sink as they flattened the tires. The phone should work if it isn't fried. Let me give it a try." Cindy and Tom hugged on the curb until the driver shouted, "They are getting the admiral on the line."

Gleason slipped into the passenger seat prepared to explain everything to the admiral. The admiral mentioned they were not on a secure line, so they should be brief and a full report could be given back at the base. The admiral wanted to get them back to the security of the base as quickly as possible, so he was dispatching a helicopter to the hospital helipad, with which his pilots were familiar. He ordered the three of them to stay with the police at the hospital until the helicopter arrived. When Tom informed Cindy of the hospital plans, she was delighted they could also check on Uncle Vinnie.

At the hospital Gleason needed the down time to prepare his explanation to the admiral. Gleason was unsure of how much the admiral knew of the sordid Azee saga and how much he should tell him.

Gleason had no hard proof that Azee was behind this attempt to end his and Cindy's lives. As a matter of fact, he was so filled with anger and hatred for Azee that he didn't need any hard proof. His gut feeling was all he needed. The CIA and the FBI would have time to develop the hard evidence against Azee that could be given to the admiral, so Gleason decided to play dumb if he were pressed for details of why he thought the attack happened.

XXXII

The president, Dr. Schmidt and White House legal counsel, Philip Wright, were having a late afternoon medical and legal consultation in the oval office. The president happily reported that Gleason was safely in U.S. hands at Sigonella naval base in Sicily for his reunion with Cindy and continued debriefing on the ongoing Azee saga. They breathed a collective sigh of relief that he was out of the unpredictable Colonel Qadafi's grasp and away from Azee's poisonous tentacles.

They would now be able to shift their focus to his medical and legal problems when he returned to the United States. It was obvious that Gleason's first priority should be to begin treatment for his AIDS with the current cocktail therapy recommended by the NIH. The president decided that Gleason would be placed on indefinite medical leave from his official Secret Service duties, while the medical and legal issues swirling around him were allowed to settle down.

The president was sure that his harshest political opponents would try to make political hay by calling for Gleason's immediate firing, and even his arrest, for any number of serious legal infractions as soon as he touched down on American soil. Fortunately, the overwhelming poll results favoring Gleason's Old West vigilante action soon muted this premature criticism and the president was emboldened to do what he felt was right for his friend and confidant. Wright was instructed by the president to contact the attorney general's office to prepare a concise legal brief of all the possible charges Gleason could face for his Azee escapade. Wright commented that the word *concise* was not in the attorney general's vocabulary, but he would try to get a legal brief speedily, which hopefully would be shortened in length because of the quick time constraints. In any case, it was certain that Gleason would face very serious legal issues, in spite of his good intentions of sparing the country the grief of Azee's protracted trial.

The president had already developed his own legal strategy for dealing with Gleason's legal quagmire when he returned, but he still wanted this preliminary legal brief from the normal governmental legal channels to provide an air of transparency for the media's benefit.

The first lady's deteriorating condition should have been an easier decision than Gleason's complicated medical and legal issues. However, since the president had entrusted Dr. Schmidt with the responsibility of maintaining the first lady's status quo as long as possible as the election drew near, he was able to pigeonhole her condition into his *to-be- dealt-with-later* brain compartment. That is, until Dr. Schmidt mentioned that she was becoming more concerned about the ethics of prolonging the first lady's totally hopeless situation, especially for political reasons.

Dr. Schmidt reviewed the results of the first lady's latest blood tests which showed no significant changes. The most recent brain scans showed that the bleeding in her brain had stopped, but there was still a small area of residual intra-cranial blood. The neurosurgeon postulated that her overall condition would not be improved even if this intra-cranial blood were not present, so there was no consideration given to surgically removing it.

She reminded the president that the first lady's Glasgow Coma Score was consistently a Three—the lowest possible score. Not meaning to complicate or confuse the issue, she mentioned that the corollary to the Glasgow Coma Scale is the predictive Glasgow Outcome Scale where the first lady's score is Two, which indicates a PVS, a Persistent Vegetative State. The only lower score in the Glasgow Outcome Scale is a One, which is death. She tried to soften the impact for the president of these numbers by saying that they were just numbers, but the president still focused on what the numbers represented—hopelessness.

When Melody was born the president rationalized that he wanted the first lady to survive a few days so that Melody, as she grew older, would never feel that her birth was the cause of her mother's death. It also allowed him and the boys time to enjoy the new baby without planning an immediate, elaborate state funeral. The first lady's life was hanging by a thread, but only time would tell, as Melody matured and lived out her adult life, whether his rationalized reasoning for not pulling the plug would achieve the desired results.

At the time of Melody's delivery, the first lady's hyperbaric oxygen treatments were cut back to once a day with no apparent deleterious effects. Dr. Schmidt closely watched the president's body language as she now recommended eliminating the hyperbaric treatment altogether. She could detect no presidential reaction to this suggestion, which she interpreted as meaning that he had no objection to the cessation of these futile treatments. She mentioned that for these hyperbaric oxygen treatments to be beneficial there has to be something for the increased oxygen levels to work on, like normal functioning brain tissue. She surmised that since there was no improvement with the intensive hyperbaric oxygen treatments, there probably wasn't enough normally functioning brain tissue to show improvement.

White House polling data of the voting electorate showed higher approval ratings if the president stayed in Washington close to his wife and new baby, so he cancelled some of his out of town campaign stops and ordered his vice president to cover the rest.

Wright mentioned that if the hyperbaric oxygen treatments were going to be discontinued it should be done without a public announcement. Sooner or later the media might find this out and, this close to the election, it hardly gets mentioned.

Wright didn't see any legal issues involved if the hyperbaric oxygen treatments were stopped since they were not improving the first lady's hopeless condition. In the final analysis this cessation was the president's personal decision, keeping in mind the first lady's medical directive that no extraordinary measures be used to keep her alive. However, for public relations consideration, the president still wondered if it would be better to start weaning her off the treatments by going to one treatment every other day rather than abruptly stopping them.

Dr. Schmidt did all she could to restrain herself at the president's political vacillation and the lawyer's usurpation of her doctor's right and obligation to do what is best for the patient. She glanced at the president to ascertain his true feelings and all she got was a shrug of his shoulders. She didn't want to make this important decision alone and then be second guessed by her boss and the media. She knew how to get the president engaged, so she brought up the fact that the Hemlock Society was getting more vociferous in their public protests on the street outside the hospital, as well as across from the White House in Lafayette Park. The Hemlock Society wanted all life sustaining technology turned off. Going a step further, they suggested giving the first lady a lethal injection if she didn't die soon after the artificial life support machines were turned off.

"They haven't protested on the hospital grounds have they?" Dr. Schmidt shook her head, knowing not to interrupt the aroused president, who was still interested in protecting his and his wife's last vestige of dignity without outsiders telling him what to do. "Life is so simple for those placard protesting bastards. Take a pill or give your loved one a shot and all troubles disappear. I'd like to give them a shot from an AK-47."

Dr. Schmidt and Wright knew that this was a time to hold their advice as the president was now in charge. "To hell with public perception! Kathy has been through enough. She isn't coming back. Let's stop the hyperbaric treatments today—cold turkey. If she survives until the election, then we'll turn off the respirator and let nature take its course, unassisted by the Hemlock Society. The nightmare needs to end for all of us."

XXXIII

There were two quiet beeps on the president's intercom from his secretary, which was their code that someone important was on the phone. Picking up the phone, he was told that Admiral Peterson was calling from Sicily. The president motioned to Dr. Schmidt and Wright to stay as they were getting up to leave and he put the incoming call on speaker phone, inviting them to share the conversation.

The admiral apologized to the president for having only minimal information provided by his staff monitoring the police radio on a restaurant fire in Messina that nearly killed Tom, Cindy and their Navy driver. He was awaiting their firsthand report after their helicopter arrived back at the base, as he didn't want the details explained on the open airwaves during their short flight back to the base.

The admiral had used his discretion in allowing Tom and Cindy off the Sigonella base when Cindy explained that her family owned a restaurant in Messina and they would like to host a quiet family party for her and Tom. The admiral assigned his most experienced Italian speaking junior officer as a driver and bodyguard. The admiral was confident in the driver, who had a black belt in karate, and he wasn't anticipating any trouble since it was not publicly known that Gleason had been sent to Sicily from Tripoli.

The Navy helicopter had picked the three of them up at the hospital helipad after Cindy visited her Uncle Vinnie. Gleason, quiet like a whipped puppy, and the Navy driver stayed in the emergency room to be checked out by the ER doctors, while Cindy went to Uncle Vinnie's room to say her goodbyes to the family. Vinnie's brother Tony and his cousin Reggie paid a quick visit to Gleason and the driver in the ER. "We'll get the bastards who did this," Tony said, loud enough for the staff beyond their curtained area to hear. "Probably from Palermo, where we have friends, too."

Gleason knew that he had to say something, but he debated how much to tell them. "Boys, don't get killed over this. They were after me because I work for the government. Vinnie saved Cindy and me by hiding us in the wine cellar. Let my government handle this."

"Don't matter who they were after. They shot Vinnie and burned down his restaurant. They will be dead before your government knows who they are. That's our way," Reggie boasted.

Gleason smiled and thought, *Go for it. You get them and I'll get Azee. You'll probably have an easier time getting them than me getting Azee, but I'll get him for what he did to Cindy and her family, if it's the last thing I do.*

The president, sensing that there was very little factual information on Gleason's latest escapade forthcoming from the admiral, asked him to call back when Gleason was there to explain things directly to him. He was trying not to blame Gleason for this serious international incident now involving Italy, one of their staunchest European allies.

If anything, the president was perturbed with the admiral for letting Tom and Cindy off the guarded confines of the Navy base, but for now he kept these thoughts to himself. It sounded to him like a case of Tom and Cindy being in the wrong place at the wrong time, as two Mafia families were settling old grudges. The admiral related that the gunman who shot Uncle Vinnie had used the word *pentito* before he shot Uncle Vinnie and that they were asking their Italian speaking translators for help on its meaning.

Counsel Wright interjected that he was very familiar with the meaning from his days as a junior prosecutor in Manhattan's federal court, where he was assigned many of the low-level extortion and racketeering cases coming out of Little Italy. He said it was a word not used lightly among the Mafia, as it carried with it the solemn obligation to kill the *pentito*, which they certainly tried to do. A *pentito* was a term of maximum disrespect for someone who collaborated with the enemy, usually the judicial system, like the famous case of Mafia hit man Joe Valachi who sang to the feds to save his own skin. Valachi, convicted of numerous crimes, had been in protective solitary confinement at Milan Federal Prison because of the Mafia's bounty on his head.

The fact that the gunman had called Uncle Vinnie a *pentito* was reason enough to shoot him for transgressions against the Family. The hit men were probably unaware of their boss's real reason, his friendship with Azee, for wanting the two Americans killed. However, when they broke into Uncle Vinnie's office asking where Tom and Cindy went, that was reason enough to call Uncle Vinnie a *pentito* for helping an enemy of the Family escape. Fortunately, the open window answered the hit men's question, thus allowing Tom and Cindy to stay hidden in the wine cellar until forced out by the fire.

The president obviously was thinking, as he vocalized a long *hmm*. Even the admiral thousands of miles away recognized that the president was getting ready to say something important. "That damned Azee is behind this. We've got to kill the bastard to stop all his bullshit." The telephone line remained silent as the president was left to explain things further. However, he didn't want to go into all the details and reasons for his suspicion of Azee with the admiral, who was not in the totality of the Azee loop. The admiral was on a need to know basis with his hosting of Tom and Cindy, and he didn't need to know any more about Azee than he already knew.

Wright, trying to justify his high government salary for legal advice, strongly suggested Tom and Cindy be put on the first flight back to the United States before the local police started investigating and determined that they were indeed the target of this Mafia hit, with an Azee connection. The president did not need Cindy, and especially Gleason, to be drawn into a protracted Italian legal system foray.

The president didn't ask the admiral how soon before the next flight to the U.S., but instead ordered that Gleason and Cindy go right from the helicopter when it landed at the navy base to a waiting plane that would get them out of Italy to a military base in a different country, where final arrangements back to the states could be arranged. As commander in chief he told the admiral that this was a direct order and that he wanted to know the exact location of Gleason and Cindy at all times. To impress on the admiral the priority of their quick and safe return to the states, he mentioned that he hoped the Air Force wouldn't have to provide the necessary flights if the Navy couldn't complete this simple mission.

The president didn't want to rattle the admiral any more by suggesting that another reason he wanted them out of Sicily immediately was because Azee and his Italian friends might have a civilian worker inside the base who could get to Gleason as their backup assassination plan for the failed restaurant hit.

The admiral didn't achieve his rank by being stubborn and stupid, at least not at the same time, so he readily agreed with the president stating that he would call the base operations office to ready a plane for immediate departure to an undetermined destination.

Cindy would be quickly escorted to the guest cottage to gather her belongings while four armed MPs would stay with Gleason until they were aboard their flight out of Italy. The admiral knew there were daily flights from Lajes Field in the Azores to the Washington D.C. area, so his plan was to personally accompany them to the Azores, which are part of the ever-supportive Portugal.

He hoped that the Azores were far enough from the European mainland that Azee's evil tentacles didn't reach there. Lajes Field is a very busy military base with flights crisscrossing the Atlantic, so it seemed to be a great location for keeping Gleason out of Azee's grasp and for getting a quick flight back to the U.S.

After they exchanged the usual goodbye pleasantries, the conference call and the oval office meeting ended. Dr. Schmidt gave the president a perfunctory hug as she quickly headed to Bethesda to stop the futile hyperbaric oxygen treatments on the first lady.

XXXIV

The president wanted to confirm his hunch that Azee was connected to the Sicilian underworld, without getting the FBI or the CIA involved, as that could led to inevitable press leaks that he didn't need with the election looming and his wife in her final days. He could think of no one better to call than Azee's best friend in the administration, Vice President Taylor. Taylor was immediately put on the defensive by the declarative way the president started the conversation. "Taylor, tell me about Azee's relationship with the Mafia."

Taylor's rambling reply was totally innocuous, as he was obviously stalling for time, hoping that the president would reveal the main reason for this rare call from the oval office. When the president felt that he was getting nothing useful from his open-ended request that had a bit of guilt-by-association for Taylor, if he wanted to pick up on it, he filled Taylor in on the details of Gleason's and Cindy's near murder in Sicily.

The mention of Sicily jogged Taylor's memory into recalling that Azee was awarded his Sistine Chapel foundation stabilization contract because a business acquaintance from Palermo knew the cardinal prefect of the Vatican's Office of Religious Works. This all-powerful church office controlled the purse strings for church building projects. Azee's Marine division had done some bulk-head and wharf repair for this person's harbor side warehouse in Palermo. They became good friends, even cruising together on the Aqua Mole to Capri, as Taylor remembered because Azee had told him that the Isle of Capri would be their first trip on a Mediterranean cruise when he was out of office. Taylor saw noth-ing to be gained by sharing Azee's unfulfilled invitation with the president.

The president wasn't surprised that Azee had powerful friends in Palermo, the reputed Italian Mafia strong-hold, who would have no problem dispatching hit men to Messina to take care of business for their old friend Azee. Before he turned this Mafia connection information over to the FBI and CIA, the president wanted a face-to-face meeting with Gleason when he got home.

Whether members of Cindy's family were part of the conspiracy to kill Gleason would come to light once a complete investigation was undertaken. The president planned on using the attack and near-death of the young Navy driver as another reason for using the full force of the United States government, after the election, to avenge Azee's attempted killing of Gleason and Cindy.

Even with Azee's Windsor office computer records and the back-up system in Tripoli destroyed, there had to be a record somewhere of construction work that GCT did in Palermo. The briefcase contents in Zurich were one possibility, and getting the local officials in Palermo to remember whom Azee had worked for was another. The latter was going to prove difficult as the families traditionally, even when fighting each other, hang together against the outside world.

XXXV

The high priority evacuation of Gleason and Cindy from Sicily to Lajes Field in the Azores gave them a chance to relax after their near-death experience in Uncle Vinnie's wine cellar. The admiral and two thick necked uniformed MPs accompanied them on the first leg of their journey back to American soil. The admiral consulted with CIA Director Hayden and decided to leave the debriefers back in Sicily, rather than continue Gleason's tedious debriefing over the Atlantic. Once airborne, the admiral sent the White House the requested message that Gleason and Cindy were safely out of Italy, beyond the reach of Azee and the Italian legal system.

One nice thing about military flights into military bases was that no visas or passports were required. When they landed at Lajes Field, the admiral realized they had time to eat at the officers' club before Gleason and Cindy jumped on their connecting flight back to the states.

Ever-thoughtful Cindy got the name of their young Navy driver in Sicily from the admiral so she could send him a thank you for taking care of them. Gleason joked to the admiral to be sure to send the White House a bill for the totaled Navy car. "Fat chance they'll pay," the admiral said. "You forget that the president is my commander in chief and I don't want to give him a reason to retire me before my time."

After dinner, the admiral and the two MPs escorted Tom and Cindy to the stairway of their military transport bound for Washington, where they expressed gratitude to the admiral for their short but memorable stay in Sicily.

Once seated on the plane, Tom reached for Cindy's hand. They held hands and took turns resting their heads on each others shoulders once airborne. He made small talk with Cindy about how much more he was enjoying this flight over the Atlantic than the one with Azee in order to stall from sharing about his one night stand in Detroit that changed his and probably the president's life forever.

Finally, he got the courage to begin, "Cindy, I'm sorry." She squeezed his hand tighter and smiled at his misty eyes. "You would be justified in never seeing me again. I let myself and you down. I went against everything I believe. Please forgive me."

"Tom, that's enough! We know that you made a terrible mistake. We can work to rebuild our relationship, but for now you have far bigger issues."

"Maybe bigger, but not more important."

"That's exactly what the president said when he asked me to meet you in Sicily. It's like you guys are soul mates."

"We think like brothers, which can be scary. I let him down big time. I hope we can still be friends."

"Don't worry; you were working for him when you did what you did in Detroit."

"Too bad our stay in Sicily didn't work out. At least we saw your family."

"Yeah, and we left them in a real mess."

Tom knew that Cindy didn't say this to intentionally inflict more guilt on his already overloaded soul. In a strange way he welcomed it, as it reinforced his commitment to get even with Azee at the first possible chance. "Someday soon, I promise that we will return to Sicily to return the love your family gave us."

"I agree, Tom, but for now you'll have to maintain a low profile until after the election. One good thing about coming home now is that Kathy might still be alive and you can be there to support the president."

"I've hardly thought of the first lady, the boys and Melody," Tom answered, with a trace of guilt and sorrow in his voice.

"That's understandable. You were in a survival mode."

"Now I have to be available to support the president, if he still wants me. We must return Azee back to the states to face the music."

"Tom, please don't get personally involved with Azee again. It will kill me. Let the system handle it."

Tom smiled at Cindy without replying. From their wedding and honeymoon in the Dominican Republic nearly twenty years ago, as well as during their married years, Cindy knew that her request for Tom to back off an issue that he was committed to was futile. Tom had become preoccupied during their Dominican Republic wedding and honeymoon, ignoring her advice at the time, and followed his hunch about a prominent Dominican businessman. After much personal and professional anguish over a period of months, Tom's hunch proved to be correct, so she learned to cut him a little more slack during their married years, and now this Azee business was probably going to fall into the same category.

They both dozed like newlyweds returning from an exhausting honeymoon, secure in their belief that things could only get better. As they were starting their descent into Andrews Air Force base, they were given a note from the cockpit informing them that the White House was dispatching a limo to pick them up. They nervously smiled at each other after they simultaneously read that the president was inviting them for a welcome home dinner. "I can't go to the White House like this," Cindy lamented, looking at her rumpled Sicily clothes.

"Well, what about me? After all, I'm the guest of honor!" Cindy's sharp elbow to his ribs doubled him over in a fit of therapeutic laughter. "I deserved that. After we land let's check your suitcase for some clothes. Anything clean is better than what we're wearing."

XXXVI

Dr. Schmidt got to Washington's Union Station early enough to have a bagel and coffee while waiting for her two CIA companions to arrive so they could board the train to New York. The president and the CIA became very concerned that Azee's Russian contact, Andre Melodny, could still deliver the bargained for nuclear materials to Iraq with or without Azee in the picture. In the days prior to this New York trip to interview Andre's younger brother, Boris, she was extensively debriefed by the CIA on her knowledge of Andre, her former Russian lover, while she was stationed at Newport Navy base over twenty years ago.

Today she was expecting a relaxing train ride to the Big Apple. Twenty years ago, she and Andre spent an idyllic weekend in New York, where she briefly met Boris, a senior dental student at New York University, who wanted to stay in the New York area to practice dentistry after he graduated. Shortly after that wonderful weekend as the romantic embers were heating up, Andre had been unmasked as a Russian spy, or so the official government report stated. He was deported out of the country without a goodbye between the two of them.

Twenty years later, at the request of her boss, the president, she had more than a jilted lover's interest in trying to locate Andre through his brother, Boris. The CIA told her that the peace and security of the western world was in serious jeopardy if Iraq got control of this nuclear material supplied by Andre. Checking New York phone books, she had tried to locate Boris without success. Now with the CIA involved there was an increased sense of urgency and they were able to locate him. He had changed his last name from Melodny to Bukharin shortly after he graduated from dental school. The name change was of great interest to the CIA, as they are always suspicious when someone tries to change his identity.

Whenever she had a few minutes to people watch in the beautifully restored Union Station, she felt that she was sitting at the crossroads of the world as every conceivable type of human being hurried past her. Years ago she noticed that train travel attracted a different type of person than airplane or bus travel. Everyone was in a hurry, carrying a weird assortment of torn shopping bags, battered briefcases, bulging suitcases with noisy wheels, and almost everyone seemed too preoccupied to quiet their fussing kids lagging behind. There were no two people dressed alike except her two CIA companions in dark suits, who arrived just in time to grab coffee and bagels as the train's departure was announced.

The three of them found bulkhead seats facing each other, so they had quiet and privacy at least on one side for the three hour trip to New York. Before the train left the dark bowels of Union Station, the older of the two CIA sleuths wondered aloud if they would be using FDR's personal railroad siding in New York with its own private elevator, which kept the wheelchair bound president out of public view when he'd visit the family home at Hyde Park for his clandestine meetings, not always of the business nature. Dr. Schmidt teased the story teller that he didn't look old enough to have been with FDR on these Eleanor-less adventures. When the younger agent joined in on the teasing of the older agent, she thought that they were going to have an entertaining three hours. The older agent admitted that the stories about this private presidential train exit ramp have been greatly amplified with each new generation of agents as they hear them and repeat them to their successors.

The younger agent, reluctant to correct his superior, finally set the record straight by saying that their train was going into Penn Station in New York and not FDR's Grand Central Station. The younger agent had made the travel arrangements for the group, so when the older agent continued to question the younger agent on their arrival station, the younger agent gave his personal account of how he and his buddies always travel by train from D.C. to attend New York Knick basketball games at Madison Square Garden, which is juxtaposed to Penn Station. The younger agent finally quieted his still doubting boss by explaining that Boris's dental office was in lower Manhattan, very near Penn Station, so that they would not have far to ride in an ulcerating yellow cab.

Observing this trivial exchange between the older and younger agent, Dr. Schmidt thought that the older agent was losing it, well past his prime, as he nodded his grey head in submission to the confident, if not cocky, younger agent. The older agent put his head on the padded neck rest and asked his younger companions to wake him when they got to Union Station, purposefully confusing it with Penn Station. Before nodding off he sleepily asked Dr. Schmidt how she got interested in a Navy career. He didn't tell her that as a newly graduated attorney he had served his tour of duty in the Navy's legal department, so he was well aware of how the Navy worked, protecting and promoting its own, especially an attractive up and coming female officer.

She innocently began a recapitulation of her Navy career starting with basic training at Newport, Rhode Island. She started to move on to her next Navy assignment without elaborating on Boris and Andre, when the older agent, without opening his eyes, groggily asked how she met these two Russian brothers. She mentioned that she met Andre at a beach volleyball game, where most of the young officers congregated on free weekend afternoons. He was standing off to the side watching the sweaty, sandy action, so she invited him to be on her team without knowing who he was. The fact that he looked athletic and was very good looking made her invitation a no-brainer. The younger agent nodded his head in understanding.

Of course, the obligatory beers after these beach volleyball games allowed Andre to become friends with the young officers. The older agent suspected, but didn't know the total depth, of Nancy's and Andre's friendship and was trying to get her to reveal it by appearing bored and sleepy as she talked. He had been able to pull up the base commander's twenty year old records and reports from that time, but ran into a brick wall when he found the admiral's terse emergency memo sent to the Pentagon, stating that Andre must be immediately deported back to Russia because of suspicious activity and creating morale problems among his officers. There was a penciled note with a date at the bottom of this urgent memo simply stating, *Deported back to Russia.*

The sly old fox nonchalantly asked what could have caused Andre to leave so abruptly. He watched out of the small slit of his drooping eye lid as her complexion turned fire engine red, signaling that he might be right about the nature of Andre's hasty departure, but still not privy to the actual reason. When he read her Navy personnel file, he noticed a highly unusual little blip in her record that stated that the base commander was reserving the right to add an addendum final report at the conclusion of her basic training. Obviously, this addendum could have been positive or negative, but the old CIA agent, with antennae that spanned the globe, would have put his money on a negative report being generated if she messed up again.

She was searching for a simple explanation of Andre's departure. The older agent, as the master inquisitor, had the seasoned forbearance to listen to a squirming respondent until the tortuous truth finally came out.

The younger agent sensed how uncomfortable she was trying to evade what on the surface should have been an innocuous question, so he mentioned that this incident was over twenty years ago and had nothing to do with their concern of the day, interviewing

Boris. The older agent bolted upright and gave the younger agent a look that said, *We'll have a talk later, if you live that long.*

Once at Penn Station, they grabbed a yellow cab to Boris's dental office, located in the Empire State Building, a few blocks away on 34th Street. Dr. Schmidt had fond memories of her only other visit to this venerable New York landmark with Andre on the same weekend that she met Boris. She remembered it as a sunny, perfectly clear day when the attendant in the 102nd floor's circular glass observatory commented that you could see over seventy miles in all directions, when her main interest was no farther than the dashingly handsome Russian diplomat at her elbow. Now, on the elevator ride up to Boris's forty-fifth floor dental office, she decided that she would not mention this previous visit to the Empire State Building, as it would just give the older CIA agent another excuse to talk about her relationship with Andre on the train ride home.

Boris agreed to meet them at his office on his afternoon off as it was convenient to Penn Station and they would have the privacy that a restaurant wouldn't allow. Boris declined the CIA's offer to meet in a conference room at the Federal Building out of a suspicion that their meeting could be recorded or picked up by the press who were always hanging around the Federal Building looking for a scoop.

Exiting the elevator, the older agent spotted a men's room, so he stated that the men had to use it as he steered the surprised younger agent through the heavy wooden door. Standing elbow to elbow at two old fashioned wall to floor yellow stained porcelain urinals, the older agent asked a question that he didn't want answered, "Didn't you take interrogation 101?" Pausing to finish his manly business, he continued, "Don't ever interrupt a witness who's struggling to answer a question. Let them hang themselves as Dr. Schmidt was about to do. Now we may never know the real reason why Andre abruptly left the country."

The chastised younger agent uttered, "Yes, sir," as he pitched his paper towel into the corner trash receptacle.

They walked past a number of small business and medical offices before they came upon the name *Boris Bukharin, D.D.S.* painted on the locked frosted glass entry door. They could see a light on in the office, so the younger agent pushed a doorbell beside the dark oak door frame. The shadow of a tall man approached to unlock the door. He locked the door behind them while introducing himself and offering robust handshakes to his three guests.

Boris suggested that they meet in the waiting room as his private office was very small. The older agent, the de facto leader, nodded his approval and commented that the rent must be very expensive as his was the only dental office they saw trying to find his office. The older agent knew that most dental offices don't generate large incomes like medical offices to be able to pay the high rent in prime buildings like the Empire State Building, so he was curious how Boris could afford it. Dr. Schmidt sat in a corner chair and put her purse on a small table that was overflowing with dog-eared magazines. There was no mistaking the distinctive pungent smell of a dental office due to the wide assortment of malodorous medications used. *This will clear my sinuses*, she thought.

The first question that the older agent wanted to address, which he thought might be a little less threatening ice breaker than getting right into discussing Andre, was Boris's reason for his name change from Melodny to Bukharin. Boris became very animated as he started giving a discourse on Russian history that the three of them thought would never end. Boris explained that his grandfather was Nikolai Bukharin.

The older agent vaguely recalled this name from his study of Russian history, which all CIA agents were required to study to give them a better understanding of their enemies during the cloak and dagger years of the Cold War. Nikolai Bukharin had been one of the founding fathers of the Russian revolution with Lenin and Trotsky, but years later, Stalin viewed him as a threat to his supreme power and purged him along with untold millions of the enemies of the USSR. Western governments were aware of these political slaughters, especially Bukharin's 1938 sham trial and execution by Stalin's order, but were powerless to stop them.

Boris's grandmother, Anna Bukharin, survived long enough to see her husband's name rehabilitated by Mikhail Gorbachev as part of the repudiation of the brutality of the Stalin years. The Bukharin family had been able to keep its name in front of each generation of U.S. State Department officials manning the Russian desk. The State Department obviously was trying to curry the favor of the changing Russian government that was repudiating the brutal Stalin years, so they went out of their way to show preferential treatment to the surviving Bukharin family, the deportation of Andre notwithstanding.

The older agent now had a mental picture of how Boris jumped over numerous bureaucratic hurdles in both Russia and the United States to attend dental school in New York when our immigration standards at the time were still restrictive for new Russian immigrants. Always suspicious, he wondered if Andre's family connection is what allowed him unprecedented access, as a low level Russian diplomat, to the Newport Naval Base where he met Dr. Schmidt. The apparent preferential treatment of the Bukharin family by the State Department could have resulted in serious security issues then and now, and he would have to inform his superiors of this connection to be sure it was not a factor in their struggle to neutralize Andre providing nuclear material to Iraq.

Boris started talking about the overthrow of the Czar and the early days of the Russian revolution and how Stalin totally destroyed the power to the people goals of the Russian revolution. The older agent was trying to derail Boris's rambling Russian history lesson, which he knew was Boris's nervous attempt to delay facing the real purpose of this meeting, so he asked, "Has anyone else in your family changed their name to Bukharin?"

The Russian history lesson ended as Boris explained his own reasons for changing his name. Most of his family still lived in Russia and it probably was not a good idea for them to change their name to Bukharin, as it would be a reminder of their grandfather's role in the communist founding of their country which the new Russia was trying to forget. The new Russia was stumbling along trying to join the western world of free enterprise and their grandfather had been one of the communistic theoreticians behind Lenin, and later Stalin, before he was put to death by Stalin.

Boris changed his name when he started his dental practice twenty years ago because he wanted to honor his grandfather who was held in total reverence by his grandmother, whom he was very close to as a boy growing up in Russia. His own father was supportive of this name change when Boris mentioned that the Bukharin name would give him more recognition among the Russian immigrants in New York, who would be the foundation of his new dental practice. Another reason for changing his name, which he reluctantly mentioned, was that it would give him a life of his own, not continuing to live in the shadow of his older brother, Andre, whom everyone knew was destined for an important government position if he wasn't killed by the Russian Mafia.

Dr. Schmidt looked around the nicely appointed office and commented that Boris had sure come a long way from the time she met him working as a waiter at the tacky Cosmic Diner in the theater district twenty years ago. He laughed and belatedly apologized for not being friendlier that night, as he was totally surprised to see Andre with a beautiful woman because he had a wife and son back in Russia. As Boris made this revelation, the older agent saw Dr. Schmidt's complexion flush again and her fists tighten. Dr. Schmidt felt totally crushed realizing that she had been used by a master spy who didn't share her feelings. He obviously would do anything to foster his own agenda and this deepened her resolve to do whatever it took to bring him down.

The older agent noticed that her face stayed flushed as she was silently struggling to control her emotions. *Justifiable rage*, he thought, as Boris must have pushed the same Andre button that he had on the train. Boris inadvertently drove the dagger deeper into her heart when he asked her, "Did you ever hear from him again after he was thrown out of the country?"

She could only meekly shake her head when the older agent,

against his own admonition to the younger agent, attempted to bail her out by asking, "Why was Andre so rapidly deported?"

"His emergency deportation was the final reason for me to change my name. I couldn't afford to get caught up in some international witch-hunt and be deported myself. The State Department suggested that I change my name to help divert that possibility. Everyone knew that Andre worked for the KGB, so I don't understand why the U.S. government gave him access to one of their most important east coast Navy bases."

"I have a copy of his file here in my briefcase," the older agent said. "It just gives a vague reason for his expulsion, stating possible espionage and suspicious behavior. Knowing how our bureaucrats think, if the reason for his expulsion was serious they would have spelled it out." He was keeping an eye on Dr. Schmidt who was still squirming in her seat, allowing her to fill in the blanks if she wanted.

Boris jumped in with the self-serving disclaimer that he didn't have any contact with Andre after the Cosmic Diner meeting for two or three years until he went back to Moscow for a family reunion. He joked that he didn't attend these family reunions frequently in hopes of avoiding the dangerous gauntlet of Russian matrons that his family lined up for him, trying to end his blissful bachelorhood.

Andre was at the last reunion with his wife and three kids when Boris, in a private moment, asked Andre why he left the United States so fast, without even a goodbye phone call. Andre made Boris promise he wouldn't tell his wife the real reason for his expulsion: he was caught naked in a whirlpool with the same female naval officer that he brought for the weekend in New York. She was a Navy doctor and the base commander was angry that a foreigner would take advantage of one of his recruits, so he was deported immediately.

The room was deathly silent as all eyes turned to the mortified Dr. Schmidt who was wishing that she could escape her corner cell and jump out a window. Finally she responded, "We don't need to go there. We need to know about Andre today, not twenty years ago."

The older agent agreed and was almost sorry that Dr. Schmidt had to be put through this public humiliation because he had a daughter about the same age, whom he hoped would never be in a similar situation. He asked Boris to give a chronological summary of Andre's career in the Russian government. The CIA file on Andre was rather sketchy, especially in the early years, since he was a low level employee below the CIA's radar.

The Chernobyl nuclear plant meltdown proved to be a big career break for Andre. After this global tragedy, the central Russia government became concerned about the lax security at its nuclear facilities: electrical power generators, weapons manufacturing plants, ICBM missile sites and waste storage facilities. They handpicked five tough minded men from the KGB to be nuclear czars over a geographic section of their sprawling country. They underwent an intensive year-long training course on the *nuclear world*, as Andre called it. These nuclear czars were given unquestioned power and authority, reporting directly to the Russian President's office. If all the men picked for this job were as cold blooded as Andre, there would never be another Chernobyl, as heads would literally roll down Red Square before it could happen again.

Boris stated that for the last few years Andre couldn't discuss his job, including where he was working, even with his wife, because there were people who would kill him if he broke this silence. Boris said the family assumed that Andre was working in one of the breakaway republics in this top secret and dangerous job, so his wife and kids were still living in Moscow where he would return for monthly visits.

While Boris gave an interesting, but factually sketchy narrative of his brother's career, the older agent was struggling on how much to reveal of the actual reason for today's visit. When Boris mentioned that the Russian government sent the Hot Five, as the nuclear czars were nicknamed, for their year-long nuclear crash course on the management of nuclear facilities, the older agent felt he had to jump in with both feet to get to the point of their meeting. He asked if Andre ever mentioned being associated with a wealthy American businessman.

Boris seemed lost in deep thought, perhaps wondering if he should betray his brother's conversation at last year's family reunion. The older agent could detect Boris's dilemma and remained silent, as did the younger agent and Dr. Schmidt, who was now off the hot seat. Boris's relieved smile preceded his proud disclosure that after the family reunion Andre's family was going to fly on a rich American's private jet to Santorini for a Greek Isle cruise aboard his private yacht, which he remembered had a funny name like Floating Mole. Boris couldn't remember if Andre mentioned this benefactor's name, but if necessary he could try to find it out from his sister-in-law in Moscow as he had no way of contacting Andre.

The older agent quickly and firmly instructed Boris that today's meeting was strictly confidential and nothing was to be relayed back to Russia, especially questions about Andre and his rich friend. He knew that if Andre became aware of the CIA's connecting the dots between him and Azee, things could get nasty. Suddenly, the older agent stood up and mentioned that he had to use the restroom and was out into the hall before he heard Boris's offer to use the office restroom.

While the older agent was gone, the three-way conversation turned rather trite and superficial, except for Boris's bold singles bar type question to Dr. Schmidt about whether she ever married after Andre was taken from her life. She wanted to go back into a dental treatment room and find a scalpel to cut out his tongue. Then she thought of the perfect way of ultimately getting back at Andre, so she coolly bounced it back to Boris, "No, I'm available. Do you want my phone number?"

The younger agent nervously cleared his throat, not believing the exchange he just heard. Before Boris could respond to the newly assertive Dr. Schmidt, the older agent returned, rubbing together his still moist hands. The younger agent could sense that all the heavy questioning of Boris was done, so he started to gather his things and close his briefcase, expecting to leave shortly whenever the older agent gave the signal.

Instead, the older agent relaxed in his chair and asked Boris a series of random open-ended questions, as if trying to kill some time. They learned what Boris's favorite New York hangouts were, how busy his dental practice was, where he liked to vacation—any place sunny and warm with a lot of beautiful women—which response brought a derisive smile from Dr. Schmidt. After an hour of this subtle disarming probing from the older agent, Dr. Schmidt realized that she knew more about Boris than she did about his older brother at the time of their ill-fated fling. Finally, the older agent perked up and asked if they could have a tour of the office and especially a view of the bustling streets of New York below them.

Boris hoped that his office tour would be the final thing on today's agenda, so he eagerly led the party back into the treatment areas of his office. He was justifiably proud of his success from his penniless waiter days at the Cosmic Diner, and yet he seemed to still have his feet on the ground as he stated more than once that he needed to work hard to keep the banks off his back and not default on his loans because he had a rich friend as a co-signer, who would have to bail him out.

The older agent meandered from room to room doing his best to appear honestly interested in Boris's little money factory high above New York. In Boris's small private office he walked behind the desk to check out a wall of photos. One of the photos he recognized as the distinctive caldera of Santorini, with a large private yacht moored near a large cruise ship that was tendering in its passengers to either ride the elevator lift up the steep rock walls, or for the more adventuresome, a donkey ride up the narrow switch backs to the summit.

Boris proudly stated that the only rule for his picture wall was that he had to have taken the picture. No stock or friend's pictures were allowed to hang beside his masterpieces. On the desk, the older agent noticed a partially filled out passport application with a photo of a clean shaven Boris, whereas he now sported a well trimmed beard. Under the desk's kneehole space a small flap of carpet was pushed aside, which was meant to cover a small floor safe.

They all diverted on the way out to catch one final parting glimpse of the Manhattan skyline from a treatment room window. The older agent gave Boris a card with his private phone number and told him to call if he remembered anything else the agency should know. The meeting wrapped up with cordial goodbyes and promises to stay in touch. To the relief of the younger agent, Boris didn't ask Dr. Schmidt for her phone number, nor did she offer it.

XXXVII

Fortunately, for the still mortified Dr. Schmidt, the elevator descent was non-stop as they were the only ones aboard. She was the first one onto 34th Street where she announced that she was going to walk to Penn Station. The two men fell in behind her for the silent parade, until the younger agent wanted to go into his favorite New York deli in the shadow of Madison Garden to get a sandwich for the train ride back to D.C.

She curtly replied that she would meet them on the train platform. She certainly wasn't looking forward to the three hour face-to-face train ride back to D.C. as she felt stripped of all her dignity by the revelation of her naked whirlpool caper with Andre, now a person of serious interest to the CIA. Moments later, the two agents carrying three deli bags found her waiting on the platform preparing to board the Metroliner back to D.C. As she walked down the narrow aisle of the train, she looked for a single seat where she could wallow in her misery. However, the older agent who boarded first found two rows of facing seats and waved for her to come. "Got you a corned beef sandwich," the older agent commented in a harsher tone than he really meant as they were settling into their seats.

"Thanks, I'll eat it later."

The two men popped their soda cans open and noisily unwrapped their overflowing deli sandwiches as the train eased out of Penn Station. They ate more as an avoidance of conversation than because they were hungry. The young agent was eager to get the older agent's opinion on how the meeting went, so he finally broke the uncomfortable silence. "I hope we didn't waste a whole day coming up here to admire the New York skyline from a dental office."

The older agent was still working on his corned beef on rye and wondered under what rock the CIA had found the young agent, so he just mumbled, "Oh," to allow the younger agent more rope to continue hanging himself.

"We could have gotten more intel from watching a Knicks – Celtics game than we did from Boris. He doesn't seem to be very close to his brother, even changed his name so as not to be associated with him. I give him credit for pulling himself up by his bootstraps to the prosperous life he now has. The American dream is alive and well."

The older agent wanted to gag on his mouthful of succulent corned beef, but he kept on chewing. Dr. Schmidt popped the lid on her diet soda and started unwrapping her sandwich as she sensed that now was not the time to join this conversation headed to hell. Clearing his mouth, the older agent played Socrates, "What should we do next?"

"First off, I'll be happy to write the report on today's meeting. It'll be short: Boris changed his name to Bukharin to honor his grandfather and to disassociate himself from his wayward brother, Andre, who has three kids. Boris has a prosperous dental practice, is single, and likes warm weather vacations with beautiful women. That's about it."

"Thanks for not mentioning why Andre left the country so quickly," Dr. Schmidt sarcastically commented to break her grand silence.

They both were waiting for the older agent to say something, but he kept them waiting even longer by walking his trash to a

receptacle at the end of the rocking train car. Maybe he was checking to see if he could pitch some bigger trash out the door of the
speeding train, so he wouldn't have to repeat his CIA 101 instructions to the over-educated, but under-smart, younger agent. By the
time he returned to his seat, he felt renewed enough to take the
backward steps necessary to proceed forward. "Why did I leave
the three of you in the waiting room? So you could talk about the
old fart while he was out taking a piss?"

"I assumed you had to use the facilities, like you said," the
younger agent answered.

"Good. I hope Boris felt the same way. I called Langley to have
them put immediate wire taps on his office and home phones. He
also has to be put under twenty-four hour surveillance."

"Aren't you overreacting?"

The older agent knew that he couldn't explain the gut feeling
from years of experience that someone is trying to snow you, so he
ignored the younger agent's stupid question. "Now, do you know
why we sat there for an hour engaging in seemingly inane conversation when you were anxious to get to the train? Langley needs
time to set this up. I guarantee that Boris contacted someone who
will be of interest to us before we got out of the elevator. What did
you notice in his private office?"

"Too small for all of us to sit in, like he said, and there's a small
floor safe under his desk to hold the day's receipts."

"There's a picture of the Azee's yacht, the Aqua Mole, anchored
at Santorini, which he took by his own admission. His calling the
Aqua Mole the Floating Mole was a big tip. He was there at the
same time as Azee and Andre. Who do you think the rich business
man is who co-signed his office loans, so he could move into his
fancy office? I'm betting that it's Azee. That'll be easy enough to
check with the bank. He's submitting a new passport application
with a picture different from the way he looks today, so he's going
to be traveling soon."

"Why didn't we pursue this with him, while we were here? We'll
just have to make another trip up here to question him more."

Dr. Schmidt wanted to jump up and help strangle the young agent, but she knew that the older agent was having too much fun to interrupt. "Don't worry, you won't ever have to come back to New York, except for a Knicks game. We'll give Boris a few days to incriminate himself and then get a court order to seize his passport and bank records. Boris can tell us a lot about Andre and Azee if we sweat him, but he'll reveal more without that hassle."

"I guess I shouldn't write the report on today's meeting. I look forward to reading your report, sir."

"It'll be shorter than you think." He turned to Dr. Schmidt and with the warmth that only the father of a daughter can express, "Today's report won't contain any reference to why Andre was expelled twenty years ago, since it doesn't affect us neutralizing him and Azee. Your life and career will go on unaffected by that incident and today's interview. To change anything would be a red flag to Boris, Andre and Azee." He turned, and with his finger pointed at the younger agent, slowly spoke through clenched teeth, "If I ever hear in the CIA gossip mill, as I surely would, about Dr. Schmidt's whirlpool incident, your career in the CIA is ended. Dead! Is this perfectly clear?"

The younger agent could only nod his head, feeling that he would be lucky to only lose his job if he revealed the salacious details of Dr. Schmidt's affair with the Russian spy.

XXXVIII

As their flight neared Andrews Air Force base, Cindy noticed Tom getting a little nervous and fidgety after their too short recuperative flight from the Azores. During his long and distinguished Secret Service career, Tom had used Andrews so many times on White House business that he instinctively went on autopilot when their plane taxied toward the secure presidential hangar. He could see Air Force One through the partially opened hangar doors as their plane rolled to a stop on the spotless tarmac where VIP passengers came and went. He waved at the limo driver waiting behind the cyclone fence. They hurried inside to use the lounge to change into different clothes for their hopefully casual White House dinner.

Once changed into clean clothes, they went out to the White House limo where they were given robust, rib cracking hugs from their Secret Service chauffeur. Gleason was so familiar with the presidential motorcade route from the suburban Andrews to the White House that he could have driven it blindfolded. He knew they would be in the area of Bethesda Naval Medical Hospital, so as much to make conversation as anything else, he mentioned, "We could pay the first lady a visit on the way by."

Cindy, taken by complete surprise, wondered, "We could?"

He picked up the limo's phone intercom and asked the driver, "What time is dinner with the president?"

"I wasn't given a time. I'll call and find out."

"Better yet, ask the White House if we have time for a quick visit to the first lady since we are close?"

Shortly, the driver was back on the intercom with the message that someone wanted to talk to him. "Welcome home, Tom. We're so relieved that you guys are okay after the fire in Sicily."

"Thank you, Mr. President. You don't know how happy we are to be back on American soil."

"Please do stop to visit Kathy. I hope you're prepared to see how much she's slipped. Don't worry about dinner. It's casual with the kids."

Cindy could tell that Tom was pleased to visit the first lady as his first act back in the states. She wondered how much guilt he still carried because everything in Detroit happened on his watch. Tom asked the driver to take them around to the guarded VIP side entrance, rather than the hospital's main front entrance. Hoping to spare Cindy the trauma of seeing the comatose first lady, he foolishly asked if she wanted to wait in the limo while he went upstairs for the quick visit.

If looks could kill, Tom would have been too dead to worry about his visit to the first lady. Cindy bounded out of the limo ahead of him and beat him to the locked double glass doors. Fortunately, the guard inside immediately recognized him, even in his casual attire, and buzzed to open the door. The guard dropped his chin and just shook his head when Tom asked how the first lady was doing.

On the elevator ride to the top floor presidential suite Tom tried to prepare himself for the first lady's deteriorated condition. He was hoping to get an update from Dr. Schmidt if she was still on duty, but she might be at the White House awaiting them for dinner. After they signed the Secret Service's log book, the duty nurse explained that Dr. Schmidt had taken a morning train to New York, hoping to meet a doctor there, the nurse assumed, who could offer advice on the first lady's condition. The nurse seemed relieved to tell them that Dr. Schmidt was taking an evening train back to D.C. and was working tomorrow morning.

Before seeing the first lady, the attending senior resident insisted on giving them a detailed report on the gradual deterioration of all the first lady's lab tests. *Too much information*, Gleason thought, as he interrupted the doctor's robotic medical briefing with the suggestion that they go in to visit her, otherwise they would be late for their White House dinner.

Gleason, struggling to keep himself upbeat and alive in his Tripoli confinement, had done a good job of blocking out the unpleasant realities of the first lady's total helplessness. Now holding Cindy's hand, hoping to get an infusion of strength, he stood silently at the first lady's bedside, thinking what a tragic waste of a wonderful life. He could still picture Kathy as the effervescent expectant mother trying to make the White House a loving home, so he tried not to focus on her deterioration since he last saw her.

The drone of the life sustaining respirator and the blipping EKG lulled him into a trance that was finally broken when Cindy suggested saying a prayer for Kathy before they left. They grasped Kathy's hands, carefully avoiding the life sustaining tubes and IVs, to form a prayer circle, as they recited the Lord's Prayer, with the chief resident doctor respectfully waiting near the door. Taking one long last look at the once beautiful first lady, they gave her soft parting kisses on her scrubbed forehead. They fought back tears as they stepped into the hall with the doctor. Tom struggled with how to verbalize his dark thoughts, so he just asked, "Any idea how much longer it will be?"

The doctor looked around and saw no one besides the three of them within hearing distance. "I can't speak for Dr. Schmidt and the president, but the respirator and meds are the only thing keeping her alive, if you call her vegetative state alive. They have to make the final decision soon, I hope."

"Aren't the hyperbaric oxygen treatments helping?"

"The president and Dr. Schmidt mercifully stopped them, as

we couldn't document that they were helping and not hurting her. So far the press hasn't picked up on this change in her treatment. Unfortunately, politics has been a major determinant in how she's been treated."

"No surprise there. I've been out of the country, so I've been out of the loop on her treatment."

"All things considered, medically and politically, this has been a very difficult case. Dr. Schmidt is totally in charge and she'll be back tomorrow after meeting today with a doctor in New York."

Tom and Cindy hurried over to the elevator as they had heard all they wanted about the first lady's hopeless condition. The hospital visit was the wake up call they needed to make them realize that they were back home with many of the same problems, plus whatever new ones they had accumulated overseas. While they were upstairs at the hospital on their call of mercy, the driver was in touch with the White House updating them on their delay. The Secret Service, to speed the drive to the White House, called the local police departments along their route to provide a police escort for the White House limousine, so they could break traffic laws to get to the White House for dinner. Even though the sirens and frequent brakings and accelerations going through traffic signals made for a hectic ride, Tom and Cindy were quietly at peace with each other and the uncertainties they faced.

XXXIX

Gleason was relieved that their driver didn't pull under the main canopied entrance of the White House off Pennsylvania Avenue that was reserved for VIP visitors. Instead, they used the side entrance that opened into the corridor where his office was located, so he quickly slipped Cindy's suitcase inside his office and noticed everything seemed to be in place. In his guilt-induced paranoia, he expected to find his office occupied by someone else and all his belongings boxed up.

Tom knew that the president would have been alerted of their arrival, so he and Cindy hurried up the back stairway to the second floor living quarters, which was near Jason and Eric's bedrooms. When the boys heard them walking by, they burst out of their rooms and put near tackling hugs on Tom, while Cindy got the leftover youthful exuberance. The president, hearing the commotion in the hall and recognizing Tom as the main culprit in the playful pushing and shoving, shouted the hollow admonition, "All you kids," obviously with special reference to Tom, "Remember that we don't own this place, so don't wreck it." The president, Tom and Cindy shared a warm three-way hug. "Great to have you home Tom and thanks Cindy, for going to rescue him. We've got a lot to talk about."

The cocktail hour was blended into the dinner, with wine and appetizers at the table for the informal family dinner that the president wanted and needed. The boys obviously had been informed of his stay in Libya, so Tom used his best judgment to avoid the gory details of the Azee saga. Hence, he only told incidents that were age appropriate for dinner table conversation. He focused on the nice doctor who had treated him and he showed them his parting picture with Colonel Qadafi, who was the head of Libya, like their dad was the President of the United States.

The president was content to let Tom carry the dinner table conversation, asking the boys what they had done in school while he was gone and how much soccer they played on the south lawn. Cindy and Tom were disappointed when the White House nanny arrived without Melody, who was still napping, to take the boys for their bedtimes. Now they would have to engage in the adult conversation that they had been able to avoid with the boys at the table. The president suggested that they move to a small sitting room away from the kitchen staff as they cleared the dining room table.

The three of them stared at the thick manila folder on the coffee table as they sat down. Tom knew that the contents of the folder would not be good news, but just how bad was the real concern in his racing mind. When the president offered a cognac in the sparkling Waterford crystal snifters in front of them, Tom was tempted to ask for a double shot to blunt the impending bad news contained in the folder. Cindy could sense the awkwardness between the two men, so she broke the silent stalemate by proposing a toast, "May Kathy have the eternal peace and rest that she deserves, and may you, Mr. President, be a continued source of strength for your children and the country." Their three glasses clinked and they momentarily savored the vintage cognac that warmed their mouth and throat.

"Thank you, Cindy, for your kind thoughts. It was very considerate of you to visit Kathy. The end of her nightmare is near."

"Since Dr. Schmidt was gone today, we talked to the attending doctor, who seemed rather discouraged."

"I know, Tom. We're all discouraged. Even Dr. Schmidt, who has been a pillar of strength through this whole ordeal, is wearing down."

"Maybe the doctor in New York whom she is visiting today will have some helpful suggestions."

The president broke out into an unrestrained laugh that caught Tom and Cindy by surprise. "Pardon me, Tom. I'm not laughing at you. That's her cover for going to New York with two CIA agents. They are interrogating Boris Bukharin, the dentist, brother of her former Russian friend, Andre. She met Boris briefly twenty years ago, so we thought he might be more inclined to talk about his brother if she was there."

"Azee was working on a deal with Andre to provide Iraq with nuclear material," Gleason said.

"We know. In your taped conversation we heard Azee admit the Iraq connection before he bailed out of the Flying Mole."

"Speaking of the devil, what's going on with Azee?"

The president paused for a minute, realizing that Tom, and especially Cindy, should not be privy to what he could say, so he just replied, "No need to worry about him now. Very soon he'll be ours, dead or alive." They all nodded their heads, knowing that this was going to be the extent of their Azee briefing. Opening the folder, the president held up a multi page legal document. "My White House Counsel, Wright, working with the attorney general, has started to prepare a list of possible charges that you could be facing, Tom. Of course, like typical lawyers, they give the disclaimer that the list can be added to or subtracted from as the situation develops."

"I'm expecting this. I'm responsible for my actions. Cindy certainly didn't do anything wrong, except perhaps caring too much for me."

"That's right, she's been a saint through all this," the president said, with a broad smile, breaking the tension. "I can give you this copy now, if you want it. Better yet, let's wait a couple days and you can sit down with Wright and he'll explain all this legalese."

"Good idea. My first priority is starting my AIDS treatment. I may not live long enough to worry about all these legal charges."

Cindy immediately interrupted Tom's morbid line of thought. "I thought that we agreed to stay focused on the positives. No more negatives!"

"Sorry," a duly chastised Tom replied. "However, one final negative, Mr. President. Effective immediately, I resign from the Secret Service to prevent continued embarrassment to you and your presidency. That is, if I haven't already been fired."

"Tom, you'll always have a job in my White House. We'll have Wright draft your retirement, not resignation, in the next couple days. After the election I will appoint you as a personal assistant in charge of special assignments. You'll have plenty of freedom in this new job to take care of your own health and anything that I need handled expeditiously and discreetly. Interested?"

"I'm overwhelmed, sir. I'll try to be worthy of your continued confidence."

"Keep your same office downstairs. We'll develop your job description as we go along. Of course, a main part of the new job will be soccer and football games with Eric and Jason on the south lawn. Tom, I really need your help and friendship to get through Kathy's final days. That's why I wanted you out of Tripoli ASAP." The room became deathly silent as the three of them dried their eyes, anticipating the emotion of the first lady's passing.

Since they had already discussed most of the important matters, Tom did not want to broach the subject of the president's own health, especially his possible AIDS contracted from his blood transfusion in Detroit. He also thought it best not to put the president in the position of talking about his own health with Cindy present. The president, sensing that his agenda had been satisfied, buzzed the kitchen for coffee and dessert to conclude Tom's welcome home party.

XL

After the president and CIA Director Hayden read the senior CIA agent's report on the interview of Boris in New York, a meeting was called at the White House. The president wanted Dr. Schmidt there along with Hayden and the senior agent, who thought that the counterproductive younger agent would be too busy emptying waste baskets to attend. Dr. Schmidt was not thrilled to be invited, or as she perceived it *ordered* to attend, for fear of what might come up in the president's presence. She had seen the older agent's report and, true to his word, it contained no mention of her whirlpool caper with Andre.

She was happy when the president opened the meeting by asking how the first lady was doing, as it took the focus off the real purpose of the meeting which could turn around to bite her. She pretended to be unhappy to report that the first lady's condition was failing and, as a matter of fact, she brought with her the hospital's standard *Do Not Resuscitate* form. She explained that the hospital administrator was insisting that a signed copy should be put with the first lady's chart so that no one, especially on the late night shift, would make the mistake of trying to revive the first lady, thinking that they were doing the right thing. The president demurred about how hard it was to die anymore, and the first lady was no exception. He signed the order expressing the hope that the form would come into play very soon as cold and cruel as that sounded.

Dr. Schmidt reported that the first lady's respirations were getting shallower, her heart rate slowing and her kidney output was declining. She also reported that the neurologist didn't see any point in continuing to come every day, since there was nothing he could do to change the first lady's slow downward spiral. The president asked if the neurologist was a Navy doctor or an outside consultant. When informed that he was a naval officer, the president went ballistic. He instructed Dr. Schmidt to convey to the neurologist the direct order from his commander in chief that he, or someone in the neurology department, was to continue checking on the first lady everyday and to record their findings in the first lady's chart. Dr. Schmidt expressed her agreement with the president's wishes, and that she would personally convey the order to the neurology department.

Hayden reported on the results of their wiretap and surveillance of Boris after the three interrogators left his office. Just as the senior agent had suspected he would, Boris made two phone calls from his office to Russia, speaking in heavily accented Russian. Hayden surmised that Boris used the office phone for his expensive international calls, so that they could be deducted as a business expense. Thus, there should be easily accessible phone records for the CIA to review that could be incriminating against Boris. The first call was to Andre's wife, exchanging small talk about the weather and her kids. She mentioned that Andre was home last weekend and wouldn't be home for another month, and she wouldn't be talking to him until then, unless he called to wish one of the children a happy birthday next week. She reminded Boris how hard it was for Andre to return phone calls.

She still gave Boris the emergency contact number where he could leave a message for Andre to return his call. This second call to Russia keep the CIA busy deciphering syllable by syllable Boris's recorded message to his brother for any hidden meaning. On the surface, it sounded innocuous as he mentioned that he just met again Andre's beautiful lady friend from twenty years ago and that she seemed interested in being in touch with him. He closed by instructing Andre to call the usual location at the usual time. The CIA was able to trace this second number into the bowels of the KGB headquarters in Moscow, but there was no hint where Andre was working in Russia or in one of the breakaway republics. Boris's return phone call instruction to Andre raised the serious question of what was so secretive in their brotherly relationship that they needed to resort to a super spy manner of clandestine communicating on non-personal phone lines.

The president perked up when he heard the mention of Andre's beautiful friend and he wondered aloud who that might be. Dr. Schmidt's complexion turned as red as the red on the American flag in the corner behind the massive presidential desk. "That was me, Mr. President, a long story from long ago."

Fortunately, the senior agent tried to rescue her as she was too upset to say any more. "Dr. Schmidt and I have discussed her friendship with Andre. That was one of the purposes of her accompanying us to question Boris, whom she briefly met twenty years ago as we told you. We thought that her presence might disarm Boris, which it did, as proven by his phone calls. I'm more interested in what Boris did after he made the phone calls from his office. The Russian restaurant where he went for a late lunch isn't very welcoming to outsiders, so our tailing agent just did a quick walk through, noticing an old fashion wooden pay phone booth in the corner on his way to the—"

"Were you in touch with Andre after he was deported back to Russia?" the curious president interrupted to ask Dr. Schmidt.

Dr. Schmidt could only shake her head no. Fortunately, the senior agent continued, "We put a wiretap on that pay phone in the corner of the bar. Also, we have hidden microphones in the restrooms—never know what sounds you might pick up there." Everyone smiled at the agent's sophomoric humor to take the focus off of Dr. Schmidt's past friendship with the dangerous Russian nuclear arms merchant.

Hayden mentioned that the U.S. embassy in Moscow was mobilized with all its CIA agents focusing on finding the where-abouts of Andre and verifying the credibility of his ability to sup-ply nuclear material to Iraq. Hayden explained the difficulty of getting an accurate reading on this dangerous game that Azee was playing because the Russian government didn't want to admit that the security around their nuclear arsenal was so defective that a high level rogue official like Andre could purloin lethal radioactive material and sell it to a wealthy buyer like Azee, who was fronting the transaction for a hostile country like Iraq. Even if a desired abduction or even a fatal hit on Azee went according to plan, the CIA was still interested in locating Andre and verifying what role his brother Boris has in this dangerous arms deal.

XLI

Azee remembered how he had been riding high when he received the news from his old Palermo contact that Gleason had landed in Sicily for a few days R and R with his ex-wife at the Sigonella naval base. He hoped that Gleason's defenses would be lowered as he'd be free to enjoy his time with Cindy.

His Palermo contact had told him that for a higher price they could even get to Gleason on the naval base as the security was laid back because there never was any trouble there. Azee told his contact that his preference was hitting Gleason, and if necessary, Cindy, off the base to make it appear to be a random crime against two American tourists gone wrong. Every look at his mangled hand was the motivation that spurred him on to make that last attempt at settling the score with Gleason, who had proven to be a more formidable opponent than he expected. Azee had given his Palermo friend carte blanche to do what had to be done, but he warned, "Don't fail or you will have to answer to me, as well as an aroused United States government."

All this became a bad memory when the message arrived at Temenos that Gleason and Cindy had survived an all-out assault by the family's most experienced killers. Azee did not need to know the details. They failed. He failed. Gleason and Cindy were probably already on their way back to the United States. He knew that he would never again have as good a chance to get even with Gleason, short of sailing a nuclear bomb up the Potomac River on a container ship and destroying Washington.

With Gleason now out of his grasp, Azee was able to focus his attention on his slowly healing hand. The local doctors from Beirut whom he brought into Temenos were able to provide palliative care, but they were unanimous in their opinions that Azee should see Dr. Lamonte in Tel Aviv for some minor follow up surgery. Azee made contact with Lamonte through one of his personal bankers in Zurich to set-up a clandestine appointment with Lamonte in Tel Aviv during his next visit to his terrorism surgical clinic. In Zurich, Lamonte was being shadowed twenty-four hours a day by only the CIA, at the suggestion of the Swiss authorities, to minimize the chances of any leaks to banking associates of Azee, and more importantly, so that the Swiss government could claim their legendary neutrality if the heat came down on one of their largest banking customers.

XLII

CIA Director Hayden elected not to come to Tel Aviv to meet his top Mideast operative, Isiah Hyman, to personally impress on him the importance of the success of their mission to capture Azee when he came to Tel Aviv for his allegedly secret appointment with Dr. Lamonte. He feared that Azee would get wind of this visit and would cancel his appointment with Dr. Lamonte. Hayden had complete confidence in Isiah to successfully carry out the most dangerous assignment of Isiah's un-chronicled clandestine CIA career.

On landing in Tel Aviv, Lamonte called his CIA contact, which was Hyman. They arranged to meet at a busy coffee shop across from the hospital parking lot. Hyman was intimately familiar with this area, and the hospital itself, as the CIA had area maps and blueprints of the highly secure, terrorist proof hospital facility. Lamonte entered this bustling java house and found a booth in the back, away from the steady stream of the takeout coffee patrons. As he was sipping his steaming coffee, a well dressed middle-aged man slipped into the booth across from him. "I'm Isiah. Isiah Hyman. Nice to finally meet you, doctor."

Lamonte instinctively retracted his delicate surgeon's hand from the strong handshake of the calloused, rough skinned grip of Hyman. He thought, *I may have a hard time passing off this bearded, stocky Isiah as a fellow surgeon.*

"I saw you enter from where I was seated on the park bench. I had to make sure that you weren't being followed." Hyman had a checklist that he needed to cover before they went across the street for introductions and a tour of the hospital.

Lamonte opened his briefcase and removed a multi-colored knit yarmulke which he held out for Hyman to feel and examine. "This is a cherished possession, knit by one of my first patients in appreciation for saving her hand. She couldn't have knitted it one-handed," he said as he covered the crown of his head with it.

When the socializing small talk was over, Hyman started with the first big test to determine if Lamonte was one hundred percent behind this mission to capture Azee, as well as to clear his name of the drug charges back home. He asked Lamonte for his passport, while watching for the slightest hesitation that might put this mission in jeopardy. Without pause, Lamonte retrieved the little red book from his briefcase and slid it across the table to the smiling Hyman, who tucked it under a napkin.

Hyman then presented the basic plan of Azee's abduction, all the time judging the content and intent of Lamonte's questions and sometimes helpful suggestions. They would have two and a half days to fine-tune the details of this high risk CIA operation. Lamonte was going to introduce Hyman and his four man team as visiting doctors, who were observing Lamonte as he went about his schedule of treating his Israeli terrorism patients before their fateful final afternoon encounter with Azee.

Hyman suggested that they leave the coffee shop separately, but meet in the guarded hospital lobby where Lamonte could assist in getting him through the hospital's security screening.

As they were gathering their things to leave, Hyman pushed the passport back to Lamonte with the simple explanation, "You passed the initial test."

While waiting in line to be frisked by an attractive no-nonsense female guard backed up by an Uzi toting commando, Hyman whispered to Lamonte, "How do doctors act?"

"I suppose you could get mad for being treated like everyone else, but better not do that here. Just relax and enjoy your frisking—but don't ask to have it done a second time." They both laughed, and their frisking and clearance through security was expedited as soon as the guards recognized the distinctive yarmulke of the often visiting Dr. Lamonte.

The hospital administrator, Ms. Rebeka, was in her office awaiting their arrival and warmly embraced Lamonte, thanking him profusely for his return visit to Tel Aviv. Hyman was introduced as Dr. Isiah Hyman. Ms. Rebeka winked her acknowledgement that she knew she was being duped and pushed the intercom button asking her secretary to come in and meet Dr. Isiah Hyman, bringing the Polaroid camera with her. After taking a passport type photo of the somber, now bespectacled Dr. Hyman, she was instructed to prepare the necessary three day passes, allowing the doctors and four of their special guests, who would be arriving later, to have unrestricted access to the entire hospital complex. Being a loyal secretary, she did not question the unusual request for the four extra unrestricted guest passes, even though she found it highly unusual that the boss would violate her own directive of no unrestricted passes to unknown people.

When the secretary departed and shut the door, the administrator mentioned that she had just gotten off the phone with the prime minister. Though they were longtime friends, it was rare for them to talk since their daily work was not directly related, unless there was a terrorist attack when the whole city was mobilized. The prime minister said that he didn't need the details of the planned abduction of Azee by the CIA and he ordered the hospital to cooperate completely with these efforts—with the strong provision that no Israeli lives be directly endangered. Hyman assured her that the mission would be aborted right up to the final moment if Israeli lives were at risk.

Ms. Rebeka reminded them that the operating room closes for the Sabbath, one hour before sundown on Friday, the day of the planned abduction, and that the whole hospital goes into a Sabbath slow down mode, so the mission must be completed by the Friday afternoon deadline. Hyman again reassured her that if all went as planned the mission would be over shortly after lunch with hours to spare before the Sabbath begins.

They agreed to meet on the Friday morning of the abduction to go over the final details. In ending the meeting, Hyman emphasized that no one, besides the three of them, were to be privy to this risky operation, as Azee certainly would have his antennae raised searching for anything suspicious prior to his appointment with Dr. Lamonte. Complete secrecy was paramount to the mission's safety and success.

XLIII

Dr. Lamonte was treated as royalty as he toured the hospital with Isiah, who was masquerading as a visiting doctor. It was hard for Lamonte, without being rude, to break off conversations with friends and colleagues wanting a piece of him like a famous rock star. All the while Isiah was trying to connect faces with the names and resumes of the key hospital personnel listed in the employee files that he had reviewed in preparation for the mission to capture Azee in three days.

Finally, they arrived at the top level fourth floor where Lamonte was always provided with a small private office connecting to the operating room assigned to him for his three days. The office was smaller than Isiah had envisioned from the hospital blueprints, but it would provide adequate hiding space for his four fellow CIA agents disguising as doctors. On signal, they would quickly enter, secure the operating room, and help carry a sedated Azee up the nearby exit stairs to the rooftop helipad. Isiah, the CIA organizer of many nefarious Mideast events that were often played by the enemies' rule book—there are no rules—had to guard against overconfidence, as no operation was ever as simple as planned on paper or in his devious mind.

When their tour took them to the rooftop helipad, they could see the backup ground level helipad near the emergency room door, convenient for incoming emergency patients. Isiah explained to Lamonte that a disguised U.S. Navy helicopter, painted white with red crosses, would land on the rooftop helipad a few minutes before Azee's ETA, so that his helicopter, incoming from Beirut, would be instructed to land on the available ground-level helipad. Six Navy SEALs, dressed in green hospital scrubs and wearing long white coats to conceal their armaments, would arrive in the rooftop helicopter and wait in the exit stairway until deployed into the fourth floor after Azee was sedated in the operating room.

They stepped to the edge of the roof and squinted into the dazzling sun as they surveyed the currently tranquil atmosphere of Tel Aviv stretching out below them. Lamonte broke their meditative silence. "There is only one thing that I can think of that could upset this well-conceived plan."

Isiah slowly turned to face Lamonte, quickly thinking that maybe he should have kept his passport to insure the doctor's complete, unquestioning cooperation. He was greeted by a question before he could get his own question out. "What if there is a terrorist attack requiring us to treat the injured victims at the same time as this planned operation?"

Isiah relaxed a bit, giving Lamonte credit for thinking like a valuable team member and worrying about all possible contingencies. "I was planning on covering that issue in our final morning meeting with the hospital administrator. Our United States president outlined this unlikely, but still possible, complication to the Israeli prime minister and they apparently had a heated discussion about this dilemma. I understand that the president was on the verge of hanging up before the prime minister finally capitulated by agreeing that this mission would take priority over all else, short of a nuclear attack on Israel."

"The hospital administrator isn't going to like this."

"She doesn't have a choice. There are no second chances in this business."

"All of a sudden I'm less excited about helping you capture Azee."

Isiah got nose-to-nose with his wavering colleague and with

teeth clenched, slowly pronounced, word-by-word, as if a voice from on high, "You don't have a choice either! Do you want me to throw you off the roof right now?"

Lamonte saw cold grey steel in Isiah's unblinking eyes and he realized that he really would do that in a heartbeat if the mission didn't go on. The operational end of the CIA in the ever shifting sands of the Mideast played hardball. Lamonte reluctantly realized that this was his first and last chance on this slippery slope, so he had better not falter. Fortunately, for the shaken Lamonte, an incoming emergency helicopter was starting its descent to the rooftop helipad, so they hurried to the stairway to clear the area.

XLIV

For two days Isiah shadowed Lamonte to get a feel for the inside operation of the hospital, and the fourth floor surgical clinic area, where Azee would be brought for the minor surgical procedures he needed, but would not receive. Isiah saw nothing to be gained by informing Lamonte that no surgery was going to be performed on Azee, even though he would be given pre-surgical sedation to aid in the abduction. He trusted Lamonte to carry out the plans as he knew them, and he didn't want to chance Lamonte's medical ethics scuttling the mission if he knew the whole plot where no surgery was going to be done on Azee.

When Dr. Lamonte started one of his lengthy surgical reconstruction cases Isiah knew that he had time to meet with the four members of the on-site extraction team, as they were calling themselves, at the coffee shop across from the hospital. The precise timetable for Azee's abduction was refined down to the minute, based on what they had observed from shadowing Lamonte.

Nothing suspicious was emanating from Azee holed up in Temenos, his seaside Beirut compound. The Israeli government had agreed to send an unmarked white Medevac helicopter to pick up Azee and two unarmed bodyguards for his transport to the Tel Aviv hospital. The Israeli government insisted that no weapons were to be brought aboard their helicopter, and Azee was in no position to countermand this condition of his safe passage to the hospital. He reassured himself that two more bodyguards would meet him at the helicopter landing at the hospital, as he never liked to be caught short handed. These two land based body-guards were to get pistols from a hospital maintenance worker, bribed by Azee, who would be trimming bushes near the helipad.

The flight plan for this short mercy flight was over the open waters of the Mediterranean coastline from Beirut to Tel Aviv. The Israeli pilots, with Azee's encouragement, since he was handsomely reimbursing Israel for its flight services, scheduled a practice run up the coast with an actual touchdown inside the Temenos com-pound the day before the real thing. The Israeli pilots were not informed of the one-way-only nature of their trip ferrying Azee to the hospital or that the U.S. Navy would have planes and helicop-ters in the air a few miles offshore to cover any contingencies that might come up.

Isiah and Lamonte shared a two bedroom suite in the doc-tors' apartment wing of the hospital that was inside the hospital's restrictive security zone. The hospital doctors had insisted that they be provided these secure sleeping rooms for when the country was on high terrorism alert and they were on twenty-four hour call. The administration always reserved the two bedroom suite for visiting VIP doctors like Lamonte, who sometimes brought his wife and family with him to share in this life-changing experience. However, this time he came alone to Tel Aviv.

The CIA did not want to allow Lamonte one free moment alone when he could contact anyone that could jeopardize their mission. Isiah insisted to his CIA boss that their hospital suite be bugged in case Lamonte tried something suspicious while he was in the shower or sleeping.

Isiah couldn't admit to Lamonte that he was also worried about a random terrorist attack that might spook Azee, or create turmoil in the Tel Aviv hospital community, in spite of the prime minister's promise that Azee's capture was number one priority for everyone. Also, any complex operation that depended on planes flying security patrol offshore and the helicopter transporting Azee to Tel Aviv and then his removal to an offshore aircraft carrier, was completely weather dependent. So far, the weather forecast was favorable. Isiah, like everyone who survives a long time in the espionage business, was a chronic worrier, but he was doing his best to conceal it from Lamonte.

The extraction team of the four additional guest doctors had the run of the hospital grounds, the surgical department and the helipad landing area, while Isiah closely shadowed Lamonte before the all important third day. They developed a good feel for the pace of the hospital's workflow, especially the fourth floor surgical area, without being too obtrusive.

On the fateful third morning, Lamonte and his five guest doctors had their scheduled meeting with the hospital administrator behind closed doors. Rebeka had insisted on a complete briefing on the details of Azee's abduction, since she would have to answer directly to the prime minister for any snafus.

They felt fortunate that no random terrorist incidents had occurred overnight to put Azee on edge and monopolize Tel Aviv's hospital resources. Since Azee was being flown from his Beirut compound in an unmarked white Israeli helicopter, the pilots would be directly in touch with the hospital for last minute landing instructions after being cleared for the hospital landing by the control tower at the Tel Aviv airport. The plan was still for the rooftop helipad to be occupied by another emergency helicopter that arrived only moments before Azee's scheduled arrival, thus forcing his helicopter to land on the ground helipad. From there, he would take the elevator to the fourth floor surgical area.

Azee's request for two more of his own, supposedly unarmed, security personnel to meet his helicopter was reluctantly granted by the hospital. Their presence on the ground level helipad to greet the arriving Azee would give him a secure feeling.

After Azee and his four-person security force were inside the hospital, the Israeli pilots were to temporarily disable the helicopter, so it could not be started without the proper reactivation steps. The pilots were then to disappear off the hospital grounds to prevent any forced escape by Azee, should there be a breakdown of the meticulously planned abduction. They wanted to leave Azee's disabled helicopter in place to prevent any other emergency helicopters from landing to avoid any extra distractions in the emergency room.

When Azee was upstairs in the surgical area, Lamonte would be allotted thirty minutes to examine and prep him for the minor surgical procedures. Once fully sedated, Azee would be carried up the back stairway away from his men in the waiting room to the evacuation helicopter on the roof-top. The four CIA pseudo doctors, after Azee's helicopter was airborne, would appear to deal with the distraught bodyguards of the vanished Azee.

Isiah did his best to stick to the best case scenario script, so as not to alarm Lamonte or Rebeka that all hell could break loose in a dangerous operation like this. He was prepared to carry out his mission that Azee be returned to the United States, dead or alive, at any cost, even his own life.

Isiah watched the body language of Lamonte during this concise briefing and was fully expecting his question, "You mean to say that I'm not doing the surgery on the sedated Azee that I promised to get him here? That's highly unethical." Lamonte stood up and walked over to the covered window and pulled back the curtain as if looking for a bolt of heavenly lightning to scuttle this operation, with which he was struggling.

Isiah wished that they were back on the roof and Lamonte would have already made his plop on the ground, four stories below. He kept one eye on the administrator, now nervously rocking in her swivel chair, and the other eye on Lamonte, pacing back and forth in front of the draped window. He learned years ago in the espionage business not to overreact when angry and upset, unless your own life is truly in danger.

Now Lamonte's life was endangered and Isiah knew that Lamonte knew it, remembering their roof discussion, so he gave

Lamonte time to either hang or save himself. Lamonte realized that he said the wrong thing and that he couldn't take it back. He didn't even try to retract it as he continued to silently pace in front of the draped window.

Finally, Isiah stood up and blocked Lamonte's pacing. He briefly parted the drawn curtains with his elbow and flicked his head toward the ground outside. Lamonte's eyes widened and his jaw dropped. "You had your chance to bail on this. Now it's too late. I think the rooftop drop is too good for you. Which is it, doctor?" Isiah didn't know or care if the others in the room understood the roof reference, as long as Lamonte did. "You will be sent back to Switzerland to be prosecuted for your drug smuggling charges. I'm sure that you have done your last case here in Tel Aviv or anywhere else." Isiah moved back to his seat, gathering his things into his briefcase, all the while watching the fidgeting administrator behind her desk.

Lamonte was sobbing as he sat down. Finally, Rebeka quietly asked, "Dr. Lamonte, what drug smuggling charges? I'm totally shocked."

As Lamonte was mumbling an incoherent answer, Isiah retrieved from his briefcase an officially embossed three page copy of the drug smuggling charges and pushed it across her desk. "Looks like serious charges to me," she said, looking at Lamonte. "I'm required to put these charges in your personnel file until they are resolved back in Switzerland. Needless to say, your hospital privileges here are revoked."

Lamonte continued his descent into his personal and professional hell for trying to make a few quick dollars in Tripoli. He didn't even try to explain the drug charges to Rebeka. He knew his only escape was to completely cooperate in Azee's abduction.

Isiah started to talk to his men about going to plan B to capture Azee. It involved air-jacking Azee's incoming helicopter with U.S. Navy planes and helicopters and escorting it to the waiting U.S. aircraft carrier offshore in the Mediterranean. The risk was that Azee and his two bodyguards would fight and cause the helicopter to crash, killing the two Israeli pilots along with themselves. Azee's self-inflicted death would be an acceptable outcome to the United States government.

Isiah made sure that he spoke loudly enough for Rebeka to hear about the collateral loss of the two Israeli pilots. The usually stoic administrator stood up and walked around her desk to face Lamonte. "Doctor, you know how we value the lives of our people, especially our brave fighters protecting our homeland. That's why we need your help with our difficult surgical cases. However, we can't risk two young Israeli pilots when you can cooperate with this planned hospital abduction. You must proceed with our original plan."

Isiah had to restrain himself from jumping up and giving a jubilant high five to the forthright administrator. Lamonte stood up and embraced the administrator and the rest of the team. "I'm sorry for being such a problem. Let's do it as planned, before I change my mind again," Lamonte said with a big smile that sent everyone, except Isiah, out of the meeting with their own happy look.

Dr. Lamonte's final morning in the clinic went quickly with mostly routine check-ups of previous cases. Physical therapy was recommended for most cases and it was his greatest frustration in Tel Aviv that it was rarely performed. He again promised himself, this time loud enough for his nurse secretary to hear and make a note of, that he was going to bring a physical therapist with him the next time he came back to Tel Aviv, after the drug smuggling charges were resolved. The Swiss therapist could work with and show the local well-intentioned, but mostly ineffective, therapists exactly what needed to be done to maximize the benefits of his delicate surgeries.

A few new patients were examined and treatments were planned for future surgeries. Isiah observed these exams as it kept him close to Lamonte until it was time for Azee's abduction. He was impressed by Lamonte's genuine empathy for the suffering of these terrorism victims due to no fault of their own. Between patients, Lamonte commented that he would be happy if all terrorism ended and people started living normal lives without the fear of being blown-up. Isiah concurred and that is precisely why it was so important to bring Azee to justice for his terrible crimes that killed and maimed many innocent victims in the United States.

The four other guest doctors were trying to look medically busy while they again ran through their precise duties when Azee arrived after lunch. They knew that Azee would be guarded by four of his own security men, and they hoped that his capture would not come down to hand-to-hand combat. However, they had the perceived advantage of hiding pistols under their white doctor coats and, of course, the numerical advantage of the six armed Navy SEALs waiting in the stairway to the rooftop heliport. The clinic nurses, except for the one helping Lamonte, were to be given extended lunch hours, so as not to be in harm's way if things turned nasty.

The CIA dispatched their most experienced, multi-lingual specialist from Germany to act as the prim clinic receptionist, whose job would be to keep an eye on Azee's bodyguards while he was back in surgical area. She would have a pistol hidden in a desk drawer that hopefully wouldn't have to be used. The team was ready, wishing they didn't have to wait the final couple hours for Azee's arrival.

XLV

While Azee was waiting at Temenos for his helicopter flight to Tel Aviv, he talked to his contact in Palermo who expressed great concern that the shooting of Vinnie and the burning of his restaurant could start a new round of intercity and interfamily violence in Sicily. The families in every city and village of Sicily were living an uneasy truce of live and let live because of the increased political pressure from the central government in Rome to stop the fratricide, as it was hurting the economy and tourism in all of Italy.

Fortunately, Vinnie survived, but his restaurant was destroyed and had to be rebuilt by the perpetrators to prevent future reprisals from the Messina families. After hanging up, Azee smiled and told Shakoor, waiting with him for the helicopter, to tell the Palermo contact where to go if he called to ask Azee to pay for their unnecessary torching of Vinnie's restaurant.

Azee was more concerned that Gleason had escaped his final vengeful grasp than he was about his own secretive visit to Tel Aviv. Gleason would assuredly be on guard for another attack back in the states and Azee had to admit to himself that he had lost the ability to stage a strong attack in the states with his Windsor office and Cripplegate estate destroyed. His last two reliable operatives were on the run in Canada to avoid extradition back to the United States. His revenge against Gleason would have to temporarily take a back seat to his own health and the nuclear arms deal with Iraq.

The white Israeli helicopter with Red Cross markings arrived right on time at Temenos. Azee was waiting with Hasnaa and their two sons under a covered portico as the young pilots skillfully landed on the white painted X in the center of the grassy soccer field inside the Temenos compound.

He gave his sons a crushing one armed bear hug and Hasnaa a gentle hug and quick kiss, promising to be back later in the day. Hasnaa had offered to go with him to Tel Aviv so that she could meet the wonderful doctor who saved his hand, but Azee declined her offer, stating that she should stay home with the boys. Besides, Tel Aviv could be a dangerous city with many unpredictable suicide bombings.

His two bodyguards gave the helicopter a quick check, both inside and out, and waved for Azee to come aboard. Before starting the noisy engine, the older of the two young pilots turned to Azee and asked the all important question, "Any guns?"

Azee, mildly irritated, looked at each of his bodyguards, and then shouted over the revving engine the answer they needed to hear, "No!" Azee didn't like to be airborne in a plane that was not under his control, but he had no choice other than to accept the hospitality and protection of the Israeli government if he were going to see Dr. Lamonte. The one hundred fifty miles from Temenos to Tel Aviv was too far to travel by road, even in an armed convoy, due to the hostile militias patrolling every little town that they would have to pass through.

Azee decided to create a diversionary distraction for anyone interested in his whereabouts by having Taajud-Deen and Abdul take a well disguised domestic worker, with his arm in a sling, out to the Beirut airport to board the Flying Mole. They filed a flight plan to Istanbul, the opposite direction of Tel Aviv, with the Flying Mole departing just minutes before his scheduled helicopter pick up.

The Navy monitored the Flying Mole's radio contacts with the tower at the Beirut airport. The commanding admiral in charge of this Azee mission decided to play along with Azee's ruse by breaking radio silence when he ordered Navy planes in Turkey to scramble and intercept the Flying Mole when it entered Turkish airspace. When Taajud-Deen heard this order, he said to Abdul, "By then we'll be headed back to Beirut, where they can't touch us."

Azee had flown along the spectacular Mediterranean coast countless times, but for one of his bodyguards it was his first time above the beautiful mingling of the azure blue sea and the baked brown sand of the endless beach. Azee gently chided him not to get too enraptured in the beauty of the moment because once they landed at the hospital they would be in a foreign, and possibly hostile, country. Azee was given a headset to monitor the radio communication between the ground and their helicopter.

Shortly after lifting off from Temenos, the control tower at Beirut's airport turned control of Special Medevac One, as the pilots identified themselves, over to the Tel Aviv airport control tower, which was in phone contact with the emergency room at the hospital. They were given an immediate straight line vector to the hospital from their coast hugging position and instructed to land on the ground level helipad as the rooftop helipad was occupied by another emergency helicopter. Azee observed medical personnel frantically working on the rooftop helipad as they started their own descent to the ground level helipad.

He was relieved when he saw his two additional bodyguards standing off to the side of the helipad waving their welcomes to him. He quickly scanned the hospital personnel wearing their full length white coats for Lamonte's face, even though Lamonte had told him that he would be upstairs preparing the surgical suite.

When the Israeli pilots saw Azee and his four bodyguards enter the elevator just inside the door, they quickly disabled the helicopter and took two small key components with them as they disappeared and were replaced by two armed Israeli commandos.

The Israelis initially wanted to fly out their helicopter once Azee was inside the hospital to prevent possible damage or destruction. However, Isiah prevailed upon them to leave it on the ground, so as not to alarm Azee that something was amiss as his return ride home disappeared. The United States' offer to replace a damaged helicopter made the plan workable for everyone.

XLVI

Azee was greeted very professionally by the imported CIA receptionist, who asked him and his four bodyguards to be seated while she notified Dr. Lamonte that his patient was here. However, Lamonte, hearing the voices in the reception area, immediately came out to greet Azee. They warmly embraced and Lamonte nervously pointed to the hallway back into the surgical area.

Azee and his men started a parade behind him. Lamonte abruptly pulled up and raised his hand as a sign for everyone to stop. He told Azee that the operating room was very small with sterile equipment everywhere and that there was not room for everyone. Azee suggested that two of his men come with him. Lamonte shook his head and held up one finger. Azee pointed back to the waiting room and gave a dismissive wave to the last three men in the procession.

The receptionist was able to close and lock the hall door without attracting attention from the returning three bodyguards. She would be responsible for monitoring and neutralizing these three waiting guards if they became suspicious about the happenings in the back room.

Azee sat on the edge of the operating table and Lamonte carefully unwrapped and examined his slowly healing hand. He pointed out to Azee areas where many small patches of dead skin were sloughing, surrounded by numerous red and very sore foci of inflammation, but he was pleased that there was no infection present. Lamonte was able to palpate three small spicules of bone that were working their way to the surface from the underlying tissue. One of the Kirchner wires seemed loose and needed to be tightened. Lamonte struggled ethically to tell Azee that these areas must be attended to, knowing full well that he would not be doing it today.

Azee reclined on the operating table and his arms were stabilized. As belated introductions, Lamonte mumbled the names of his masked assistant, Dr. Hyman and the nurse giving the IV sedation to render Azee unconscious.

The bodyguard, upon learning that Azee's operation would take an hour and that it would be rather bloody, asked if he could wait in the reception area with his cohorts as he didn't like the sight of blood. A relieved Isiah escorted him to the door and quickly closed and relocked it. The presence of a bodyguard in the operating room had been one of Isiah's biggest concerns and now it was not a factor as the unsuspecting bodyguard willingly left.

Isiah saw that Azee was quickly in never-never land from his IV sedation, so he opened the doors to the small doctor's office and to the rooftop stairway. The four white coated doctors with guns drawn blocked the hallway to the reception room and the six armed Navy SEALs came out of the rooftop stairway.

The SEALs quickly strapped Azee to a stretcher for the quick ascent up to the waiting helicopter. This evacuation was made more difficult because Isiah insisted on keeping the IV sedation going. Any unusual noise during this quick removal of Azee was their enemy, as Azee's bodyguards would be alerted that something was amiss back in the surgical area.

Disconsolate, Lamonte saw, through teary eyes, the worn soles of Azee's shoes as the stretcher was hustled up the stairs. He appeased his conscience by murmuring, "I tried, I tried."

The roof exit door was secured and two of the Navy SEALs

waited until the last second to climb aboard as the helicopter lifted off. The noise from the helicopter taking off reached Azee's body-guards in the waiting room. Their hard knocking on the hall door was followed by a loud crash as one of them put his shoulder into the door, springing it open.

With a raised pistol, the first in line of the hallway guards shouted, "Halt! Hands up over your heads." Azee's four body-guards instinctively started to back pedal into the reception room until the same command was repeated behind them by a softer feminine voice. The secretary thought she saw one of the bodyguards reaching for some thing under his shirt. *They were supposed to be unarmed*, she thought, *but did anyone actually frisk them?* A shot rang out and she hit the floor, as did everyone trapped in the narrow hallway.

The forward guard hopped over Azee's four prostrated body-guards. He found the secretary on the floor crouched behind an overturned wicker chair, as if that would be any protection in a face-to-face gun battle. "Are you okay?" he asked, as he didn't see any blood on her. "I had to shoot him. I saw him reaching under his shirt for what looked like a gun. I was worried about hitting you out here if I missed him."

"You must have hit him," she said, as there was moaning and faint crying coming from the heap of stunned bodyguards on the floor. Blood was starting to soak into the carpet from under the pile of bodies.

"Get Dr. Lamonte out here. It looks like he'll get to operate after all," one of the guards shouted.

The three uninjured bodyguards were hand and ankle cuffed and given wheelchair rides to the ground level. An armored per-sonnel carrier was waiting to drive them to the Lebanon border, where they could figure out how to get back to Beirut. Since they had committed no crime, outside of working for a wanted terror-ist, Israel was anxious to release them immediately to avoid an international incident over what was essentially a United States operation. Nevertheless, Israel was still going to be blamed by the radical Arab states for allowing the United States to kidnap a Lebanese citizen on their soil. The United States rarely called in any of its markers from Israel, but when it did, Israel had little choice but to cooperate, while hoping to minimize collateral damage with its less radical Arab neighbors.

Lamonte examined the wounded bodyguard's upper arm and was able to stop the bleeding with a tourniquet and cold compresses. He ordered an x-ray to be sure that there was no bone damage and that the bullet had exited the body.

At the all clear signal, the hospital administrator was immediately on the scene. She was relieved that the worst case scenario of multiple injuries and a destroyed surgical suite did not materialize. The only damage appeared to be the bloody carpet and a bullet hole in a wall magazine rack, only inches from where the secretary had been standing. Rebeka embraced the still upset Dr. Lamonte, whose only comment was, "I should have been allowed to do the surgery on Azee."

She held his trembling hands in front of her and looked into his misty eyes. "Yes, in a perfect world, you should have. Azee is a casualty of a bigger war, and war is messy as you know. Every time you come to Israel, you clean up a little bit of our wartime mess. Please don't stop coming. We need you."

"I won't stop coming. I need you, too."

Moving out of the way of the litter taking the bodyguard for his x-ray, they embraced again until she was brought back to reality by looking at the large black institutional wall clock. "We have to get you to the airport for your flight back to Zurich. I'll have one of our surgeons patch up the bodyguard's wound before we drive him to the Lebanon border. You'll be accompanied on your flight by one of our security officers, and the Swiss authorities are meeting your flight when you land in Zurich. They will provide protection for you and your family as long as necessary. Even though Azee is off the streets, he still has rich, powerful friends in Zurich."

"I need to put this whole Azee business behind me as quickly as possible. I can't live in a cocoon forever."

"You're right. Put Azee out of your mind after you dictate your report of today's medical findings and treatment recommendations for Azee. I'll fax it to our prime minister to forward to the president of the United States for his immediate attention. The United States at least owes us this, that Azee be treated as a casualty of war and be given the required treatment that you recommend. Then you have to forget him, like the other surgical cases you've done, and move on with your life."

Dr. Lamonte repositioned the colorful yarmulke on his head without contradicting her as she continued, "I'll also be in touch with Isiah with a copy of your report. He is personally guarding Azee all the way back to the United States."

While Isiah and the Navy SEALs kept guard over the still sedated Azee, a Navy SEAL doctor rewrapped his injured hand, shaking his head in wonderment, as he had never seen such an intricate surgical case. It was like a fledging artist admiring the genius of a Picasso. It looked so simple, but he knew it wasn't. Their orders were to keep Azee sedated until the helicopter touched down on its aircraft carrier home base, where he would be transferred to the fully equipped hospital below deck.

Azee was starting to stir from his sedation as the helicopter touched down on the gently pitching deck of the aircraft carrier that was ten miles offshore from Israel in international waters. He was quickly moved two decks below to the hospital ward, where he was transferred to a bed with his ankles and one good arm securely cuffed to the bed frame.

A Navy corpsman backed away from the bed as Azee was fighting to regain consciousness. He was blinking his still heavy eyelids trying to focus on his unfamiliar surroundings. Isiah was standing silently beside the bed, waiting to see if Azee recognized him. "Where am I?" Isiah knew that Azee wasn't fully awake and wouldn't remember anything he was told. He instructed a corpsman to give Azee a sip of ice water. "Why am I strapped to this bed? Where are my men?" With the corpsmen in their scrubs,

Azee had little way of knowing that he wasn't still in the Tel Aviv hospital. "Why doesn't my hand hurt after the surgery?"

Finally, Isiah broke the cruel silence when he decided that Azee was now awake enough to process his answer. "Your hand wasn't operated on, that's why it doesn't hurt."

"Where's Dr. Lamonte? I paid him very well to fix my hand. I demand that he finish my operation."

"Sorry, Azee. The U.S. government has other plans for you, like standing trial in Detroit. Dr. Lamonte is in Tel Aviv and you're cruising the Mediterranean, courtesy of the United States Navy."

"I remember you. You were in the operating room."

"That's right. Now my final job is to deliver you back to the United States for your trial."

"Good luck. Better men than you have tried to beat me."

"Azee, I have unlimited authorization from your friend, the president, to bring you back, dead or alive. It makes no difference to me. Like you, I have no conscience. Killing enemies of my country is my job and I'm very good at it."

"I've heard of you. You should be working for me. What's your name?"

"For this operation, my name is Isiah, and if you ever again mention me working for you, I will kill you." Isiah spun around and motioned for the corpsmen to attend to Azee.

XLVII

In the final days before the election, the White House political operatives closely monitored the polling services. The president's favorable polling results continued to grow, so their strategy became one of maintaining the status quo. Gleason was kept out of the public spotlight and the whereabouts of the captured Azee was a closely held secret due to security concerns.

The president's landslide reelection emboldened him to disregard the political fallout of keeping the publicly tainted Gleason on his staff. The president's post-election full pardon of Gleason, calling him a national hero, freed Gleason from the legal quagmire that would have consumed his meager retirement savings to defend himself. Gleason's retirement from the Secret Service allowed him time to focus on his AIDS health issues, while still serving at the president's beck and call.

He kept his same office in the lower level of the White House, so everyone knew that he was the president's go-to man, especially since he was given the title *Special Presidential Assistant*. Gleason was available for private presidential assignments and to spend time with Jason and Eric, as their special friend and surrogate father. He was also appointed the White House liaison with the FBI, CIA, Attorney General and the Federal Bureau of Prisons, for all things pertaining to Azee and his future trial in Detroit Federal Court.

How much the tragedy in Detroit and the sympathy vote for his comatose wife contributed to his overwhelming victory would be left to the historians to decide. It was a hollow victory as the day after the election the first lady started to experience additional lung and heart complications. The president was called early in the morning and informed that a Navy Chaplain had been summoned to administer the last rites of the Catholic Church to the failing first lady.

Gleason accompanied the president and his sons for a consultation with Dr. Schmidt, where all cried and prayed that the first lady's hellish nightmare would soon be over when the respirator was disconnected. The president was concerned with how it would look politically to discontinue her life support the day after the election. Dr. Schmidt found the courage to suggest that it was no longer about anything other than the first lady. The election was over and she deserved to die in dignity, as she had not responded to the best treatment that modern medicine could offer.

The president, cradling both sobbing boys on his lap, nodded his head in agreement with Dr. Schmidt's forthright professional opinion. Dr. Schmidt and Gleason both moved to sit on the couch next to the president and his sons for a group snuggle. They were interrupted by a call from Cardinal Rourke, which the president took and cut short with the mention that the White House would be in touch with him soon about the first lady's funeral arrangements.

The first lady succumbed thirty minutes after her respirator was disconnected to validate the medical opinion that she was in an irreversible coma. With his own health issues and the reelection campaign, the president hadn't focused on planning a funeral for his wife.

Fortunately, Gleason had taken it upon himself to research the protocol for a first lady's funeral with the bottom line being that the president could do whatever he wanted in staying true to his wife's wishes. Gleason reminded the president how much Kathy tried to make the White House a true family home, in spite of all the media attention that went with living there. The president decided that after a day of public visitation under the rotunda at the Capital, she would be returned to the White House for a final visitation night with family and close friends and a private prayer service, where fond remembrances of Kathy could be shared.

Gleason used the computer password that Kathy had given him to access her personal diary. He found emotionally moving short paragraphs on love of family that she wrote the days after Jason and Eric were born. He printed them out for the president to share on that remembrance night. Gleason knew that the president needed help sharing the loving, emotional side of Kathy, so no better way than to use her own words.

The president was committed to making Kathy's funeral as easy as possible on the boys, so he wanted no long slow street procession that would keep the boys in the public spotlight. He had no desire for his sons to be part of a public spectacle, as moving and touching as the picture of little John John Kennedy was saluting his father's passing casket.

Gleason was dispatched to talk to his old seminary professor, the easily irascible Cardinal Rourke, about the first lady's final church services before her burial at Arlington, where the president insisted that she be buried, so that he and the boys could easily visit her grave while he was still in the White House for the next four years.

The Cardinal, figuring on a large, grandiose state funeral, had his staff prepare complete reports on the pros and cons of holding the funeral mass at either St. Mathews Cathedral near the White House, where the first lady often worshipped, or at the larger Shrine of the Immaculate Conception on the campus of Catholic University. The Cardinal pushed these thick files across the desk to Gleason, but he didn't pick them up much to the cardinal's nervous consternation.

Gleason looked down at the untouched folders, afraid to make eye contact with the fidgeting Cardinal who was tapping a pencil eraser like a drum stick on the polished desk top. Finally, Gleason got the courage to say that these reports wouldn't be needed as neither of these magnificent Catholic churches was under consideration for the funeral mass. Before the Cardinal's legendary Irish temper erupted, Gleason mentioned what type of funeral service the president wanted for the sake of the boys and not for the edification of the country: a simple service in a church near the White House.

The cardinal moved from behind his desk to a large wall map of the District of Columbia that had numerous green pins in seemingly random locations. He explained that the pins were the locations of the Catholic churches in the Washington Archdiocese. Gleason, standing beside the Cardinal, could see that there was no Catholic church closer to the White House than the church that the president wanted to use. He was trying to think of a graceful way to inform the Cardinal that the president wanted to use the small Protestant Saint John's Church, a stone's throw across Lafayette Park from the White House, so he just said, "Saint John's Church?"

Gleason could hear the Cardinal's surprised, "Oh," as he sat down behind his desk. Gleason wanted to preempt the Cardinal's certain objection so he mentioned that he had already talked to the rector of Saint John's and that he would be honored to host the first lady's funeral service. Gleason knew that the Cardinal was doing a slow burn that would certainly erupt into a major conflagration if not adroitly handled. However, the Cardinal started a monologue that Gleason knew not to interrupt. His main concern was that Saint John's was not a Roman Catholic Church, but an Anglican Church, and since the first lady was Roman Catholic she should be buried by her own church.

Gleason did not want to get into a theological argument with his former professor, so he mentioned that the rector of Saint John's had offered to step aside to allow the Cardinal to celebrate the traditional Catholic funeral liturgy in the church that the president desired. While the Cardinal was mulling over the rector's offer, and before he could raise other objections, Gleason pointed out that Saint John's prides itself on being the church of the presidents and their families, as every president since Madison has worshipped there. Madison in a rare case of presidential humility eschewed the front pew and sat eight pews back in what is now labeled the President's Pew. All the presidents are remembered by their own red velvet kneeling cushion with their embroidered name, term of office and the presidential seal. Gleason struggled to keep explaining the practical reasons for using this little yellow church across Lafayette Park from the White House to forestall the Cardinal from exploding.

The Cardinal held up a quivering hand as a signal that he had heard enough. He prayerfully folded his hands, his fingertips touching his chin as he prepared to speak his peace. "The first lady, the president and the nation have suffered enough. If this is what the president wants, I'll be honored to celebrate her funeral service in the shadow of her White House home. We bury our fallen heroes during times of war in open fields without a church, so who am I to say that this historic little church isn't right for the first lady? I'll call the rector and invite him to share the altar with me." The Cardinal came around the desk and gave Gleason a crushing hug. He said, "Tell the president that the Cardinal does have feelings." Gleason heard this final statement as permission for the modest funeral arrangements that the president desired.

XLVIII

Azee was on the proverbial slow boat to China, except he was headed to an undisclosed East Coast Navy base. After his abrupt snatching in Tel Aviv and his short helicopter flight to the offshore aircraft carrier, the wheels of justice were set in motion for his return to the United States after the election.

The president had been interested in having Azee face the full wrath and fury of the federal judicial system, hopefully resulting in a sure and speedy death sentence. To accomplish this desired objective he took the calculated gamble of a failed kidnapping attempt and the subsequent international ridicule that would follow. He had rolled the dice, betting on the CIA's best Mideast operative, Isiah, to capture Azee and return him to American soil to face justice.

Azee with the best international defense team that money could buy was appealing his illegal kidnapping to the International Court at the Hague. The justice department lawyers gave this lawsuit little chance of succeeding. Even on the rare chance that it succeeded, the president had no intention of honoring its decision to release Azee. To the bleeding hearts who questioned the legality of Azee's abduction, the president quoted the old real estate maxim, *possession is nine-tenths of the law*. The United States now possessed Azee. End of discussion.

The administration privately welcomed the delay that Azee's appeal to the International Court at the Hague caused, as it provided an excuse for keeping Azee offshore and away from the media glare while trial preparations were underway at the Justice Department. The Hague legalities effectively put Azee's murder and treason trial in Detroit on indefinite hold. The media speculated that he was being held offshore until the International Court rendered its decision.

Even after the president easily won his reelection, there was no urgency in sharing Azee's exact whereabouts until he was in his secure onshore location awaiting trial.

However, Gleason could see the frustration over Azee's uncertain legal timetable building in his boss, so on a relatively quiet morning he invited him to have coffee in Kathy's favorite secluded garden spot overlooking the south lawn of the White House.

Gleason had been struggling to conceal his deep personal hatred of Azee, who had turned his and the president's lives upside down. Gleason knew that the AIDS-infected casino hostess, Misty, worked for Azee at the time that she passed AIDS on to him. The final straw was Azee's desperate attack in Sicily on himself and especially on Cindy. All Gleason's frustrations emboldened him to surprise the president. "Mr. President, I'd like to take another run at Azee when we finally get him ashore. You could be out of office before he comes to trial with his unlimited resources to hire the best attorneys."

The president sipped his coffee contemplating Gleason's open ended offer. "Tom, you're the best friend the boys and I have. You could have been killed in your first run at Azee on his airplane. That would have been more than I could take coupled with Azee killing Kathy and nearly me."

Gleason did not know how he would deal with his own hatred of Azee if the president denied his request for personal revenge, so he added, "This time I'll not be physically endangered. You need not know the details so you can have deniability."

The president poured coffee refills for Tom and himself. He walked among the garden plantings that Kathy so loved, observing their fading fall colors. The stark white Washington Monument soaring heavenward carried his thoughts to Kathy and their first meeting during a protest march at the base of the monument. Statue-like, he stared contemplatively at the better times of their unrecoverable past. Tom finished his coffee, not disturbing the pensive president. They set their empty coffee cups on the white wrought iron table. Turning toward Tom, the misty-eyed president was barely able to whisper his ascent. "Azee took Kathy from me. Do it."

IL

Gleason could not believe how everything in his life seemed to be coming together. His cocktail treatments for AIDS gave him and his NIH doctors hope that he could live a normal life. Being freed of the minute-to-minute responsibility of protecting the president was a load off his shoulders that he never realized was there until it was gone. His favorite time of the day was when Jason and Eric returned from school and were looking for something to do on the expansive south lawn. Occasionally, the president would join them for a little two-on-two soccer, football or whatever sport was in season. Gleason felt it was a shame that it took the death of the first lady to make the president realize what was really important.

He and Cindy jump-started a casual open-ended dating relationship that they both seemed to be enjoying. However, Cindy was wise enough to know that he still had major unresolved issues as she now also had with what happened to Uncle Vinnie and the family restaurant in Sicily. She was in weekly contact with her family there and the good news was that Uncle Vinnie was on his way to a full recovery. The bad news was that she could sense the family's frustration that the Italian law enforcement agencies were not making progress in identifying the culprits, even though everyone knew that the trigger men were Mafia from Palermo.

Her family had gone *legit* two generations ago, but she understood that revenge and retribution were only a phone call away. She dreaded that idea and was trying to shed the guilt that she and Tom could be the cause of a new Mafia war engulfing Sicily. Even though Gleason was able to enlist the help of various United States government agencies in the investigation of their attack, their role was limited by the pride of the Italian government which felt that they could handle their own turf wars.

Although Tom was sorry for being the target of the surprise attack, he convinced Cindy there was nothing that they could do personally to identify and apprehend the perpetrators. The Italian authorities had a vested interest in not having another Mafia war, so they should move the investigation along.

He mentioned to Cindy that once Azee was on U.S. soil, the rules of the game would change since he was the instigator of their near death in Sicily. She did not want to know what the current Azee rules were and especially what the new rules would be once Azee was ashore. Tom didn't dare share with Cindy that the president threw out the rule book, which allowed Tom to formulate one more final solution to the Azee saga.

Gleason needed expert help to terminate Azee, so he spent an afternoon at Langley in the CIA biological lab picking their devious brains for a solution to his non-specified problem of chemically killing someone without leaving behind any telltale evidence. Being given a printout of the macabre history of lethal drug development starting with Socrates' hemlock, he wondered how many CIA field agents had been given this same briefing and left with the same lethal handout. The coldly dispassionate briefing technician highlighted the printout's page on potassium chloride and explained that it was difficult to detect post mortem because it is naturally found in the body, unlike many of the newer synthetic killing agents that leave behind telltale chemical markers.

L

The Hague International Tribunal ruled that they did not have jurisdiction over Azee's abduction in Tel Aviv. The issue was really between the U.S. and Israel, since the abduction happened inside Israeli borders. With both countries cooperating on Azee's abduction, its legality was not an issue.

After the Hague ruling, Azee's aircraft carrier headed for Norfolk to start his legal proceedings in the United States. Since the federal crimes of attacking the president and killing the first lady happened in Michigan, his trial would be held in the federal court in Detroit. The justice department decided that Azee would be housed at the Milan Federal Reformatory, an hour west of the federal courthouse in Detroit. He would be shuttled back and forth to the federal courthouse in Detroit for the motions and preliminary hearings locked inside an armored Federal Bureau of Prisons bus capable of transporting twenty criminals in the most secure environment possible. This windowless rolling prison was the bureau of prisons' usual method of transferring prisoners, securely shackled to their seats, from prison to prison across the country. There would be several armed federal marshals guarding the one shackled high-profile prisoner in the smelly bus as it made its round trips to and from the federal courthouse in Detroit.

Milan Federal Reformatory had experience in housing high profile criminals such as Mafia informant Joe Valachi. They kept him alive for the sole purpose that he could continue his suicidal singing about the Mafia. When word of Azee's new residency at the Milan Reformatory became known, Gleason did a background check on everyone working in the small ten bed prison hospital, knowing that sooner or later Azee would need medical and certainly surgical treatment on his injured hand.

The United States Public Health Service provides the professional staff—physicians, dentists, psychologists, and medical and laboratory technicians—needed to run the small Federal prison hospital at Milan. Gleason thought it was a good idea to meet with the professional staff's boss, the Surgeon General, to give him a heads up that Azee was about to come under his care. Gleason brought a summary chart of Azee's medical conditions to the Surgeon General. To impress on him the seriousness of his new caretaker role over Azee, Gleason presented a hand written memo from the president stating that the care and safety of Azee was the Public Health Service's number one priority while he was confined at Milan, and that no expense was to be spared to assure that Azee stayed healthy for his long trial.

There was one name, Richard Benz, on the hospital work roster provided by the Surgeon General that Gleason thought he recognized from their hellish Navy basic training days. Benz was from Michigan and retired as a senior medical technician from the Navy, so it made sense that he could be supplementing his Navy pension by working in the Milan prison hospital, near where he was raised. His Navy personnel file contained numerous commendations from various commanding officers for staunch patriotism and service above and beyond the call of duty. Gleason's background check of Benz revealed that he was a former member of the Michigan Militia, but that he no longer appeared actively involved in their bizarre activities.

Before Azee arrived at Milan, Gleason called him out of the blue and sure enough, Benz remembered him from their basic training days. Benz was quick to mention that he had read about his failed heroics over the Atlantic in trying to singlehandedly bring Azee to justice. Benz's final comment, "Let me know if there's anything I can do to help finish what you started," was the opening Gleason needed to again get close to Azee to take care of unfinished business.

When Azee's floating prison docked at Norfolk, he was taken to the naval airbase for an immediate flight to Detroit Metro Airport. He was handcuffed by his good wrist to super CIA agent Isiah, who was still under presidential order not to let Azee out of his sight until turning him over to the U.S. Marshals at Detroit Metro Airport.

At Metro, they disembarked at a distant freight terminal to avoid a media circus at the main terminal. A cohort of Federal Marshals was waiting on the tarmac for the tethered pair of Azee and Isiah to descend the steep airplane stairway.

Isiah smiled at Azee while fumbling for the handcuff key in his pants pocket. Azee returned the smile with the comment, "I told you that you should be working for me."

"And I told you that I would kill you if you ever mentioned it again. Lucky for you, the federal marshals are here to save your sorry ass." Isiah headed into the small freight terminal to get away from Azee before he fulfilled his deadly promise.

Since Azee's arrival on U.S. soil and his immediate transfer to Detroit were unannounced, the Federal Marshal's service felt confident that one armored vehicle for the prisoner with two additional support vehicles would be adequate to securely transport him the short distance from Detroit Metro to the Milan Federal Reformatory, his home for the duration of the federal proceedings in Detroit.

Even though Milan Prison was classified as a reformatory, which meant that it housed a young inmate population capable of being rehabilitated, it was also a very secure facility for a high profile prisoner like Azee. The guard towers at the four corners of the double rows of electrified cyclone fences were manned by sharp-shooting guards with orders to shoot to kill if the perimeter were breached by an escape-minded inmate.

Gleason, aware of the small plane that crashed into the roof of the White House, suggested that the air space above and around the reformatory should be declared a No Fly Zone to negate any possible helicopter escape attempt by Azee, as well as TV news helicopters that would do anything for a scoop. With the high profile Azee joining the prison population, the reformatory was declared a No Fly Zone and the tower guards had new instructions to watch for any aircraft venturing into this restricted area and to shoot it down.

LI

The final day of the month for the dental clinic at Milan Reformatory was always extra busy for a good bureaucratic reason: the dentists had to elevate their month-end statistics to reach a mandated monthly quota of patients before submitting their monthly clinic statistics to their Bureau of Prison headquarters in Washington. The dental chief for the Federal Bureau of Prisons in Washington was mainly interested in the number of patient visits per month and not the quantity or quality of treatment provided. Thus, at the end of the month, the two dentists always scheduled a number of tongue blade exams, merely moving the patient's tongue aside to verify that teeth were present in the one hundred patients scheduled for this needless examination. This thirty-second exam counted as a patient visit for the monthly report, so their Washington boss was happy even though no meaningful treatment was performed.

The correctional staff hated these month-end extra busy days as they had to make sure that the inmate patients kept these dental appointments and weren't loitering around the prison unsupervised. It was very time consuming for the guards to physically escort this many patients to the dental clinic to keep the inmates from getting lost on their way or causing problems on the compound. The dental clinic operated with a shot of adrenaline on these month-end padding days and the call from the warden's office was not good news to the two hustling dentists.

Milan Federal Reformatory operated on *Warden Time*, so when they were ordered to report to his office immediately, they knew they should have been there ten minutes earlier. However, they did take time to wash their hands before hurrying out the dental clinic because the warden always offered a robust handshake. The chief dental officer, Dr. Ragman, poked his head into the hospital administrator's office with the terse comment, "We've been called out front so keep an eye on things."

The officer behind the bulletproof glass, manning the double gated control center in the corridor leading to the warden's office, waved them through. When the occasion called for it, Warden Jack Baldridge could charm the knife from a mass murderer's bloody hands. Today was one such occasion and the dentists recognized that the warden was going to ask them for a favor, although he certainly could have ordered it by an interdepartmental memo, as there was no questioning his absolute power.

The younger dentist, Dr. Joe Capino, kept glancing at the minutes ticking away on the black institutional wall clock behind the warden's desk, as he was anxious to get back to the clinic to complete his month-end exams. His boss, Dr. Ragman, seemed to enjoy bantering with the warden about their latest scores in the reformatory skeet shooting league and the hopeless state of Detroit Tiger baseball. Capino, being a big city boy from Boston, had little interest in the Tigers or guns, especially since a young inmate was shot off the prison's perimeter fencing the day after he reported for active duty.

A few days later, he overheard a group of prison guards discussing the biggest tragedy of this killing was that the shooting officer would be restricted to the usually uneventful, totally boring tower duty for the rest of his working career. They gave no consideration to the young victim, who in their judgment, got what he deserved for being so stupid to challenge the authority of a man in the guard tower with a high power rifle. The shooting guard's identity was common knowledge among the inmates on the compound and would be passed on to incoming inmates so that if he ever worked inside the prison again, he wouldn't do it for very long, as a homemade knife would puncture his ribcage in revenge for killing one of their own. Tower guard duty was rotated monthly among the correctional officers to allow them to keep their sanity, so heaven help that shooting officer who would have his hands on a high power rifle for the rest of his working career.

Finally, Warden Baldridge picked up a skinny gold Cross pen and tapped it on the highly polished cherry desktop as a signal that BS time was over. "Men, we have a problem..." He let this short sentence hang, hoping for a reaction.

Capino was tempted to say that he was just following orders doing these meaningless month-end tongue blade exams. Ragman had enough years in the United States Public Health Service to retire, so no problem was too big for his retirement mindset to avoid if he could.

Getting no response, the warden got to the reason for this meeting. "As I'm sure that you've heard, the notorious Mr. Azee is now a guest of the federal government upstairs in a secure isolation room. He's guarded around the clock, while under continuous video and audio surveillance from the control center. He has a toothache and the federal court in Detroit has ordered us to provide the appropriate treatment. Dr. Ragman, as you remember, we had the same high security issue with Joe Valachi."

"We'll be happy to treat Azee like we did Valachi. Azee must have bypassed the usual admission process with the required initial dental exam, so I have no idea what his problem could be."

"That's right. He went right into isolation when he arrived. The process will be the same with Azee as it was with Valachi, but with even tighter security. At no time will Azee be out of his solitary confinement when the general prison population is free to harm him. Many inmates would try to kill him for their fifteen minutes of fame. Like Valachi, we are mandated to keep Azee healthy and alive so he can have his day, or I should say months, if not years, in court. I'll have a guard escort you upstairs to determine his problem when you leave here. Don't be offended when you are frisked, and even guarded, inside Azee's locked cell."

Dr. Ragman nodded his head in understanding of what the warden just said, but also in anticipation of the marching orders about to come from the warden. "If your exam today shows that you need to see Azee in the dental clinic to treat his problem, we'll use the same procedure as we did with Valachi. I'll call you sometime in the next week after midnight. When you answer the phone, I'll say *yes* and hang up. You are to be here in thirty minutes and we will have Azee waiting in the dental clinic when you arrive. No one else is to know of this arrangement."

"Can I bring Dr. Capino?"

"No."

"I could use his help if I run into trouble."

"I said no. Use the on-duty night med tech if you need help. I believe he had some dental training in the Navy. The entire hospital staff has been cleared to have contact with Azee. Call me after you check Azee if we need to activate the late night plan for his dental clinic visit." The door opened behind them as the escorting guard entered to take them upstairs to see their hurting patient.

LII

While waiting between the double gates at the control center that monitors access to the inside of the prison, Ragman tried to minimize the warden's rejection of Capino. "Joe, don't take the warden's denial personally. Protecting Azee is job one for the warden. He has to have everything connected with Azee, like with Valachi, approved by the Federal Court in Detroit. Any failures with Azee mean the warden would be retired at an early age. Count your blessings that you don't have to get up in the middle of the night to treat the likes of Azee."

After going through heavy locked metal doors at the bottom and top of the stairway to Azee's abode, they arrived in a small hall with a heavier metal door with a small wire reinforced glass window. There was a rectangular slot large enough to pass a food tray through or to reach inside to handcuff the inmate backed up to the door.

The guard seated on a stool high enough to constantly observe Azee through the door window was glad to have someone to talk to, as he was ordered to have no unnecessary conversation with Azee. A voice activated video camera feeding into the control center was the enforcement tool that kept everyone on their toes in this solitary guard duty that was even more boring than the tower duty. The guard checked their sequentially numbered pass bearing the warden's signature to verify that this was a permissible visit to Azee.

The dentists emptied their pockets into small plastic bowls for later retrieval and the guards took turns patting them down. The guard on duty rattled a pair of handcuffs and the Pavlovian trained Azee backed up to the door to have his hands cuffed behind his back. Ragman caught a glimpse of Azee's surgically saved, but still grossly deformed, right hand so he questioned, "Is this necessary?"

"Probably not, just following orders. Talk to the warden if you have a problem with it," the on-duty guard answered.

"We never cuffed Valachi when I checked his teeth."

"Valachi was a small potato compared to Azee. Besides, he was an old man by the time he was here."

Recalling Valachi, Ragman remembered thinking that he wouldn't want to meet him in a narrow alley on a moonless night. An old black and white TV blasting mindless soap operas, a set of scuffed-up bar bells rolled under the rusty black metal bed frame were the only diversions for the Mafia killer of too many victims to count. His shirtless seventy year old washboard torso and chiseled biceps still said, *don't mess with me*. Ragman didn't get this feeling looking at the smaller Azee with the deformed hand. Azee sat on the edge of the bed and opened his mouth for the dentists. With just a flashlight, the dentists were able to see a lower molar that was broken off at the gum line and yellow pus oozing out from around the stubby roots of a once proud tooth.

"I broke a beautiful gold crown off that tooth a year ago and I've been too busy to have it fixed. Can you save it?"

"Some night soon we'll get you down to the dental clinic for an x-ray. From what I see today, I doubt that we can save the tooth because it's infected."

"You know money is no object if you want to bring in a specialist to save it."

"The warden won't approve any outside consultant seeing you."

"Fuck the warden."

"Nice meeting you, Mr. Azee. We'll arrange to pull this bad tooth after you've been on antibiotics for a couple days," Ragman concluded.

LIII

Once free of their accompanying guard on their way back from seeing Azee to the dental clinic, the enthusiastic Capino mentioned that a root canal on Azee's bad molar would be a piece of cake and a new crown could be made that would last Azee for years.

"That would be too many early morning appointments for the warden," Ragman answered. "Maybe you haven't heard that the federal prosecutor is asking for the death penalty, so Azee may not live long enough to justify all that treatment."

Rounding the corner to the dental clinic, the dentists expected to see patients lined up into the hallway waiting for their exams, but no one was there. No one was in the waiting room of the dental clinic either, so Ragman barked, "Trimble, where the hell is everyone? We need to finish the month-end exams."

Inmate Trimble, seated behind the beat-up institutional grey metal desk, was the best receptionist that Ragman had worked with in his thirty years of prison dentistry. The timid reply, "Captain Birkmeyer," accompanied by a finger pointed toward their private office, answered the question.

Here we go again, Ragman thought, pausing to compose himself before confronting Milan's diminutive answer to Napoleon. *That little bastard has screwed up my monthly report to Washington* was the best thought that he could conjure up before entering his office. "Captain, mind if I sit in my own chair behind my desk?"

Defiantly slow, the captain surrendered the chair and sat next to Capino in a smaller side chair. "I was looking for a pen and paper to write the warden a memo." Ragman shrugged his shoulders, which threw gasoline on the simmering coals. "You left at least thirty inmates unsupervised in and round the dental clinic for God knows how long. If I hadn't arrived, there would have been a riot. That's how a prison riot starts, unsupervised inmates screwing around. Have you ever been in a prison riot?" Ragman, a decorated Marine captain, continued to ignore this pesky little nuisance with every bit of restraint he had. "Give me a pen and paper for my memo to the warden," the captain demanded.

After silently staring the captain down, Ragman stood up and headed out of the office. "Follow me," he ordered the captain. At hospital administrator Sevenson's hallway door, Ragman hollered in, "Call the warden's office. Tell him that the captain and I are on the way."

Between the two control center gates, Captain Birkmeyer tried to change the direction they were headed. "Let's talk a minute."

"The warden's expecting us," Ragman said. In prison there are inherently multiple sources of tension between the staff in the various departments. The professional hospital staff, trying to compassionately treat the institutionalized inmates as if they were real patients in a real world setting, often butted heads with the paranoid, security-conscious correctional staff headed by Captain Birkmeyer. He was third in command at Milan behind the warden and assistant warden; so unfortunately, he was a force to be reckoned with in trying to render quality, compassionate care to their inmate patients, even the persona-non-grata locked upstairs in solitary confinement. The inmate population was helplessly caught in the middle of this institutional power struggle that had no purpose beyond ego gratification.

The warden's secretary ushered them into the inner sanctum. "I'm saving the captain the trouble of writing you a memo, sir,"

Ragman said to open the meeting with the warden.

"What's the problem, captain?"

"It's really not so important that you have to use your valuable time to address. Doc and I can work it out," the captain rationalized.

"Give it to me. I'll decide if it's important."

The captain started to explain how he came upon unsupervised inmates in the hall outside the dental clinic, and even in the dental clinic itself. Inmates were on the verge of starting a riot because the dentists were out running around the prison when they should have been in their clinic. Ragman had all he could do to not throttle the self-promoting captain. However, he knew that the warden would call the captain short on his wayward thinking.

"Excuse me captain, but the dentists were following my orders by checking on our new guest on the second floor. The hospital administrator called needing to know how much longer they were going to be detained because his med tech, watching the dental clinic, had to get his meds put up for sick call. So, what's the problem, captain?"

"Nothing sir, the way you explained it."

"Thank you, captain, you can go now. Doctor, what did you find out from examining Azee?"

Ragman smiled at the exiting captain before beginning. "Azee has an infected lower molar tooth, broken off at the gum line. If we do nothing, withholding antibiotics, he could die of this infection."

"Not too bad a choice. It would save the taxpayers a lot of money on the trial and his room and board here at Milan. However, probably not going to happen this way after the Federal court in Detroit hears about his infection."

"Our next choice would be to try to save it with a root canal and a new crown like he had on it before it broke apart. He offered to pay an outside specialist for this many appointment treatment. If this was your tooth, that's what you would want done."

The warden laughed at the absurdity of this option. "One

important difference: I'm not facing the death penalty, like him. Forget this."

"Then the infected tooth has to be extracted. I'll start him on antibiotics today, so we can extract it when you call me."

"Thanks, Doc," the warden replied. "I'll call you after I get the required court approval. We're still waiting for permission from the court to give Azee a new steroid inhaler for his asthma, which isn't being helped by his dank, dark cell. I'll tell the court that this infected tooth is a matter of life and death, so they get off their butt and give permission to extract it before it's too late. By the way, Doc, don't be too tough on the captain. He has the hardest job in the prison, keeping five hundred inmates and two hundred staff safe on a minute-to-minute basis. I deal with the big picture of running this joint. He's the heart and soul of the prison's day-to-day operation."

LIV

Ragman returned to the clinic to fill out his month-end report to Washington. He was tempted to put a captain's upward adjustment on his numbers since he ran off most of the dental clinic's patients. However, he had never fudged the numbers before and he wasn't going to let a small-minded captain be the cause of doing it now. Filling out the report brought him a sense of relief because he was another month closer to retirement. The report was what it was and Washington could deal with it.

On his way home for the day, he brought the monthly dental report to Sevenson, who beckoned him to sit down. He always found his paper boss a steadying influence in all the institutional turf wars being fought. As a former Navy medic, who climbed the ranks to become a Navy hospital administrator, he could relate to the petty fights always raging in the closed prison environment. "Everything go okay with the warden?"

"The captain stood down when the warden explained that Capino and I were doing his business examining the patient upstairs and that you had the dental clinic covered in our absence. I may have won this battle, but I'll probably lose the war with the captain."

"Let me be your go-between with the captain. I already have my Navy retirement and I took this job to keep me off the golf course seven days a week. I've dealt with admirals who make the captain look like a shoe shine boy, although don't tell him that."

Ragman appreciated this fatherly advice. Remembering the warden's stern secrecy warning, he debated how much to reveal about his impending late night hospital visit to treat Azee. He thought it best by beginning with a question. "Have you been upstairs to visit Azee?"

"I saw him with the physician for his admittance physical. We didn't have time to call you for the dental exam portion, which you can complete when you treat him in the dental clinic. I have to co-sign everything connected with Azee. The government isn't taking any chances with him. Things are much tighter with him than they were with Valachi."

"Capino and I saw him for an infected tooth. I prescribed an antibiotic for him to take until the tooth is pulled." He stopped there, letting the sage administrator fill in the rest of the treatment sequence.

"I know. I had to co-sign for the antibiotic before sending it up to him. I'm surprised that we got it approved by the court so quickly. I guess that speaks to the wonder of the fax machine versus the pony express. We're still waiting to get approval for his asthma inhaler, which we'll then have to requisition from the medical center in Springfield. Azee could be tried and found guilty before we get the damned inhaler. I'll let my night nurse know that you'll be coming in, so that he doesn't think he's seeing a ghost at that hour of the night."

"Don't say too much. This is supposed to be top secret."

LV

The good news of Azee's toothache kicked Gleason's contingency plan into high gear. He got on the first flight to Detroit Metro. For this secret mission his usual VIP White House travel was out of the question. He traveled under an assumed ID, provided by the same reliable non-governmental back street source that supplied him with two time-released glass cartridges of potassium chloride. He was met at Detroit Metro by Benz in his dusty pickup truck. They immediately recognized each other and their years apart were bridged by their now laughable basic training horror stories. Gleason, riding shotgun, was searching for a fast food restaurant without surveillance cameras. Finally, they ordered coffee in an outside drive-up lane and brought it inside to a back booth away from the cameras at the ordering counter.

Gleason had less than three hours before his turnaround flight to D.C. so he decided to roll the dice with minimum ice-breaking delays. Benz appeared to be a super patriot who had no stomach for the treachery of Azee or any other traitors who were trying to destroy the America he risked his life for in his service years.

Opening his folded white handkerchief, Gleason revealed a small brown coin envelope inside a plastic baggie that did little to conceal its narrow contents, a little shorter than a small golf pencil. He explained the details of Azee's upcoming tooth extraction, which would fit perfectly with Benz's third shift duty as the only nurse staffing the sleeping hospital. Gleason emphasized the need to burn the baggie to destroy all fingerprints and to wear latex gloves when handling the small brown coin envelope and its lethal contents. Benz had worked in an aircraft carrier dental clinic as part of the Navy's obsession with cross-training all hospital personnel, so he was familiar with how the anesthetic cartridges would slip into the metal syringe for the numbing injections. Benz reassured Gleason that he was familiar with the dental clinic needle security procedures and that substitution of the two lethal cartridges for the regular dental anesthetic cartridges would be no problem.

Pulling up to Gleason's departure area, Benz thanked him for allowing him a chance to finish what an old Navy buddy started, ridding the world of a scourge worse than the devil incarnate. Gleason had no choice but to trust his newfound accomplice with completing the deadly deal that he and the president concluded was the best way to honor the deceased first lady's memory.

He tried to stay inconspicuous while waiting to board his return flight to Washington by sitting for a half hour in a stall of the men's room near his departure gate. Once airborne, he rested his head on the cool window frame in a feeble attempt to sleep, but more to avoid conversation with his adjoining passenger, a nervous elderly lady who could never seem to find what she was looking for in her bulging purse. Gleason's flight back from Detroit to Washington encountered as much turbulence as he was experiencing inside his troubled mind so he was not able to offer much comfort to the nervous lady seated beside him. He was working hard to assuage his conscience aboard another airplane that he again was doing the right and necessary thing by taking another run at Azee. He finally dozed off for a few minutes only to awaken in a cold sweat. As much as he hated Azee, especially for his nearly successful attempt on Cindy's and his life in Sicily, his desire for revenge was being tempered by the realization that he had backed his friend, the president, into his same perverted corner where their only escape was killing Azee outside the boundaries of the legal system.

He felt that he owed the president one final chance to still back away from the *Azee Solution*, which, upon many sleepless nights of deep introspections, had become his personal vendetta against Azee. He didn't want his friend and boss, the president, to be sucked into his personal maelstrom of depravity.

For the next few days before leaving the dental clinic, Ragman checked that his inmate assistant had laid out a surgical tooth extraction setup for possible after hours use. The sterile setup contained everything, including two anesthetic cartridges that he anticipated using to numb Azee's infected tooth. However, per bureau of prison directives, the injection needle was kept locked up until the moment of usage. Medical needles were highly coveted contraband in the widespread prison drug scene, so they had to be closely accounted for and destroyed after every usage. The inmate dental assistant didn't have to be told who the set up was for because the only previous time this regimen was followed was the Valachi case. In spite of the warden's caveat about no discussion of Azee's late night dental visit, there were few secrets in prison.

LVI

Gleason was in his White House office earlier than usual the next morning to check the president's schedule for the day. He needed to meet early before he lost his nerve to bring the *Azee Solution* to the president. Deep down Gleason was hoping that the president would solve his growing moral dilemma that the end does not justify the means needed to achieve it. Gleason had no doubt that a dead Azee would be a good thing. However, the means to achieve it were contrary to his fundamental values.

He was having a cup of coffee in the outer office with the president's secretary when she received the signal that he was leaving the upstairs residence and would be in his office momentarily. Gleason stood up and nervously paced in front of her desk until she motioned for him to go into the oval office.

Gleason felt that he had better come quickly to the point of his surprise visit. Without going into the specific details of how Azee was going to meet his maker, he explained to a pensive president that all of the macabre plans were in place.

Finally, the president broke his silence, "Are you sure we still want to do this?"

"Not so sure, anymore," Gleason quietly stated.

"Please explain your change of heart."

"It's hard to explain. I feel that I unfairly dragged you into my personal war with Azee. I'm convinced that we can get away with it, but it doesn't seem right on all levels."

The president was silent again as he reached for a tissue on the credenza behind his desk. "The birth of Melody has changed me, softened me if you will. I want all the killing to stop. Let's call it off. The courts can take care of Azee."

"I agree, Mr. President. I'll get your order to our man at Milan."

Gleason hurried to his office to make this emergency call to Milan on a secure, non-traceable phone line. He left a terse message at Benz's number. "Our deal is cancelled by the boss. Return unused merchandise."

LVII

On the home front, the only discussion Ragman had with his wife was not to be alarmed at a late night call notifying him to immediately come to the prison to treat an emergency patient. He would be home in an hour to get a few more hours of sleep.

At 2 a.m. on the fourth night of the Azee watch the *yes call* came. Ragman opted to wear jeans and a faded University of Michigan sweatshirt in place of the uncomfortable Navy uniform that members of the public health service wear during regular work hours. Observing all speed limits while monitoring if he was being followed, he arrived at the quiet prison parking lot under the watchful eyes of the guard in the main tower. He cleared security at the control center and entered the dental clinic simultaneously with the shackled patient, who was also aroused from his slumber.

Azee seemed to express sincere appreciation when he greeted Ragman, "Sorry to get you up in the middle of the night."

"That's why I get paid the big bucks! I hope you go back to sleep when we're done."

"Let's go for it, Doc. I hate shots, especially in the mouth."

"First, I need to get an x-ray to check the shape of the roots." The night nurse, Richard Benz, welcomed this dental clinic change of pace from his boring night watch of only one patient, a post-surgical tattoo removal case, sleeping in the hospital. Benz brought the developed x-ray for Ragman's quick check before proceeding with what should be a simple extraction.

Ragman had to ask the hovering custodial officer to step back, so he could get at the locked needle drawer at his elbow. He retrieved a long 27 gauge needle and twisted it onto a metal syringe. Two anesthetic cartridges were on the sterile surgical set up and he slid one into the syringe away from Azee's nervously darting eyes. He needed to do a deep muscle nerve block on the lower jaw, as well as infiltrating the outside gum line nerves, so he used both cartridges that were on the surgical tray. Waiting a few minutes, Ragman asked Azee if his tongue or lip were feeling numb. His wordless head shake sent Benz reaching for two more cartridges for Ragman to load into the syringe. Ragman apologized to Azee for having to re-inject him, but everything would be over soon as the x-ray showed normal roots. This second set of injections took effect almost immediately. Benz efficiently cleared away the dirty gauze and the empty anesthetic cartridges, so the operation could begin with an uncluttered surgical tray.

Relief of pain is the main thrust of prison dentistry. The prison's morning sick call, run by Benz and his fellow nurses and medical technicians, usually generated four or five patients a day for the dental clinic. Most of these hurting patients needed relief of pain, so too many extractions were done on teeth that could be saved with root canal and crowns, if the Bureau of Prison's dental procedure manual permitted. Ragman, at lunch recently with the just arriving Capino, roughly calculated that he had done over ten thousand extractions in his thirty year prison dental career, so Azee's extraction was the least of his worries. After curetting the oozing gum line and elevating the doomed molar roots, a gentle tug on the forceps delivered the intact roots.

Biting on a folded gauze pad, Azee was able to quickly control the bleeding. Azee stated that he was feeling a little disoriented, so he wanted to get back to the familiar setting of his cell to sleep it off. Ragman promised Azee that he would come up to check him later that afternoon.

Ragman put Azee's chart and x-ray on his office desk, resolving to fill it out first thing when he returned for his regular work day. Benz scrubbed the blood off the instruments and left them for the inmate assistants to bag and sterilize in the morning. With gloved hands, Benz carefully unscrewed the long needle from the metal syringe and put it into the red biohazard destroyer to render it useless in the needle hungry prison. Benz left the remaining empty cartridges on the dirty surgical tray to be discovered in the morning. He covered the tray with a small towel and turned out the lights.

Ragman headed back to his Ann Arbor home to catch a little more sleep, but his relaxed drive was interrupted by the flashing strobe lights and obnoxious sirens of an ambulance and fire rescue unit headed in the direction he was coming from. Pulling into his driveway, he noticed the porch light on and the front door ajar. Opening the screen door he was greeted by his hysterical wife with the phone at her ear, "What happened?"

Grabbing the phone from her, he heard an echoing voice from the speaker phone in the the prison control center. "I have audio and video from Azee's cell where the EMTs are trying to get a pulse on Azee, who is not breathing. Benz was summoned from the hospital and performed CPR before the EMTs arrived. The warden said that he wants Azee taken to the emergency room at the University of Michigan Hospital in Ann Arbor. One of the EMTs just said that Azee is dead."

"Oh my God!" Ragman dropped the phone and collapsed onto the sofa, trying to figure out what went wrong.

The warden adamantly insisted that Azee's lifeless remains be rushed to the University of Michigan Hospital emergency room. Maintaining continuous radio contact with the emergency room doctors, the ambulance EMTs were able to give Azee most of the same heart starting treatment that he would have gotten in the hospital emergency room, except for the open chest direct heart massage. Numerous attempts at shocking the heart with the defibrillator and multiple injections of adrenaline directly into the heart muscle stimulated no heartbeat.

Nevertheless, CPR was maintained during the speedy trip to Ann Arbor. The EMTs, not knowing whom they were transporting, were relieved to turn their non-responsive patient over to the emergency room doctors, who were fully mobilized and informed by the warden who their arriving patient was.

After their quick evaluation and review of the EMT's futile efforts, the doctors consulted with the warden and decided to do an immediate cut down to expose the heart for direct manual cardiac message. The doctors worked feverishly against impossible odds to no avail. Azee was pronounced officially dead at the University of Michigan Hospital, not at the Milan Federal Reformatory. A visibly upset Ragman had arrived and was at the warden's side when this news was delivered by a somber ER doctor. A federal marshal agreed to stand guard over the corpse in the morgue until the federal judge issued further instructions.

Gleason was immediately notified of Azee's death by the federal marshal's office that was in charge of Azee when he was off the prison site. His body would be kept indefinitely until the mystery of his death was solved or until released back to the family by the Federal Court in Detroit.

Immediate cremation with the ashes spread to the four winds would have been Gleason's choice for his old nemesis to eliminate any possible evidence, but he knew that wasn't going to happen. Ultimately, he couldn't care less what happened to Azee's corpse and he wondered if Azee's family would feel the same.

Gleason's pressing question was whether to awaken the president or let him get three or four more hours of sleep before learning the good news of Azee's death. He decided on a compromise of waiting two more hours before disturbing him, in case any additional information came in from Ann Arbor. He wasn't expecting to hear from Benz as they had agreed when they said goodbye at the airport that they should not be in contact.

LVIII

The president was informed that, in spite of the valiant efforts of Benz's initial CPR, the ambulance EMTs shocking and injecting Azee's heart and the full force of the University of Michigan Hospital, there was no reviving Azee. Later in the morning, the Federal Court in Detroit ordered two independent autopsies. Ragman and Warden Baldridge had the most at stake, professionally and personally, in the results of these high profile autopsies. Their heads could roll depending on the findings of the autopsies. They became better friends during the prolonged wait for the autopsy results as they sought mutual support for what happened, but more importantly, what could happen when the results were unveiled.

With each passing day that the country waited for the autopsy results, the more the realization grew that Azee was dead as dead could be. Not everyone really needed or wanted to know the cause of his death. The traitor was dead and that was answer enough. The autopsy results were delayed as the pathologists left no stone unturned. They wanted the medical history and reports of Azee's hand surgeries in both Tripoli and the aborted efforts in Tel Aviv, mainly to check on the medications and drugs that were used. They were trying to rule out an anaphylactic drug reaction, which triggers the immune system to fatally shut down the body the second time a drug is received. Gleason was able to supply the name of Dr. Rahmat in Tripoli, but he suggested that they contact Dr. Lamonte in Zurich for detailed medical information on both Tripoli and Tel Aviv. Lamonte still had a vested interest in cooperating with the government because his legal entanglements for drug smuggling were not yet dismissed by the Swiss authorities, who were doing extensive background investigations so they couldn't be accused of letting a wealthy, high profile smuggler off the hook. Gleason felt a little tinge of guilt when he heard of Lamonte's continuing legal problems generated by the CIA-planted drugs. One thing that would never be admitted was that Lamonte had been entrapped with the planted drugs, so the case would have to proceed through the normal Swiss legal channels.

The warden and Ragman continued their weekly skeet shooting league with gradually fading interest in the unanswered deadly enigma of Azee's death. Still, their unproductive introspections sent them on fruitless guilt trips of what they could have done to make things different.

The long awaited autopsy findings were reviewed by the Federal Court in Detroit with copies sent to Gleason at the White House and the Federal Bureau of Prisons before being released to the public. An enlarged heart, not uncommon in a person as vigorously active as Azee, who used a steroid inhaler for his asthma before his imprisonment was the only unusual finding of the autopsy besides the extensive post mortem notes on his repaired hand. No needle marks or banned substances were found in his body, which was always a consideration in prison deaths. Idiopathic cardiac arrest was ruled as the cause of death.

Ragman submitted his resignation to his Washington office, with his regular monthly report, the same day the exonerating autopsy results were announced. Warden Baldridge accepted a transfer to the maximum security Leavenworth Federal Prison as assistant warden to be less accessible to the still inquisitive press. Richard Benz, the forgotten man in the Azee saga, retired again to have more time to devote to his hunting, fishing and paramilitary militia activities.

Ten days after Azee's autopsy was released, Gleason received in his White House mail a padded brown envelope mailed from Anchorage, Alaska containing two full dental anesthetic cartridges.

Epilogue

Azee's cremains were released to Misty, his loyal casino hostess, since no family member claimed them. She took them to Arlington National Cemetery and spread them on the grave of the First Lady for his final resting place with the unobtainable love of his life.

Acknowledgments

Writing a novel is an exciting thing for the author as I hope that reading it is for the reader. The author's discovery of new ideas ultimately resulting in the completed book keeps both author and reader engaged.

The readers of the first drafts helped make this a better book and I am grateful for their suggestions. Donald A Scofield, John and Kathy Snider, my brother Neil Mullally and my niece, Shannon Mullally, PhD, were early readers who encouraged and stimulated me.

My cousin, Richard Mullally, using his enormous teaching skills, was my instructor as he reviewed the manuscript for those final issues that can go undetected. Thank you, Rich.

My webmaster Bob Wright and his wife Terri deserve my appreciation for bringing my books to the world of the internet.

A special note of appreciation is due to retired Michigan State University professor, Frances Schattenberg, PhD. She went over the manuscript with the helpful eye of a university creative writing instructor. The final manuscript is a testimony to her tenacious belief that good can always become better.

To the countless readers of *The First Lady Sleeps,* who kept inquiring about the progress of this sequel, a big thank you as it kept me on task to get it done in a timely fashion.

Finally, to my family, I express my appreciation for encouraging me to keep on this writing journey—final destination yet undetermined.

Please turn this page for an excerpt from
John Mullally's next novel

A DOMINICAN REPUBLIC WEDDING

LEADS TO INTERNATIONAL INTRIGUE

A DOMINICAN REPUBLIC WEDDING

LEADS TO INTERNATIONAL INTRIGUE

I

Tom leaned over Cindy to catch a glimpse of the spectacular Dominican Republic shoreline as their jumbo jet began its descent into Puerto Plata. They were getting an aerial view of the glistening silver water that sparked the Spanish explorers to so name this tropical paradise the silver port.

The pilot moments earlier had pointed out the unmistakable border of Haiti and the Dominican Republic. The Haitian side, dark brown from having been stripped of its vegetation, looked like one big mud slide: past, present and future. In contrast the rolling Dominican side was verdant with large cultivated fields of sugar cane stretching as far as they could see from their rapidly descending jet that was delivering them for their wedding at the luxurious Iberostar resort later in the week.

They were arriving before the rest of their guests to make sure that all the arrangements were in place for their marriage, which Tom lamely joked should be just a KISS. Cindy, getting the first and last word about the male shunned preparations, agreed as long as he remembered that KISS meant: Keep It Short, Stupid. In spite of his steely, business-like Secret Service appearance, Tom was the romantic of the two and Cindy did not want to be caught off guard by one of his surprise romantic pranks, so she daily reinforced the KISS principle with him while exercising autocratic control over all facets of the wedding.

The only thing not under her all-pervasive purview was the bachelor party that Tom was quietly planning for tomorrow after the rest of the wedding party arrived. It took all of Cindy's restraint not to ask Tom or the best man Neil Gibson what was planned for their last fling on the island.

Tom's comment of, "You'd be surprised what we're going to do," only heightened her anxiety about what she didn't know or have control over. Tom brought his golf clubs and went through the pretense of making tee times at the Jack Tar golf course next to their Iberostar resort to divert Cindy's attention to this harmless golf outing that she could not object to. Tom threw a little gasoline on the fire by asking Cindy whether they should take male or the bikini clad female caddies for the boys' round of golf. Her comment that his game was already bad enough without the female distraction was uttered without cracking a smile so he realized that she was operating with a very short fuse and he had better not push his luck with his demonic Irish charm.

Cindy had held the line on agreeing to their marriage until she was sure that Tom was a changed person from the person she met three years ago. Tom, to reinforce his less work obsessed, newly changed person, had insisted that they go through a formal three month pre-cana program like every other engaged couple was required to do. Tom so badly wanted to win Cindy that he even voluntarily went to the couple's pre-cana weekend retreat without the slightest protest. Cindy stalled off the wedding plans as long as she could trying to assess if Tom was truly changed or just jumping through the hoops to get her to the altar, or in this case a beach-side table under a colorful umbrella. She needed time to decipher what was real and permanent in their relationship. She finally acquiesced as she gradually determined that Tom was now really different than the man she first met three years ago. Hence, they were marrying in front of a few close friends in the tropical paradise of the Dominican Republic. Cindy always joked that everything goes downhill after the honeymoon, so they decided to start on the high note of the Dominican Republic wedding and honeymoon.

II

Cindy and her wedding attendants were relieved when the men left the resort for their bachelor party. Now they could get down to the necessary 'girl things' for tomorrow's wedding. One supposed advantage of a destination wedding is that everything is taken care of, thus freeing the wedding party to enjoy their beautiful tropical setting. Yesterday, Tom and Cindy checked on the resort's list of responsibilities and everything seemed organized that they had contracted and paid for.

Today, Cindy wanted her bridal party to try on their outfits to be sure that everyone had everything they needed with no last minutes panic shopping trips as there were no bridal stores in Puerto Plata. After the giggles and laughter of the three women, wiggling and pushing each other into tomorrow's clothes, subsided, Cindy announced, "Let's go shopping, and you have to wear your bathing suits." The women all laughed, knowing about the non-existent shopping around the resort, but nevertheless they agreed to meet in fifteen minutes at the pool to begin their bachelorette party.

Cindy was wearing a broad brimmed straw hat to protect her face from the searing tropical sun because of tomorrow's pictures. Only the maid of honor had the courage and the physique to wear a skimpy bikini as the ladies met at the Iberostar's free formed meandering pool that probably would have stretched out to be a block long if straightened out. "We're going to the Orange Mall," Cindy announced like a true girl scout leader. They each tucked their pesos into areas of their swimming suits that only they dared to venture.

At the sparkling beach, Cindy pointed to her right toward a distant faded orange building that almost could be a mirage caused by the brilliant sun reflecting off the sand and scrub foliage on either side of a little river emptying into the ocean.

About halfway to this intriguing Orange Mall, Joanne, the obviously athletic maid of honor, commented that she felt funny wearing her bikini. The other ladies, looking down at their own modest one piece suits, poorly disguising their prematurely sagging physiques, reassured her that she looked fantastic and that she was the only one of them who could get away with wearing such a revealing suit. "No, that's not the problem," she said. "I fell funny walking past all these flabby women sunning on the beach who are only wearing a monokini. "If they can get away with it, so can I." She no sooner finished saying this than her hand undid the little clasp holding her top on. Cindy nonchalantly mentioned that she might need to put her top back on when they got to the mall to avoid a traffic jam from male gawkers.

The three of them splashed in and out of the shallow water at the edge of the beach to avoid the scorching sand on their feet as they headed toward the euphemistically named Orange Mall. Approaching the mall they walked past a large estate that had a guard seated on a bench at the top of the low barrier dune. He was armed with a camera with a long telephoto lens pointed at them. Before Joanne could put her top back on the camera man smiled and lowered the camera, obviously having already taken pictures of the embarrassed, topless Joanne.

The girls thought for a minute about confronting him, but had second thoughts when they saw the rifle across his legs and another security guard on the deck of the ocean front mansion behind him. "So much for having a little fun," Joanne commented as she too late became a bikini lady again.

The old Quonset hut that had been sprayed orange to make it visible for miles up and down the beach was partitioned into booths and stalls that allowed the local crafters and artisans to display their wares. Cindy called a huddle with Joanne and Mary before they entered the mall. She extracted her money from one of those feminine hiding spots and gave Joanne and Mary each 50 pesos to buy their bridesmaid's gift. Ever the practical one, Cindy explained that she didn't have room to carry any gifts from home and this way they could each get a local gift as a remembrance of the wedding weekend. The girls had a group hug before beginning their shopping. Cindy decided that she had better keep an eye on Joanne to keep her from getting backed into a corner by a Caribbean lover boy who viewed her skimpy bikini as an invitation for a little fun.

The girls perused the local handicrafts that had a distinctive Dominican flavor. The hand decorated wicker baskets, purses and hats provided many a laugh as they modeled them with brightly colored muumuus and scarves. Of courses the exquisite hand made jewelry made their splurge decisions even more difficult.

They were thinking of finishing their shopping, when an unshaven, uniformed man with a camera hanging from a broad neck-strap, approached Joanne. "You come with me," he ordered in halting English.

She crossed her arms across her chest, trying for a degree of modesty as the man's dark eyes avoided eye contact and bore into her chest. "Why," was the only response that she could come up with?

"Have pictures of you naked, walking on my private beach," he said as he took the camera off his neck as if handing it to her.

"So? Many other women were not wearing tops," she replied while turning away to find the other girls.

He put his hand on her bare shoulder, trying to turn her

around to face him, which he didn't have to do as she freely spun around and buried her knee in his groin. He doubled up in agony, falling to his knees as his camera went bouncing on the sandy concrete, "Bitch, you pay bitch."

The other girls heard the commotion and came to Joanne's side as a circle of curious tourists and shopkeepers formed around them. Joanne picked up the camera that had landed at her feet. The camera back had sprung open when it bounced on the concrete, exposing the roll of film to the bright afternoon sun rendering it useless. Another uniformed guard appeared out of the crowd and bent over his still moaning colleague. Cindy grabbed a tie-dyed tee shirt from the nearest booth for Joanne to slip on to lessen the distraction caused by her skimpy bikini. Joanne's practiced eye immediately noticed that the uniforms of the two cops were different. The fallen officer's seemed to be of the rent-a-cop variety, while the other seemed to be an official police uniform with a badge, handcuffs and a pistol hanging from a large belt that was already strained to hold the protuberant belly above it.

"Let's get back to the hotel," Cindy whispered to the girls. "We can finish shopping later." She tossed 10 pesos to the lady behind the tee shirt booth. "Keep the change."

"Stay," the real officer barked as he saw the girls trying to back out of the every growing circle. "Why did you assault this officer? You can be arrested."

"He assaulted me. Nobody touches me without my permission. Nobody," Joanne screamed as she calmly handed him the camera with the now useless film. The entire circle started to back up anticipating further confrontation while the girls formed their own tighter huddle.

The injured cop slowly rose to his feet, still painfully bending over trying to avoid grabbing his throbbing crotch. Joanne had difficulty suppressing a smile as her CIA training achieved its desired effect. A well dressed, distinguished man wearing a name tag indicating that he was the mall manager rushed over to the two officers and after a brief conference announced, "All okay. Please, everybody, go back to shopping."

The crowd slowly dispersed and the mall manager approached the girls who felt in a state of limbo with the two cops still glaring at them. Joanne was relieved to see that the injured rent-a-cop was not armed and that the film in the camera was now useless as evidence. "Who does he work for," Joanne asked the mall manager?

"He is the guard for a very important person who owns the big house where no nude bathing is permitted on his private beach. Our European vacationers are the ones who usually get in trouble on his private beach, as it is their custom to sun bathe topless. You are the first Americans to violate the law on his property. You will have to talk to the police when they come to your hotel to possibly arrest you. This is the way the police handle these cases."

Joanne had all she could do to restrain herself from drop kicking the mall manager as the real cop approached them. Looking at the girls' blue Iberostar wrist bands he said, "I will meet you in the Iberostar lobby tomorrow night at 6 p.m. for you to plead guilty and pay your fine of 50 pesos and 50 pesos for my expenses."

Cindy moved in front of the still fuming and about to erupt Joanne to prevent her from taking on the real cop, which would have landed all of them in a dreaded Caribbean jail. "Sorry, she can't meet you tomorrow. She is the maid of honor at my wedding. How about the next day?"

The rent-a-cop, now standing a little more erect, overheard Cindy's offer of postponed justice and interjected, "Mr. Walther isn't going to like this delay. His camera has been ruined by this American bitch. She must pay!"

Cindy shuffled sideways a couple steps to stay between Joanne and the reenergized rent-a-cop. She slipped her prescription Reva sunglasses off and looked straight in the faces of both cops. "Look at me. Don't you know who I am? I don't think you want to mess with us too much more."

The realization that this incident may be getting a little beyond his pay grade brought out the cop's conciliatory offer. "We can settle this case here and now for 200 pesos and this case disappears."

Cindy reached into her swim suit top and retrieved her stash of sweaty and sandy folded bills. "Looks like I am a little short."

As she was starting to hand the money to the over-eager cop, who probably would have settled for any amount of money, Mary the unobtrusive third member of the beleaguered trio, pushed Cindy's outstretched arm back to her side. "No. Don't give it to them. This is a scam, an illegal shakedown. I'll fight it in court. They have no evidence, the film is ruined." Mary took one step toward the two cops. "Come to the hotel with your legal paperwork and we'll settle the case then." The girls quickly headed to the beach for the hike back to their hotel.

They walked with a quickened pace, with one eye over their shoulders. Joanne kept tugging down on her festive tie-dyed shirt so that it was starting to be long enough for a sleeping shirt by the time they were passing the scene of the crime. The beach front voyeur with the smashed camera was probably in the house icing his privates to keep down the swelling from Joanne's well placed knee, but they could see his cohort still on the mansion's expansive deck with a pair of binoculars and a camera zeroed in on them. "Should we tell the men about our little adventure," Cindy threw out, not knowing what answer to expect from the other girls?

"I can't wait to tell Neil. He'll be so proud of me executing the disabling knee thrust just like he trained me in our CIA self-defense class. This was the first time I've done it to anyone not having extra padding in the crotch. Wow, it really works!"

"I agree we have to tell them, but let's wait until after the wedding tomorrow so that we don't take away from your day."

"Don't worry about me, Mary. The wedding will go off as planned," Cindy deadpanned.

"That may be true," Mary agreed, "but let's just wait until

after the wedding. We told these jokers not to come tomorrow. They probably won't show up at all."

The three of them nodded their heads in agreement to this post-wedding confession, when they would all be together to share this unbelievable story of making a mountain out of a molehill.

• • • • •